The Pools Of Silence

by

H. De Vere Stacpoole

Double 9 BOOKS

The Pools Of Silence

by H. De Vere Stacpoole

ISBN: 978-93-70425-69-9

Published by

DOUBLE 9 BOOKS
2/13-B, Ansari Road
Daryaganj, New Delhi – 110002
info@double9books.com
www.double9books.com
Tel. 011-40042856

ABOUT THE AUTHOR

Henry de Vere Stacpoole was an Irish author known for his romantic and adventure novels. Born on April 9, 1863, in Dún Laoghaire, Ireland, he became widely recognized for his 1908 novel The Blue Lagoon, which was later adapted into multiple films. Stacpoole wrote under his real name and occasionally used the pseudonym Tyler de Saix. His works often centered around themes of love, survival, and human nature, blending elements of romance with captivating adventures. Throughout his career, Stacpoole gained a following for his lyrical storytelling and the timeless appeal of his narratives. In addition to his literary works, he had an intriguing life that involved travel and romantic entanglements. Stacpoole was partnered with Florence Robson from 1938, and earlier with Margaret de Vere Stacpoole, whom he was with from 1907. His parents, William Church Stacpoole and Charlotte Augusta Mountjoy, were part of his early life influence. Stacpoole lived to the age of 88, passing away on April 12, 1951, in Shanklin, United Kingdom. His legacy endures through his works, particularly The Blue Lagoon.

CONTENTS

PART THREE

PART FOUR

PART ONE

CHAPTER I
A LECTURE OF THENARD'S

The sun was setting over Paris, a blood-red and violent-looking sun, like the face of a bully staring in at the window of a vast chill room.

The bank of cloud above the west, corrugated by the wind, seemed not unlike the lowermost slats of a Venetian blind; one might have fancied that a great finger had tilted them up whilst the red, callous, cruel face took a last peep at the frost-bitten city, the frost-bound country—Montmartre and its windows, winking and bloodshot; Bercy and its barges; Notre Dame, where icicles, large as carrots, hung from the lips of the gargoyles, and the Seine clipping the *cité* and flowing to the clean but distant sea.

It was the fourth of January and the last day of Félix Thénard's post-graduate course of lectures at the Beaujon Hospital.

Post-graduate lectures are intended not for students, using the word in its limited sense, but for fully fledged men who wish for extra training in some special subject, and Thénard, the famous neurologist of the Beaujon, had a class which practically represented the whole continent of Europe and half the world. Men from Vienna and Madrid, Germany and Japan, London and New York, crowded the benches of his lecture room. Even the Republic of Liberia was represented by a large gentleman, who seemed carved from solid night and polished with palm oil.

Dr. Paul Quincy Adams, one of the representatives of America at the lectures of Thénard, was just reaching the entrance of the Beaujon as the last rays of sunset were touching the heights of Montmartre and the first lamps of Paris were springing alight.

He had walked all the way from his rooms in the Rue Dijon, for omnibuses were slow and uncomfortable, cabs were dear, and money was, just at present, the most unpleasant thing that money can convert itself into—an object.

Adams was six feet two, a Vermonter, an American gentleman whose chest measurements were big, almost, as his instincts were fine. He had fought his way up, literally from the soil, putting in terms as seaside *café* waiter to help to pay his college fees; putting aside everything but honour in his grand struggle to freedom and individual existence, and finishing his college career with a travelling scholarship which brought him to Paris.

Individualism, the thing that lends something of greatness to each American, but which does not tend to the greatness of the nation, was the mainspring of this big man whom Nature had undoubtedly designed with her eye on the vast plains, virgin forests, and unfordable rivers, and across whose shoulder one half divined the invisible axe of the pioneer.

He was just twenty-three years of age, yet he looked thirty: plain enough as far as features go, his face was a face to remember in time of trouble. It was of the American type that approximates to the Red Indian, and you guessed the power that lay behind it by the set of the cheek-bones, the breadth of the chin and the restfulness of the eyes. Like the Red Indian, Paul Quincy Adams was slow of speech. A silent man with his tongue.

He entered the hospital and passed down a long corridor to the cloakroom, where he left his overcoat and from there, by another corridor, he found his way to the swing-door of the lecture theatre. It wanted five minutes to the hour. He peeped over the muffing of the glass; the place was nearly full, so he went in and took his seat, choosing one at the right hand end of the first row of the stalls—students' vernacular for the lowest row of the theatre benches.

The theatre was lit with gas. It had whitewashed walls bare as the walls of a barn; a permanent blackboard faced the audience, and the air was suffocatingly hot after the crisp, cold air of the streets. It would be like this till about the middle of the lecture, when Alphonse the porter would pull the rope of the skylight and ventilate the place with an arctic blast.

This room, which had once been an anatomical theatre, and always a lecture room, had known the erect form of Lisfranc; the stooping shoulders of Majendie had cast their shadow on its walls; Flourens had lectured here on that subject of which he had so profound a knowledge—the brain; the echoes of this room had heard the foundations of Medicine shift and change, the rank heresies of yesterday voiced as the facts of to-day—and *vice versa*.

Adams, having opened his notebook and sharpened his pencil, sat listening to the gas sizzling above his head; then he turned for a moment and glanced at the men behind him: the doctor from Vienna in a broadly braided frock-coat with satin facings, betraying himself to all men by the end of the clinical thermometer protruding from his waistcoat pocket; the two Japanese gentlemen—brown, incurious, and inscrutable—men from another world, come to look on; the republican from Liberia, and the rest. Then he turned his head, for the door on the floor of the theatre had opened, giving entrance to Thénard.

Thénard was a smallish man in a rather shabby frock-coat; his beard was scant, pointed, and gray-tinged; he had a depressed expression, the general air of a second-rate tradesman on the verge of bankruptcy; and as he entered and crossed to the *estrade* where the lecture table stood and the glass of water, he shouted some words vehemently and harshly to Alphonse, the theatre attendant, who, it seemed, had forgotten to place the box of coloured chalks on the table—the sacred chalks which the lecturer used for colouring his diagrams on the blackboard.

One instantly took a dislike to this shabby-looking *bourgeois*, with the harsh, irritable voice, but after awhile, as the lecture went on, one forgot him. It was not the profundity of the man's knowledge, great though it was, that impressed one; or the subtlety of his reasoning or the lucidity of his expression, but his earnestness, his obvious disregard for everything earthly but Truth.

This was borne in on one by every expression of his face, every gesture of his body, every word and every tone and inflection of his voice.

This was the twelfth and last lecture of the course. It was on the "Brain Conceived as a Machine Pure and Simple."

It was a cold and pitiless lecture, striking at the root of poetry and romance, speaking of religions, not religion, and utterly ignoring the idea which stands poised like a white-winged Victory over all other ideas—the Soul.

It was pitiless because it did these things, and it was terrible because it was spoken by Thénard, for he was just standing there, a little, oldish man, terribly convincing in his simplicity, absolutely without prejudice, as ready to acknowledge the soul and its attributes as to refuse them, standing there twiddling his horsehair watch-chain, and speaking from the profundity of his knowledge with, at his elbow, a huge army of facts, instances, and cases, not one of which did not support his logical deductions.

I wish I could print his lecture in full. I can only give some few sentences taken at haphazard from the peroration.

"The fundamental basis of all morality can be expressed by the words Left—or Right. 'Shall I take the path to the right, when my child is being threatened with death by a pterodactyl, or shall I take the path to the left when a mastodon is threatening to put a foot on my dinner?'

"The prehistoric man asking himself that question in the dawn of time laid the foundation of the world's morality. Do we know how he answered it? Yes—undoubtedly he saved his dinner.

"The prehistoric woman crouching in the ferns, wakened from sleep by the cries of her child on the left and the shouting of her man on the right, found herself face to face with the question, 'Shall I court self-destruction in attempting to save *It*, or shall I seek safety with *Him*?' Do we know how she answered that question? Undoubtedly she took the path to the left.

"The woman's Right was the man's Left, and she took it not from any motive of goodness but just because her child appealed to her as powerfully as his dinner appealed to the man. And which was the nobler instinct? In prehistoric times, gentlemen, they were both equally noble, for the instinct of the man was as essential to the fact that you and I are here gathered together in enlightened Paris, as the instinct of the woman.

"Right or Left? That is still the essence of morals—all the rest is embroidery. Whilst I am talking to you now, service is being held at the Madeleine, the Bourse is closed (looking at his watch), but other gaming houses are opening. The *Café de Paris* is filling, the Little Sisters of the Poor are visiting the sick.

"We feel keenly that some people are doing good and some people are doing evil. We wonder at the origin of it all, and the answer comes from the prehistoric forest.

"'I am Determination. I can choose the Right or I can choose the Left. Whilst dwelling in the man's heart my choice lies *that* way, in the woman's heart *that* way.

"'I am not religion, but between the man and the woman I have created an essential antagonism of motive which will be the basis of all future religions and systems of ethics. I have already dimly demarcated a line between ferocity and greed, and a thing which has yet no name, but which will in future ages be called Love.

"'*I* am a constant quantity, but the dim plan I have traced in the plastic brain will be used by the ever-building years; spires and domes shall fret the skies, priests unroll their scrolls of papyri, infinite developments of the simple basic Right and Left laid down by me shall combine to build a Pantheon of a million shrines to a million gods—who are yet only three: the tramp of the mastodon, the cry of the child in the pterodactyl's grip, and myself, who in future years shall be the only surviving god of the three—Determination.'

"The Pineal Gland had no known function, so Descartes declared it to be the seat of the soul. 'There is nothing in here. Let us put something in,' and he put in the idea of the soul. That was the old method.

"Morphology teaches us now that the Pineal Gland is the last vestige of an eye which once belonged to a reptile long extinct. That is the new method; the results are not so pretty, but they are more exact."

"You have finished your post-graduate work, and I suppose you are about to leave Paris like the others. Have you any plans?"

The lecture was over, the audience was pouring out of the theatre, and Adams was talking to Thénard, whom he knew personally.

"Well, no," said Adams. "None very fixed just at present. Of course I shall practise in my own country, but I can't quite see the opening yet."

CHAPTER II
DR. DUTHIL

Thénard, with his case-book and a bundle of papers under his arm, stood for a moment in thought. Then he suddenly raised his chin.

"How would you like to go on a big-game shooting expedition to the Congo?"

"Ask a child would it like pie," said the American, speaking in English. Then, in French, "Immensely, monsieur. Only it is impossible."

"Why?"

"Money."

"Ah, that's just it," said Thénard. "A patient of mine, Captain Berselius, is starting on a big-game shooting expedition to the Congo. He requires a medical man to accompany him, and the salary is two thousand francs a month and all things found——"

Adams's eyes lit up.

"Two thousand a month!"

"Yes; he is a very rich man. His wife is a patient of mine. When I was visiting her yesterday the Captain put the thing before me—in fact, gave me *carte blanche* to choose for him. He requires the services of a medical man—an Englishman if possible——"

"But I'm an American," said Adams.

"It is the same thing," replied Thénard, with a little laugh. "You are all big and strong and fond of guns and danger."

He had taken Adams by the arm and was leading him down the passage toward the entrance hall of the hospital.

"The primitive man is strong in you all, and that is why you are so vital and important, you Anglo-Saxons, Anglo-Celts, and Anglo-Teutons. Come in here."

He opened the door of one of the house-surgeon's rooms.

A youngish looking man, with a straw-coloured beard, was seated before the fire, with a cigarette between his lips.

He rose to greet Thénard, was introduced to Adams, and, drawing an old couch a bit from the wall, he bade his guests be seated.

The armchair he retained himself. One of the legs was loose, and he was the only man in the Beaujon who had the art of sitting on it without smashing it. This he explained whilst offering cigarettes.

Thénard, like many another French professor, unofficially was quite one with the students. He would snatch a moment from his work to smoke a cigarette with them; he would sometimes look in at their little parties. I have seen him at a birthday party where the cakes and ale, to say nothing of the cigarettes and the unpawned banjo, were the direct products of a pawned microscope. I have seen him, I say, at a party like this, drinking a health to the microscope as the giver of all the good things on the table—he, the great Thénard, with an income of fifteen to twenty thousand pounds a year, and a reputation solid as the four massive text-books that stood to his name.

"Duthil," said Thénard, "I have secured, I believe, a man for our friend Berselius." He indicated Adams with a half laugh, and Dr. Duthil, turning in his chair, regarded anew the colossus from the States. The great, large-hewn, cast-iron visaged Adams, beside whom Thénard looked like a shrivelled monkey and Duthil like a big baby with a beard.

"Good," said Duthil.

"A better man than Bauchardy," said Thénard.

"Much," replied Duthil.

"Who, then, was Bauchardy?" asked Adams, amused rather by the way in which the two others were discussing him.

"Bauchardy?" said Duthil. "Why, he was the last man Berselius killed."

"Silence," said Thénard, then turning to Adams, "Berselius is a perfectly straight man. On these hunting expeditions of his he invariably takes a doctor with him; he is not a man who fears death in the least, but he has had bitter experience of being without medical assistance, so he takes a doctor. He pays well and is entirely to be trusted to do the right thing, as far as money goes. On that side the contract is all right. But there is another side—the character of Berselius. A man, to be the companion of Captain Berselius, needs to be big and strong in body and mind, or he would be crushed by the hand of Captain Berselius. Yes, he is a terrible man in a way—*un homme affreux*—a man of the tiger type—and he is going to the country of the big baboons, where there is the freedom of action that the soul of such a man desires— —"

"In fact," said Adams, "he is a villain, this Captain Berselius?"

"Oh, no," said Thénard, "not in the least. Be quiet, Duthil, you do not know the man as I do. I have studied him; he is a Primitive— —"

"An Apache," said Duthil. "Come, dear master, confess that from the moment you heard that this Berselius was intent on another expedition, you determined to throw a foreigner into the breach. 'No more French doctors, if possible,' said you. Is not that so?"

Thénard laughed the laugh of cynical confession, buttoning his overcoat at the same time and preparing to go.

"Well, there may be something in what you say, Duthil. However, there the offer is—a sound one financially. Yes. I must say I dread that two thousand francs a month will prove a fatal attraction, and, if Mr. Adams does not go, some weaker man will. Well, I must be off."

"One moment," said Adams. "Will you give me this man's address? I don't say I will take the post, but I might at least go and see him."

"Certainly," replied Thénard, and taking one of his own cards from his pocket, he scribbled on the back of it—

CAPTAIN ARMAND BERSELIUS

14 AVENUE MALAKOFF

Then he went off to a consultation at the Hotel Bristol on a Balkan prince, whose malady, hitherto expressed by evil living, had suddenly taken an acute and terrible turn and Adams found himself alone with Dr. Duthil.

"That is Thénard all over," said Duthil. "He is the high priest of modernism. He and all the rest of the neurologists have divided up devilment into provinces, and labelled each province with names all ending in *enia* or *itis*. Berselius is a Primitive, it seems; this Balkan prince is—I don't know what they call him—sure to be something Latin, which does not interfere in the least with the fact that he ought to be boiled alive in an antiseptic solution. Have another cigarette."

"Do you know anything special against Captain Berselius?" asked Adams, taking the cigarette.

"I have never even seen the man," replied Duthil, "but from what I have heard, he is a regular buccaneer of the old type, who values human life not one hair. Bauchardy, that last doctor he took with him, was a friend of mine.

Perhaps that is why I feel vicious about the man, for he killed Bauchardy as sure as I didn't."

"Killed him?"

"Yes; with hardship and overwork."

"Overwork?"

"*Mon Dieu,* yes. Dragged him through swamps after his infernal monkeys and tigers, and Bauchardy died in the hospital at Marseilles of spinal meningitis, brought on by the hardships of the expedition—died as mad as Berselius himself."

"As mad as Berselius?"

"Yes; this infernal Berselius seemed to have infected him with his own hunting fever, and Bauchardy—*mon Dieu,* you should have seen him during his illness, shooting imaginary elephants, and calling for Berselius."

"What I want to get at is this," said Adams. "Was Bauchardy driven into these swamps you speak of, and made to hunt against his will—treated cruelly, in fact—or did Berselius take his own share of the hardships?"

"His own share! Why, from what I can understand, he did all the hunting. A man of iron with the ferocity of a tiger—a very devil, who made others follow him as poor Bauchardy did, to his death——"

"Well," said Adams, "this man interests me somehow, and I intend to have a look at him."

"The pay is good," said Duthil, "but I have warned you fully, if Thénard hasn't. Good evening."

The Rue Dijon, where Adams lived, was a good way from the Beaujon. He made his way there on foot, studying the proposition as he went.

The sporting nature of the proposal coming from the sedate Thénard rather tickled him.

"He wants to pit me against this Berselius," said Adams to himself, "same as if we were dogs. That's the long and short of it. Yes, I can understand his meaning in part; he's afraid if Berselius engages some week-kneed individual, he'll give the weak-kneed individual more than he can take. He wants to stick a six-foot Yankee in the breach, instead of a five-foot froggie, all absinthe and cigarette ends. Well, he was frank, at all events. Hum, I don't like the proposition—and yet there's something—there's something—there's something about it I *do* like. Then there's the two thousand francs a month, and not a penny out of pocket, and there's the

Congo, and the guggly-wuggly alligators, and the great big hairy apes, and the feel of a gun in one's hand again. Oh, my!"

"All the same, it's funny," he went on, as he drew near the Boulevard St. Michel. "When Thénard spoke of Berselius there was something more than absence of friendship in his tone. Can old man Thénard have a down on this Berselius and does he in his heart of hearts imagine that by allotting P. Quincy Adams to the post of physician extraordinary to the expedition, he will get even with the Captain? My friend, remember that hymn the English Salvationists were yelling last Sunday outside the American Presbyterian Church in the Rue de Berry—'Christian, walk carefully, danger is near.' Not a bad motto for Paris, and I will take it."

He walked into the *Café d'Italie,* which, as everyone knows, is next to Mouton's, the pork shop, on the left-hand side of the Boul' Miche, as you go from the Seine; called for a boc, and then plunged into a game of dominoes with an art student in a magenta necktie, whom he had never met before, and whom, after the game, he would, a million to one, never meet again.

That night, when he had blown out his candle, he reviewed Thénard's proposition in the dark. The more he looked at it the more attraction it had for him, and—"Whatever comes of it," said he to himself, "I will go and see this Captain Berselius to-morrow. The animal seems worth the trouble of inspection."

CHAPTER III
CAPTAIN BERSELIUS

Next morning was chill and a white Seine mist wrapped Paris in its folds. It clung to the trees of the Avenue Champs Elysées, and it half veiled the Avenue Malakoff as Adams's *fiacre* turned into that thoroughfare and drew up at No. 14, a house with a carriage drive, a porter's lodge, and wrought-iron gates.

The American paid off his cab, rang at the porter's lodge, was instantly admitted, and found himself in an enormous courtyard domed in with glass. He noted the orange and aloe trees growing in tubs of porcelain, as the porter led him to the big double glass doors giving entrance to the house.

"He's got the money," thought Adams, as the glass swing-door was opened by a flunkey as magnificent as a Lord Mayor's footman, who took the visitor's card and the card of M. Thénard and presented them to a functionary with a large pale face, who was seated at a table close to the door.

This personage, who was as soberly dressed as an archbishop, and had altogether a pontifical air, raised himself to his feet and approached the visitor.

"Has monsieur an appointment— —"

"No," said Adams. "I have come to see your master on business. You can take him my card—yes, that one—Dr. Adams, introduced by Dr. Thénard."

The functionary seemed perplexed; the early hour, the size of the visitor, his decided manner, all taken together, were out of routine. Only for a moment he hesitated, then leading the way across the warm and flower-scented hall, he opened a door and said, "Will monsieur take a seat?" Adams entered a big room, half library, half museum; the door closed behind him, and he found himself alone.

The four walls of the room showed a few books, but were mostly covered with arms and trophies of the chase. Japanese swords in solid ivory scabbards, swords of the old Samurai so keen that a touch of the edge would divide a suspended hair. Malay krisses, double-handed Chinese execution swords; old pepper-pot revolvers, such as may still be found on the African coast; knob-kerries, assegais, steel-spiked balls swinging from whips of raw hide; weapons wild and savage and primitive as those with which Attila drove before him the hordes of the Huns, and modern weapons of to-day and yesterday; the big elephant gun which has been supplanted by the express rifle; the deadly magazine rifle, the latest products of Schaunard of the Rue de la Paix and Westley Richards of London.

Adams forgot time as he stood examining these things; then he turned his attention to the trophies, mounted by Borchard of Berlin, that prince of taxidermists. Here stood a great ape, six feet and over—*monstrum horrendum*—head flung back, mouth open, shouting aloud to the imagination of the gazer in the language that was spoken ere the earliest man lifted his face to the chill mystery of the stars. In the right fist was clutched the branch of a M'bina tree, ready lifted to dash your brains out—the whole thing a miracle of the taxidermist's art. Here crawled an alligator on a slab of granitic rock; an alligator—that is to say, the despair of the taxidermist—for you can make nothing out of an alligator; alive and not in motion he looks stuffed, stuffed, he looks just the same. Hartbeest, reedbuck, the maned and huge-eared roan antelope, gazelle, and bush-buck, all were here, skull or mask, dominated by the vast head of the wildebeest, with ponderous sickle-curved horns.

Adams had half completed the tour of the walls when the door of the library opened and Captain Berselius came in. Tall, black-bearded and ferocious looking—that was the description of man Adams was prepared to meet. But Captain Berselius was a little man in a frock-coat, rather worn, and slippers. He had evidently been in *négligé* and, to meet the visitor, slipped into the frock-coat, or possibly he was careless, taken up with abstractions, dreams, business affairs, plans. He was rather stout, with an oval, egg-shaped face; his beard, sparse and pointed and tinged with gray, had originally been light of hue; he had pale blue eyes, and he had a perpetual smile.

It is to be understood by this that Captain Berselius's smile was, so to speak, hung on a hair-trigger; there was always a trace of it on his face round the lips, and in conversation it became accentuated.

At first sight, during your first moments of meeting with Captain Berselius, you would have said, "What a happy-faced and jolly little man!"

Adams, completely taken aback by the apparition before him, bowed.

"I have the pleasure of speaking to Dr. Adams, introduced by Dr. Thénard?" said Captain Berselius, motioning the visitor to a chair. "Pray take a seat, take a seat—yes——" He took a seat opposite the American, crossed his legs in a comfortable manner, caressed his chin, and whilst chatting on general subjects stared full at the newcomer, as though Adams had been a statue, examining him, without the least insolence, but in that thorough manner with which a purchaser examines the horse he is about to buy or the physician of an insurance company a proposer.

It was now that Adams felt he had to deal with no common man in Captain Berselius.

Never before had he conversed with a person so calmly authoritative, so perfectly at ease, and so commanding. This little commonplace-looking, negligently dressed man, talking easily in his armchair, made the spacious Adams feel small and of little account in the world. Captain Berselius filled all the space. He was *the* person in that room; Adams, though he had personality enough, was nowhere. And now he noticed that the perpetual smile of the Captain had no relation to mirth or kindliness, it was not worn as a mask, for Captain Berselius had no need for masks; it was a mysterious and unaccountable thing that was there.

"You know M. Thénard intimately?" said Captain Berselius, turning suddenly from some remarks he was making on the United States.

"Oh, no," said Adams. "I have attended his clinics; beyond that— —"

"Just so," said the other. "Are you a good shot?"

"Fair, with the rifle."

"You have had to do with big game?"

"I have shot bear."

"These are some of my trophies," said the Captain, rising to his feet. He took his stand before the great ape and contemplated it for a moment. "I shot him near M'Bassa on the West Coast two years ago. The natives at the village where we were camping said there was a big monkey in a tree near by. They seemed very much frightened, but they led me to the tree. He knew what a gun was; he knew what a man was, too. He knew that his hour of death had arrived, and he came roaring out of the tree to meet me. But when he was on the ground, with the muzzle of my Mannlicher two yards from his head, all his rage vanished. He saw death, and to shut out the sight he put his big hands before his face— —"

"And you?"

"I shot him through the heart. This room does not represent all my work. The billiard room and the hall contain many of my trophies; they are interesting to me, for each has a history. That tiger skin there in front of the fireplace once covered a thing very much alive. He was a full-sized brute, and I met him in a rice field near Benares. I had not even time to raise my gun when he charged. Then I was on my back and he was on top of me. He had overshot the mark a bit—I was not even scratched. I lay looking up at his whiskers; they seemed thick as quills, and I counted them. I was dead to all intents and purposes, so I felt no fear. That was the lesson this gentleman taught me; it is as natural to be dead as to be alive. I have never been afraid of death since. Well, something must have distracted his attention and frightened him, for he lifted himself, passed over me like a cloud, and was gone. Well, so much for the tiger. And now for business. Are you prepared to act as medical attendant to my new expedition?"

"Well," said Adams, "I would like a little time to consider——"

"Certainly," said Captain Berselius, taking out his watch. "I will give you five minutes, as a matter of form. Thénard, in a note to me this morning, informs me he has given you all details as to salary."

"Yes, he gave me the details. As you give me so short a time to make my decision about you, I suppose you have already made your decision about me?"

"Absolutely," said Berselius. "Two minutes have passed. Why waste the other three? For you have already made up your mind to come."

Adams sat down in a chair for a moment, and in that moment he did a great deal of thinking.

He had never met a man before at all like Berselius. He had never before come across a man with such a tremendous personality. Berselius fascinated yet repelled him. That there was evil in this man he felt, but he felt also that there was good. Much evil and much good. And beyond this he divined an animal ferocity latent—the ferocity of a tiger—a cold and pitiless and utterly divorced from reason ferociousness, the passion of a primitive man, who had never known law except the law of the axe wielded by the strongest. And yet there was something in the man that he liked. He knew by Berselius's manner that if he did not take the offer now, he would lose it. He reckoned with lightning swiftness that the expedition would bring him in solid cash enough to start in a small way in the States. He was as poor as Job, as hungry for adventure as a schoolboy, and he only had a moment to decide in.

"How many men are making up your party?" suddenly asked Adams.

"You and I alone," replied Berselius, putting his watch in his pocket to indicate that the time was almost expired.

"I will come," said Adams, and it seemed to him that he said the words against his will.

Captain Berselius went to a writing table, took a sheet of paper and wrote carefully and with consideration for the space of some five minutes. Then he handed the paper to Adams. "These are the things you want," said he. "I am an old campaigner in the wilds, so you will excuse me for specifying them. Go for your outfit where you will, but for your guns to Schaunard, for he is the best. Order all accounts to be sent in to my secretary, M. Pinchon. He will settle them. Your salary you can take how you will. If it is useful to you, I can give you a cheque now on the Crédit Lyonnais, if you will state the amount."

"Thank you, thank you," said Adams. "I have quite sufficient money for my needs, and, if it is the same to you, I would rather pay for my outfit myself."

"As you please," said Captain Berselius, quite indifferently. "But Schaunard's account and the account for drugs and instruments you will please send to M. Pinchon; they are part of the expedition. And now," looking at his watch, "will you do me the pleasure of staying to *déjeuner*?"

Adams bowed.

"I will notify you to-night at your address the exact date we start," said Captain Berselius as he led the way from the room. "It will be within a fortnight. My yacht is lying at Marseilles, and will take us to Matadi, which will be our base. She will be faster than the mail-boats and very much more comfortable."

They crossed the hall, Captain Berselius opened a door, motioned his companion to enter, and Adams found himself in a room, half morning room, half boudoir. A bright log fire was burning, and on either side of the fireplace two women—a girl of about eighteen and a woman of thirty-five or so—were seated.

The elder woman, Madame Berselius, a Parisienne, pale, stout, yet well-proportioned, with almond-shaped eyes; full lips exquisitely cut in the form of the true cupid's bow; and with a face vigorous enough, but veiled by an expression at once mulish, blindish, and indolent—was a type.

The type of the poodle woman, the parasite. With the insolent expression of a Japanese lady of rank, an insult herself to the human race, you will see her everywhere in the highest social ranks of society. At the Zoölogical Gardens of Madrid on a Sunday, when the grandees of Spain take their pleasure amidst the animals at Longchamps, in Rotten Row, Washington

Square, Unter den Linden, wherever money is, growing like an evil fungus, she flourishes.

Opposite Madame Berselius sat her daughter, Maxine.

Adams, after his first glance at the two women, saw only Maxine.

Maxine had golden-brown hair, worn after the fashion of Cléo de Mérode's, gray eyes, and a wide mouth, with pomegranate-red lips. Goethe's dictum that the highest beauty is unobtainable without something of disproportion was exemplified in the case of Maxine Berselius. "Her mouth is too wide," said the women, who, knowing nothing of the philosophy of art, hit upon the defect that was Maxine's main charm.

Berselius introduced Adams to his wife and daughter, and scarcely had he done so than a servant, in the blue-and-gold livery of the house, flung open the door and announced that *déjeuner* was served.

Adams scarcely noticed the room into which they passed; a room whose scheme of colour was that watery green which we associate with the scenery of early spring, the call of the cuckoo, and the river echoes where the weir foams and the willow droops.

The tapestry hanging upon the walls did not distract from this scheme. Taken from some château of Provence, and old almost as the story of Nicolete, it showed ladies listening to shepherds who played on flutes, capering lambs, daffodils blowing to the winds of early spring under a sky gray and broken by rifts of blue.

Adams scarcely noticed the room, or the tapestry, or the food placed before him; he was entirely absorbed by two things, Maxine and Captain Berselius.

Berselius's presence at the table evidently cast silence and a cloak of restraint upon the women. You could see that the servants who served him dreaded him to the very tips of their fingers, and, though he was chatting easily and in an almost paternal manner, his wife and daughter had almost the air of children, nervous, and on their very best behaviour. This was noticeable, especially, in Madame Berselius. The beautiful, indolent, arrogant face became a very humble face indeed when she turned it on the man who was evidently, literally, her lord and master. Maxine, though oppressed by the presence, wore a different air; she seemed abstracted and utterly unconscious of what a beautiful picture she made against the old-world tapestry of spring.

Her eyes sometimes met the American's. They scarcely spoke to each other once during the meal, yet their eyes met almost as frequently as though they had been conversing. As a matter of fact, Adams was a new type of man to her, and on that account interesting; very different was this son of Anak, with the restful, forceful face, to the curled and scented dandies of the Chaussée d'Antin, the "captains with the little moustaches," the frequenters of the *foyer de Ballet*, the cigarette-dried mummies of the Grand Club. It was like the view of a mountain to a person who had only known hills.

Maxine, in her turn, was a new type of woman to Adams. This perfect flower from the Parisian hot-house was the rarest and most beautiful thing he had met in the way of womanhood. She seemed to him a rose only just unfolded, unconscious of its own freshness and beauty as of the dew upon its petals, and saying to the world, by the voice of its own loveliness, "Behold me!"

"Well," said Captain Berselius, as he took leave of his guest in the smoking room, "I will let you know to-night the day and hour of our departure. All my business in Paris will be settled this afternoon. You had better come and see me the day before we start, so that we can make our last arrangements. *Au revoir.*"

CHAPTER IV
SCHAUNARD

The young man turned down the Avenue Malakoff, after he had left Berselius's house, in the direction of the Avenue des Champs Elysées.

In twenty-four hours a complete change had taken place in his life. His line of travel had taken a new and most unexpected course; it was as though a train on the North German had, suddenly, by some mysterious arrangement of points and tracks, found itself on the Paris-Lyons and Mediterranean Railway.

Yesterday afternoon the prospect before him, though vague enough, was American. A practice in some big central American town. It would be a hard fight, for money was scanty, and in medicine, especially in the States, advertisement counts for very much.

All that was changed now, and the hard, definite prospect that had elbowed itself out of vagueness stood before him: Africa, its palms and poisonous forests, the Congo—Berselius.

Something else besides these things also stood before him very definitely and almost casting them into shade. Maxine.

Up to this, a woman had never stood before him as a possible part of his future, if we except Mary Eliza Summers, the eleven-year-old daughter of old Abe Summers, who kept the store in Dodgeville, Vermont, years ago—that is to say, when Paul Quincy Adams was twelve, an orchard-robbing hooligan, whose chief worry in life was that, though he could thrash his eldest brother left-handed, he was condemned by the law of entail to wear his old pants.

When a man falls in love with a woman—really in love—though the attainment of his desire be all but impossible, he has reached the goal of life; no tide can take him higher toward the Absolute. He has reached life's zenith, and never will he rise higher, even though he live to wield a sceptre or rule armies.

Adams reached the Place de la Concorde on foot, walking and taking his way mechanically, and utterly unconscious of the passers-by.

He was studying in minute detail Maxine Berselius, the pose of her head outlined against the tapestry, the curves of her lips that could speak so well without speaking, the little shell-like ears, the brown-gold coils of her hair, her hands, her dress.

He was standing undetermined as to his route, and whether he would cross over to the Rue St. Honoré or turn toward the Seine, when someone gripped his arm from behind, and, turning, he found himself face to face with Dr. Stenhouse, an English physician who had set up in Paris, practising in the Boulevard Haussmann and flourishing exceedingly.

"Well, this is luck," said Stenhouse. "I lost your address, or I would have written, asking you to come and see us. I remembered it was over on the other side of the water somewhere, but where exactly I could not remember. What are you doing with yourself?"

"Nothing, just at present."

"Well, see here. I'm going to the Rue du Mont Thabor to see a patient; walk along with me—it's quite close, just behind the Rue St. Honoré."

They crossed the Place de la Concorde.

"You have finished your post-graduate work, I expect," said Stenhouse. "Are you going to practise in the States?"

"Ultimately, I may," replied Adams. "I have always intended doing so; but I have to feel my way very cautiously, for the money market is not in a particularly flourishing state with me."

"Good heavens!" said Stenhouse, "when is it with a medical man, especially when he is just starting? I've been through that. See here, why don't you start in Paris?"

"Paris?"

"Yes, this is the place to make money. You say you are thinking of starting in some American city; well, let me tell you, there are very few American cities so full of rich Americans as Paris."

"Well," said Adams, "the idea is not a bad one, but just for the present I am fixed. I am going on a big-game shooting expedition to the Congo."

"As doctor?"

"Yes, and the salary is not bad—two thousand francs a month and everything found, to say nothing of the fun."

"And the malaria?"

"Oh, one has to run risks."

"Whom are you going with?"

"A man called Berselius."

"Not Captain Berselius?" asked Stenhouse, stopping dead.

"Yes, Captain Berselius, of No. 14 Avenue Malakoff. I have just returned from having *déjeuner* with him."

Stenhouse whistled. They were in the Rue du Mont Thabor by this, in front of a small *café*.

"Well," said Adams, "what's wrong?"

"Everything," replied the other. "This is the house where my patient lives. Wait for me, for a moment, like a good fellow. I shan't detain you long, and then we can finish our talk, for I have something to tell you."

He darted into the *café* and Adams waited, watching the passers-by and somewhat perturbed in mind. Stenhouse's manner impressed him uncomfortably, for, if Captain Berselius had been the devil, the Englishman could not have put more disfavour into his tone. And he (Adams) had made a compact with Captain Berselius.

The Rue du Mont Thabor is a somewhat gloomy little street, and it fitted Adams's mood as he waited, watching the passers-by and the small affairs of the little shops.

At the end of five minutes Stenhouse returned.

"Well?" said Adams.

"I have had no luncheon yet," replied Stenhouse. "I have been so rushed. Come with me to a little place I know in the Rue St. Honoré, where I can get a cup of tea and a bun. We will talk then."

"Now," said Stenhouse, when he was seated at a little marble-topped table with the cup of tea and the bun before him. "You say you have engaged yourself to go to the Congo with Captain Berselius."

"Yes. What do you know about him?"

"That's just the difficulty. I can only say this, and it's between ourselves, the man's name is a byword for a brute and a devil."

"That's cheerful," said Adams.

"Mind you," said Stenhouse, "he is in the very best society. I have met him at a reception at the Elysée. He goes everywhere. He belongs to the best clubs; he's a *persona grata* at more courts than one, and an intimate friend of King Leopold of Belgium. His immense wealth, or part of it, comes from the rubber industry—motor tires and so forth. And he's mad after big game.

That's his pleasure—killing. He's a killer. That is the best description of the man. The lust of blood is in him, and the astounding thing, to my mind, is that he is not a murderer. He has killed two men in duels, and they say that it is a sight to see him fighting. Mind you, when I say 'murderer,' I do not mean to imply that he is a man who would murder for money. Give the devil his due. I mean that he is quite beyond reason when aroused, and if you were to hit Captain Berselius in the face he would kill you as certain as I'll get indigestion from that bun I have just swallowed. The last doctor he took with him to Africa died at Marseilles from the hardships he went through—not at the hands of Berselius, for that would have aroused inquiry, but simply from the hardships of the expedition; but he gave frightful accounts to the hospital authorities of the way this Berselius had treated the natives. He drove that expedition right away from Libreville, in the French Congo, to God knows where. He had it under martial law the whole time, clubbing and thrashing the niggers at the least offence, and shooting with his own hand two of them who tried to desert."

"You must remember," said Adams, taking up the cudgels for Berselius and almost surprised himself at so doing, "that an expedition like that, if it is not held together by a firm hand, goes to pieces, and the result is disaster for everyone. And you know what niggers are."

"There you are," laughed Stenhouse. "The man has obsessed you already, and you'll come back, if you go, like Bauchardy, the man who died in the hospital at Marseilles, cursing Berselius, yet so magnetized by the power of the chap that you would be ready to follow him again if he said 'Come,' and you had the legs to stand on. That is how Bauchardy was."

"The man, undoubtedly, has a great individuality," said Adams. "Passing him in the street one might take him for a very ordinary person. Meeting him for the first time, he looks all good nature; that smile——"

"Always," said Stenhouse. "Beware of a man with a perpetual smile on his face."

"Yes, I know that, but this smile of Berselius's is not worn as a cloak. It seems quite natural to the man, yet somehow bad, as if it came from a profound and natural cynicism directed against all things—including all things good."

"You have put it," said Stenhouse, "in four words."

"But, in spite of everything," said Adams, "I believe the man to have great good qualities: some instinct tells me so."

"My dear sir," said Stenhouse, "did you ever meet a bad man worth twopence at his trade who had not good qualities? The bad man who is half good—so to speak—is a much more dangerous villain than the barrier bully without heart or soul. When hell makes a super-excellent devil, the devil puts goodness in just as a baker puts soda in his bread to make it rise. Look at Verlaine."

"Well," said Adams, "I have promised Berselius, and I will have to go. Besides, there are other considerations."

He was thinking of Maxine, and a smile lit up his face.

"You seem happy enough about it," said Stenhouse, rising to go. "Well, 'he who will to Cupar maun to Cupar.' When do you start?"

"I don't know yet, but I shall hear to-night."

They passed out into the Rue St. Honoré, where they parted.

"Good luck," said Stenhouse, getting into a *fiacre*.

"Good-bye," replied Adams, waving his hand.

Being in that quarter of the town, and having nothing especial to do, he determined to go to Schaunard's in the Rue de la Paix, and see about his guns.

Schaunard personally superintends his own shop, which is the first gun-shop on the Continent of Europe. Emperors visit him in person and he receives them as an equal, though far superior to them in the science of sport. An old man now, with a long white beard, he remembers the fowling-pieces and rifles which he supplied to the Emperor Maximilian before that unfortunate gentleman started on his fatal expedition in search of a throne. He is a mathematician as well as a maker of guns; his telescopic sights and wind gauges are second to none in the world, and his shop front in the Rue de la Paix exposes no wares—it has just a wire blind, on which are blazoned the arms of Russia, England, and Spain.

But, inside, the place is a joy to a rightly constituted man. Behind glass cases the long processions of guns and rifles, smooth, sleek, nut-brown and deadly, are a sight for the eyes of a sportsman.

The duelling pistol is still a factor in Continental life, and the cases containing them at Schaunard's are worth lingering over, for the modern duelling pistol is a thing of beauty, very different from the murderous hair-trigger machines of Count Considine—though just as deadly.

To Schaunard, pottering amongst his wares, appeared Adams.

The swing-door closed, shutting out the sound of the Rue de la Paix, and the old gun-merchant came forward through the silence of his shop to meet his visitor.

Adams explained his business. He had come to buy some rifles for a big-game expedition. Captain Berselius had recommended him.

"Ah! Captain Berselius?" said Schaunard, and an interested look came into his face. "True, he is a customer of mine. As a matter of fact, his guns for his new expedition are already boxed and directed for Marseilles. Ah, yes—you require a complete outfit, I suppose?"

"Yes," said Adams. "I am going with him."

"Going with Captain Berselius as a friend?"

"No, as a doctor."

"True, he generally takes a doctor with him," said Schaunard, running his fingers through his beard. "Have you had much experience amidst big game, and can you make out your own list of requirements, or shall I help you with my advice?"

"I should be very glad of your advice. No, I have not had much experience in big-game shooting. I have shot bears, that's all——"

"Armand!" cried Schaunard, and a pale-faced young man came forward from the back part of the shop.

"Open me this case."

Armand opened a case, and the deft hand of the old man took down a double-barrelled cordite rifle, light-looking and of exquisite workmanship.

"These are the guns we shoot elephants with nowadays," said Schaunard, handling the weapon lovingly. "A child could carry it, and there is nothing living it will not kill." He laughed softly to himself, and then directed Armand to bring forward an elephant gun of the old pattern. In an instant the young man returned, staggering under the weight of the immense rifle, shod with a heel of india-rubber an inch thick.

Adams laughed, took the thing up with one hand, and raised it to his shoulder as though it had been a featherweight.

"Ah!" said he, "here's a gun worth shooting with."

Schaunard looked on with admiration at the giant handling the gigantic gun.

"Oh, for you," said he, "it's all very well. *Ma foi,* but you suit one another, you both are of another day."

"God bless you," said Adams, "you can pick me up by the bushel in the States. I'm *small*. Say, how much is this thing?"

"*That!*" cried Schaunard. "Why, what on earth could you want with such an obsolete weapon as that?"

"Tell me—does this thing hit harder, gun for gun—not weight for weight, mind you—but gun for gun—than that double-barrel you are holding in your hands?"

"Oh, yes," said Schaunard, "it hits harder, just as a cannon would hit harder, but——"

"I'll have her," said Adams. "I've taken a fancy to her. See here, Captain Berselius is paying for my guns; they are his, part of the expedition—I want this as my own, and I'll pay you for her out of my own pocket. How much is she?"

Schaunard, whose fifty years of trading had explained to him the fact that when an American takes a whim into his head it is best for all parties to let him have his own way, ran his fingers through his beard.

"The thing has no price," said he. "It is a curiosity. But if you must have it—well, I will let you have it for two hundred francs."

"Done," said Adams. "Have you any cartridges?"

"Oh, yes," replied Schaunard. "Heaps. That is to say, I have the old cartridges, and I can have a couple of hundred of them emptied and re-filled and percussioned. Ah, well, monsieur, you must have your own way. Armand, take the gun; have it attended to and packed. And now that monsieur has his play-toy," finished the old man, with one of his silent little laughs, "let us come to business."

They did, and nearly an hour was spent whilst the American chose a double hammerless-ejector cordite rifle and a .256 sporting Mannlicher, for Schaunard was a man who, when he took an interest in a customer, could be very interesting.

When business was concluded Schaunard gave his customer various tips as to the treatment of guns. "And now," said he, opening the door as Adams was taking his departure, "I will give you one more piece of advice about this expedition. It is a piece of private advice, and I will trust you not to tell the Captain that I gave it to you."

"Yes. What is the advice?"

"Don't go."

Adams laughed as he turned on his heel, and Schaunard laughed as he closed the door.

A passer-by might have imagined that the two men had just exchanged a good joke.

Before Adams had taken three steps, the door of the shop re-opened, and Schaunard's voice called again.

"Monsieur."

"Yes?" said Adams, turning.

"You need not pay me for the gun till you come back."

"Right," said Adams, laughing. "I will call in and pay you for it when I come back. *Au revoir.*"

"Adieu."

CHAPTER V
MARSEILLES

On the day of departure Berselius was entertained at *déjeuner* by the Cerele Militaire. He brought Adams with him as a guest.

Nearly all the sporting members of the great club were present to speed the man who after Schillings was reckoned on the Continent the most adventurous big-game hunter in the world.

Despite what Stenhouse, Duthil, and Schaunard had said, Adams by this time inclined to a half-liking for Berselius; the man seemed so far from and unconscious of the little things of the world, so destitute of pettiness, that the half liking which always accompanies respect could not but find a place in Adams's mind.

Guest at a table surrounded by sixty of the wealthiest and most powerful officers of a military nation, Berselius did not forget his companion, but introduced him with painstaking care to the chief men present, included him in his speech of thanks, and made him feel that though he was taking Berselius's pay, he was his friend and on a perfect social equality with him.

Adams felt this keenly. On qualifying first he had obtained an appointment as travelling physician to an American, a prominent member of the New York smart set, a man of twenty-two, a motorist, a yachtsman, clean shaved as an actor and smug as a butler, one of those men who make the great American nation so small in the eyes of the world—the world that cannot see beyond the servants' hall antics of New York society to the great plains where the Adamses hew the wood and draw the water, build the cities and bridge the rivers, and lay the iron roads, making rail-heads of the roar of the Atlantic and the thunder of the Pacific.

This gentleman treated Adams as a paid attendant and in such a manner that Adams one morning lifted him from his bed by the slack of his silk pajamas and all but drowned him in his own bath.

He could not but remember the incident as he sat watching Berselius so calm, so courtly, so absolutely destitute of mannerism, so incontestably the superior, in some magnetic way, of all the other men who were present.

Maxine and M. Pinchon, the secretary, were to accompany them to Marseilles.

A cold, white Paris fog covered the city that night as they drove to the station, and the fog detonators and horns followed them as they glided out slowly from beneath the great glass roof. Slowly at first, then more swiftly over rumbling bridges and clicking point, more swiftly still, breaking from the fog-banked Seine valley, through snarling tunnel and chattering cutting, faster now and freer, by long lines of poplar trees, mist-strewn, and moonlit ponds and fields, spectral white roads, little winking towns; and now, as if drawn by the magnetic south, swaying to the rock-a-bye of speed, aiming for the lights of Dijon far away south, to the tune of the wheels, "seventy-miles-an-hour—seventy-miles-an-hour."

Civilization, whatever else she has done, has written one poem, the "Rapide." True to herself, she makes it pay a dividend, and prostitutes it to the service of stockbrokers, society folk, and gamblers bound for Monaco—but what a poem it is that we snore through between a day in Paris and a day in Marseilles. A poem, swiftly moving, musical with speed, a song built up of songs, telling of Paris, its chill and winter fog, of the winter fields, the poplar trees and mist; vineyards of the Côte d'Or; Provence with the dawn upon it, Tarascon blowing its morning bugle to the sun; the Rhone, and the vineyards, and the olives, and the white, white roads; ending at last in that triumphant blast of music, light and colour, Marseilles.

La Joconde, Berselius's yacht, was berthed at the Messagerie wharf, and after *déjeuner* at the Hotel Noailles, they took their way there on foot.

Adams had never seen the south before as Marseilles shows it. The vivid light and the black shadows, the variegated crowd of the Canabier Prolongue had for him an "Arabian Nights" fascination, but the wharves held a deeper fascination still.

Marseilles draws its most subtle charm from far away in the past. Beaked triremes have rubbed their girding cables against the wharves of the old Phocée; the sunshine of a thousand years has left some trace of its gold, a mirage in the air chilled by the mistral and perfumed by the ocean.

At Marseilles took place the meeting between Mary Magdalen and Laeta Acilia, so delightfully fabled by Anatole France. The Count of Monte Cristo landed here after he had discovered his treasure, and here Caderouse after the infamy at "La Reservée" watched old Dantès starving to death.

Multitudes of ships, fabled and real, have passed from the harbour to countries curious and strange, but never one of them to a stranger country than that to which *La Joconde* was to bear Berselius and his companion.

Gay as Naples with colour, piercing the blue sky with a thousand spars, fluttering the flags of all nations to the wind, shot through with the sharp rattle of winch-chains, and perfumed with garlic, vanilla, fumes of coal tar, and the tang of the sea, the wharves of Marseilles lay before the travellers, a great counter eternally vibrating to the thunder of trade; bales of carpets from the Levant, tons of cheeses from Holland, wood from Norway, copra, rice, tobacco, corn, silks from China and Japan, cotton from Lancashire; all pouring in to the tune of the winch-pauls, the cry of the stevedores, and the bugles of Port Saint Jean, shrill beneath the blue sky and triumphant as the crowing of the Gallic cock.

Between the breaks in the shipping one could see the sea-gulls fishing and the harbour flashing, here spangled with coal tar, here whipped to deepest sapphire by the mistral; the junk shops, grog shops, parrot shops, rope-walks, ships' stores and factories lining the quays, each lending a perfume, a voice, or a scrap of colour to the air vibrating with light, vibrating with sound, shot through with voices; hammer blows from the copper sheathers in the dry docks, the rolling of drums from Port St. Nicholas, the roaring of grain elevators, rattling of winch-chains, trumpeting of ship sirens, mewing of gulls, the bells of Notre Dame and the bells of St. Victor, all fused, orchestrated, into one triumphant symphony beneath the clear blue sky and the trade flags of the world.

La Joconde was berthed beside a Messagerie boat which they had to cross to reach her.

She was a palatial cruising yacht of twelve hundred tons' burden, built somewhat on the lines of Drexel's *La Margharita,* but with less width of funnel.

It was two o'clock in the afternoon when they went on board; all the luggage had arrived, steam was up, the port arrangements had been made, and Berselius determined to start at once.

Maxine kissed him, then she turned to Adams.

"Bon voyage."

"Good-bye," said Adams.

He held her hand for a fraction of a second after his grasp had relaxed.

Then she was standing on the deck of the Messagerie boat, waving good-bye across the lane of blue water widening between *La Joconde* and her berth mate.

At the harbour mouth, looking back across the blue wind-swept water, he fancied he could still see her, a microscopic speck in the great picture of terraced Marseilles, with its windows, houses, flags, and domes glittering and burning in the sun.

Then the swell of the Gulf of Lyons took *La Joconde* as a nurse takes an infant and rocks it on her knee, and France and civilization were slowly wrapped from sight under the veils of distance.

PART TWO

CHAPTER VI
MATADI

It was evening. *La Joconde*, Berselius's yacht, lay moored at the wharf of Matadi; warpling against the starboard plates, whimpering, wimpling, here smooth as glass, here eddied and frosted, a sea of golden light, a gliding mirror, went the Congo.

A faint, faint haze dulled the palms away on the other side; from the wharf, where ships were loading up with rubber, ivory, palm-oil, and bales of gum copal, the roar and rattle of steam-winches went across the water, far away across the glittering water, where the red flamingoes were flying, to that other shore where the palm trees showed their fringe of hot and hazy green.

The impression of heat which green, the coolest of all colours, can produce, damp heat, heart-weakening heat, that is the master impression produced by the Congo on the mind of man. All the other impressions are—to paraphrase Thénard—embroideries on this.

Yet how many other impressions there are! The Congo is Africa in a frank mood. Africa, laying her hand on her heart and speaking, or rather, whispering the truth.

This great river flooding from Stanley Pool and far away beyond, draws with it, like a moving dream, the pictures of the roaring rapids and the silent pools, the swamps filled with darkness of vegetation and murderous life; the unutterable loneliness of vast forests. The water brook of the hartbeest and antelope, it brings with it their quiet reflections, just as it brings the awful horn and the pig-like face of the rhinoceros. What things have not slaked their thirst in this quiet water flooding past Matadi—and wallowed in it? Its faint perfume hints at that.

On the deck of the yacht, under the double awning, Berselius was seated, and, close to him, Adams. They had arrived only yesterday, and to-morrow they were proceeding by rail to Leopoldville, which was to be the real base of the expedition, leaving *La Joconde* behind at Matadi.

The yacht would return to France.

"What a lot of stuff they are loading on those ships," said Adams, turning in his chair as the roar and rattle of the winch chains, that had ceased for a moment, flared up again like a flame of sound. "What are the exports here?"

"Gum copal—nuts—rubber—tusks—everything you can get out of there," answered Berselius, lazily waving a hand to indicate the Congo basin.

Adams, leaning back in his deck chair, followed with his eyes the sweep of Berselius's hand, "over there"; little did he dream of what those words held in their magic.

Then Berselius went below.

The moon rose; lights speckled the misty wharf and a broad road of silver lay stretched across the moving water to the other bank that, under the moonlight, lay like a line of cotton-wool. It was the mist tangled by and tangling the trees.

Adams paced the deck, smoking and occasionally pausing to flip off his cigar-ash on the bulwark rail. He was thinking of Maxine Berselius. She had come to Marseilles to see them off, and——

Not a word had been exchanged between them that a third person did not hear or might not have heard, yet they had told each other the whole of that delightful story in which the hero is I and the heroine You.

Adams on his side and Maxine on hers did not in the least contemplate possibilities. A social river, wide as the Congo, and flowing from as mysterious a source, lay between them. Maxine was rich—so rich that the contrast of her wealth with his own poverty shut the door for Adams on the idea of marriage. He could not hope to take his true place in the world for years, and he would not stoop to take a woman's money or assistance.

He was too big to go through a back door. No, he would enter the social temple by walking between the pillars of the portico, or smashing an entrance way through the wall with his fist.

He was a type of the true American man, the individual who trusts in himself; an unpleasant person very often, but the most essentially male creation in Nature.

Though he could not contemplate Maxine as a wife, he did as a woman. In a state of savagery he would have carried her off in his arms; surrounded as he was by the trammels of civilization, he contented himself with imagining her in that position.

It is quite possible that no other woman would ever inspire the same passion in him. He knew this, yet he did not grumble; for he was practical, and his practical nature had a part in his wildest dreams.

Go to New York and look at the twenty-storied, sky-scrapers built by the Adamses. They look like houses out of a story by Dean Swift. The wildest dreams of architecture. Yet they don't fall down; they serve their purpose, for the dreamers who built them were at bottom practical men.

As he paced the deck, smoking and contemplating the moonlit river, Maxine gave place in his mind to her father.

Berselius up to this had shown himself in no unfavourable light. Up to this he had been almost companionable.

Almost! They had dined together, paced the deck together, discussed all sorts of subjects, yet not by the fraction of an inch had he advanced in his knowledge of the man. A wall of ice divided Berselius from his fellow-men. Between him and them a great gulf was fixed, a gulf narrow enough to speak across, but of an impenetrable depth. Berselius was always so assured, so impassively calm, so authoritative, his conversation so penetrative, so lit by intuition and acquired knowledge, that Adams sometimes in his company felt that elation which comes to us when we find ourselves in the presence of a supreme mind. At other times this overpowering personality weighed upon him so much that he would leave the saloon and pace the deck so as to become himself again.

Next morning they left by rail for Leopoldville, where they found waiting for them the *Leopold*, a shallow-draught steamer of some two hundred tons.

CHAPTER VII
YANDJALI

The *Leopold* was officered entirely by Belgians, and it would have been almost impossible to find a pleasanter set of men. Tilkins, the captain, especially, won Adams's regard. He was a huge man, with a wife and family in Antwerp, and he was eternally damning the Congo and wishing himself back in Antwerp.

They transhipped to a smaller boat, the *Couronne*, and one morning shortly after breakfast three strokes on the steamer bell announced their approach to Yandjali.

Imagine a rough landing-stage, a handful of houses, mostly mud-built, the funereal heat-green of palm and banana, a flood of tropical sunshine lighting the little wharf, crammed with bales of merchandise.

Such was Yandjali, and beyond Yandjali lay the forest, and in front of Yandjali flowed the river, and years ago *boom-boom* down the river's shining surface, from away up there where the great palms gave place to reeds and water-grass, you might have heard the sound of the hippopotami bellowing to the sun, a deep organ note, unlike the sound emitted by any other creature on earth. You do not hear it now. The great brutes have long ago been driven away by man.

On the wharf to greet the steamer stood the District Commissioner, Commander Verhaeren; behind him six or seven half-naked, savage-looking blacks, each topped with a red fez and armed with an Albini rifle, stood gazing straight before them with wrinkled eyes at the approaching boat.

Verhaeren and Berselius were seemingly old friends; they shook hands and Berselius introduced Adams; then the three left the wharf and walked up to the District Commissioner's house, a frame building surrounded by palm trees and some distance from the mud huts of the soldiers and porters.

The Yandjali of this story, not to be confounded with Yandjali notorious in Congo history for its massacre, is not in a rubber district, though on the fringe of one; it is a game district and produces cassava. The Congo State has parcelled out its territory. There are the rubber districts, the gum copal districts, the food districts, and the districts where ivory is obtained. In each of these districts the natives are made to work and bring in rubber, gum copal, food, or ivory, as a tax. The District Commissioner, or *Chef de Poste*, in each district draws up a schedule of what is required. Such and such a village must produce and hand over so many kilos of rubber, or copal, so much cassava, so many tusks, etc.

Verhaeren was a stout, pale-faced man, with a jet-black beard, a good-tempered looking man, with that strange, lazy, semi-Oriental look which the Belgian face takes when the owner of it is fixed to a post, with nothing to do but oversee trade, and when the post is on the confines of civilization.

Away up country, lost in the dim, green, heat-laden wilderness, you will find a different type of man; more alert and nervy, a man who never smiles, a preoccupied looking man who, ten years or five years ago, lost his berth in an office for misconduct, or his commission in the army. A *déclassé*. He is the man who really drives the Congo machine, the last wheel in the engine, but the most important; the man whose deeds are not to be written.

Verhaeren's living room in the frame house was furnished with steamer deck chairs, a table and some shelves. Pinned to the wall and curling up at the corners was a page torn from *La Gaudriole*, the picture of a girl in tights; on one of the shelves lay a stack of old newspapers, on another a stack of official papers, reports from subordinates, invoices, and those eternal "official letters," with which the Congo Government deluges its employees, and whose everlasting purport is "Get more ivory, get more rubber, get more copal."

Verhaeren brought out some excellent cigars and a bottle of Vanderhum, and the three men smoked and talked. He had acted as Berselius's agent for the expedition, and had collected all the gun-bearers and porters necessary, and a guide. It was Berselius's intention to strike a hundred miles west up river almost parallel to the Congo, and then south into the heart of the elephant country. They talked of the expedition, but Verhaeren showed little knowledge of the work and no enthusiasm. The Belgians of the Congo have no feeling for sport. They never hunt the game at their doors, except for food.

When they had discussed matters, Verhaeren led the way out for Berselius to inspect his arrangements.

The porters were called up. There were *forty* of them, and Adams thought that he had never before seen such a collection of depressed looking individuals; they were muscular enough, but there was something in their faces, their movements and their attitude, that told a tale of spirits broken to servitude by terror.

The four gun-bearers and the headman were very different. The headman was a Zappo Zap, a ferocious looking nigger, fez-tipped, who could speak twenty words of French, and who was nicknamed Félix. The gun-bearers were recruited from the "soldiers" of the state by special leave from headquarters.

Adams looked with astonishment at the immense amount of luggage they were bringing. "Chop boxes," such as are used on the east coast, contained stores; two big tents, a couple of "Roorkee" chairs, folding-beds and tables, cork mattresses, cooking utensils, made up the pile, to say nothing of the guns which had just been taken from their cases.

"What did you bring this thing for?" asked Berselius, pointing to Adams's elephant gun, which the Zappo Zap headman was just stripping from its covering.

"To shoot with," said Adams, laughing.

Berselius looked at the big man handling the big gun, and gave a short laugh.

"Well, bring it," said he; "but I don't envy your gun-bearers."

But Félix, the headman, did not seem of the same opinion. The enormous rifle evidently appealed to his ferocious heart. It was a god-gun this, and no mistake, and its lustre evidently spread to Adams, the owner of it.

Félix was a very big man, almost as big as Adams: a member of the great cannibal fighting tribe of Zappo Zaps, he had followed Verhaeren, who had once held a post in the Bena Pianga country, to Yandjali; he had a sort of attachment for Verhaeren, which showed that he possessed some sort of heart. All the Zappo Zaps have been enrolled by the Congo Government as "soldiers"; they have a bad name and cause a lot of heart-searching to the Brussels administration, for when they are used in punitive expeditions to burn villages of recalcitrant rubber-getters, they, to use a local expression, "*will* eat when they have killed." When they are used *en masse*, the old cannibal instinct breaks out; when the killing is over they go for the killed, furious as dogs over bones. God help the man who would come between them and their food!

Of these men Félix was a fine specimen. A nature man, ever ready to slay, and cruel as Death. A man from the beginning of the world.

If Félix had possessed a wife, he and she might have stood for the man and woman mentioned by Thénard in his lecture.

The basic man and woman in whose dim brains Determination had begun to work, sketching the vague line on either side of which lies the Right and Left of moral action.

A true savage, never to be really civilized. For it is the fate of the savage that he will never become one of us. Do what you will and pray how you will, you will never make up for the million years that have passed him by, the million years during which the dim sketch which is the basis of all ethics has lain in his brain undeveloped, or developed only into a few fantastic and abortive God shapes and devil shapes.

He will never become one of us. Extraordinary paradox—he never can become a Leopold or a Félix Fuchs!

Berselius disbanded the porters with a wave of the hand, and he and his companions began a round of the station. Verhaeren, with a cigar in his mouth, led the way.

He opened the door of a go-down, and Adams in the dim light, saw bale upon bale of stuff; gum copal it proved to be, for Yandjali tapped a huge district where this stuff is found, and which lies forty miles to the south. There was also cassava in large quantities, and the place had a heady smell, as if fermentation were going on amidst the bales.

Verhaeren shut the door and led on till, rounding a corner, a puff of hot air brought a stench which caused Adams to choke and spit.

Verhaeren laughed.

It was the Hostage House that sent its poisonous breath to meet them.

A native corporal and two soldiers stood at the palisade which circled the Hostage House. The women and children had just been driven back from the fields where they had been digging and weeding, and they had been served with their wretched dinners. They were eating these scraps of food like animals, some in the sun amidst the tufts of grass and mounds of ordure in the little yard, some in the shadow of the house.

There were old, old women like shrivelled monkeys; girls of twelve and fifteen, some almost comely; middle-aged women, women about to become mothers, and a woman who had become a mother during the past night lying there in the shelter of the Hostage House. There were little pot-bellied nigger children, tiny black dots, who had to do their bit of work in the fields with the others; and when the strangers appeared and looked over the rail, these folk set up a crying and chattering, and ran about distractedly, not knowing what new thing was in store for them. They were the female folk and children of a village, ten miles away south; they were here as "hostages," because the village had not produced its full tale of cassava. They had been here over a month.

The soldiers laughed, and struck with the butts of their rifles on the palisading, as if to increase the confusion. Adams noticed that the young girls and women were of all the terrified crowd seemingly the most terrified. He did not know the reason; he could not even guess it. A good man himself, and believing in a God in heaven, he could not guess the truth. He knew nothing of the reason of these women's terror, and he looked with disgust at the scene before him, not entirely comprehending. Those creatures, so filthy, so animal-like, created in his mind such abhorrence that he forgot to make allowances for the fact that they were penned like swine, and that perchance in their own native state, free in their own villages, they might be cleaner and less revolting. He could not hear the dismal cry of the "Congo niggers," who of all people on the earth are the most miserable, the most abused, the most sorrow-stricken, the most dumb. He did not know that he was looking at one of the filthy acts in the great drama that a hundred years hence will be read with horror by a more enlightened world.

They turned from the degrading sight and went back to Verhaeren's house for dinner.

CHAPTER VIII
THE VOICE OF THE CONGO FOREST

Just after daybreak next morning the expedition started.

Berselius, Adams, the gun-bearers and Félix headed the line; a long way after came the porters and their loads, shepherded by half a dozen soldiers of the state specially hired for the business.

Before they had gone a mile on their route the sun was blazing strongly, sharp bird-calls came from the trees, and from the porters tramping under their loads a hum like the hum of an awakened beehive. These people will talk and chatter when the sun rises; club them, or threaten them, or load them with burdens as much as you please, the old instinct of the birds and beasts remains.

At first the way led through cassava and manioc fields and past clumps of palms; then, all at once, and like plunging under a green veil or into the heart of a green wave, they entered the forest.

The night chill was just leaving the forest, the great green gloom, festooned with fantastic rope-like tendrils, was drinking the sunlight with a million tongues; you could hear the rustle and snap of branches straightening themselves and sighing toward heaven after the long, damp, chilly night. The tropical forest at daybreak flings its arms up to the sun as if to embrace him, and all the teeming life it holds gives tongue. Flights of coloured and extraordinary birds rise like smoke wreaths from the steaming leaves, and the drone of a million, million insects from the sonorous depths comes like the sound of life in ferment.

The river lay a few miles to their left, and faintly from it, muffled by the trees, they could hear the shrill whistling of the river steamboat. It was like the "good-bye" of civilization.

The road they were pursuing through the forest was just a dim track beaten down by the feet of the copal and cassava gatherers bearing their loads to Yandjali. Here and there the forest thinned out and a riot of umbrella thorns, vicious, sword-like grass and tall, dull purple flowers, like hollyhocks made a scrub that choked the way and tangled the foot; then the trees would thicken up, and with the green gloom of a mighty wave the forest would fall upon the travellers and swallow them up.

Adams, tramping beside Berselius, tried vainly to analyze the extraordinary and new sensations to which this place gave birth in him.

The forest had taken him. It seemed to him, on entering it, that he had died to all the things he had ever known. At Yandjali he had felt himself in a foreign country, but still in touch with Europe and the past; a mile deep in the forest and Yandjali itself, savage as it was, seemed part of the civilization and the life he had left behind him.

The forests of the old world may be vast, but their trees are familiar. One may lose one's direction, but one can never lose *oneself* amidst the friendly pines, the beeches, the oaks, whose forms have been known to us from childhood.

But here, where the beard-moss hangs from unknown trees, as we tramp through the sweltering sap-scented gloom, we feel ourselves not in a forest but under a cover.

There is nothing of the perfume of the pine, nothing of the breeze in the branches, nothing of the beauty of the forest twilight here. We are in a great green room, festooned with vines and tendrils and hung about with leaves. Nothing is beautiful here, but everything is curious. It is a curiosity shop, where one pays with the sweat of one's brow, with the languor of one's body, and the remembrance of one's past, for the sight of an orchid shaped like a bird, or a flower shaped like a jug, or a bird whose flight is a flash of sapphire dust.

A great green room, where echo sounds of things unknown.

You can see nothing but the foliage, and the tree boles just around, yet the place is full of life and war and danger.

That crash followed by the shrieking of birds—you cannot tell whether it is half a mile away or quite close, or to the right, or to the left, or whether it is caused by a branch torn from a tree by some huge hand, or a tree a hundred years old felled at last by Time.

Time is the woodman of the Congo forests. Nobody else could do the work, and he works in his own lazy fashion, leaving things to right themselves and find their own salvation.

Just as there is eternal war to the death between the beasts of this jungle, so there is war to the death between the trees, the vines, and the weeds. A frightful battle between the vegetable things is going on; we scarcely recognize it, because the processes are so slow, but if five years of the jungle could be photographed week by week, and the whole series be run rapidly off on some huge cinematograph machine, you would see a heaving and rending struggle for existence, vegetation fed by the roaring tropical rains rising like a giant and flinging itself on the vegetation of yesterday; vines lengthening like snakes, tree felling tree, and weed choking weed.

Even in the quietude of a moment, standing and looking before one at the moss-bearded trees and the python-like loops of the lianas, one can see the struggle crystallized, just as in the still marble of the Laocoon one sees the struggle of life with death.

In this place which covers an unthinkable area of the earth, a vast population has dwelt since the beginning of time. Think of it. Shut off from the world which has progressed toward civilization, alone with the beasts and the trees, they have lived here without a guide and without a God. The instinct which teaches the birds to build nests taught them to build huts; the herd-instinct drove them into tribes.

Then, ages ago, before Christ was crucified, before Moses was born, began the terrible and pathetic attempt of a predamned people to raise their heads and walk erect. The first lifting of purblind eyes destined never to see even the face of Art.

Yet there was a germ of civilization amongst them. They had villages and vague laws and art of a sort; the ferocious tribes drew to one side, hunting beasts and warring with each other, and the others, the milder and kindlier tribes, led their own comparatively quiet life; and Mohammed was born somewhere in the unknown North, and they knew nothing of the fact till the Arab slavers raided them, and robbed them of men and women and children, just as boys rob an orchard.

But the birth of Christ and the foundation of Christendom was the event which in far distant years was destined to be this unhappy people's last undoing.

They had known the beasts of the forests, the storms, the rains, the Arab raiders, but Fate had reserved a new thing for them to know. The Christians. Alas! that one should have to say it, but here the fact is, that white men, Christian men, have taken these people, have drawn under the banner of Christianity and under Christian pay all the warlike tribes, armed them, and set them as task-masters over the humble and meek. And never in the history of the world has such a state of servitude been known as at present exists in the country of this forlorn people.

They had been marching some three hours when, from ahead came a sound as of some huge animal approaching. Berselius half turned to his gun-bearer for his rifle, but Félix reassured him.

"Cassava bearers," said Félix.

It was, in fact, a crowd of natives; some thirty or forty, bearing loads of Kwanga (cassava cakes) to Yandjali. They were coming along the forest path in single file, their burdens on their heads, and when the leaders saw the white men they stopped dead. A great chattering broke out. One could hear it going back all along the unseen line, a rattlesnake of sound. Then Félix called out to them; the gun-bearers and the white men stood aside, and the cassava bearers, taking heart, advanced.

They were heavily laden, for most of them had from ten to twenty Kwanga on their heads, and besides this burden—they were mostly women—several of them had babies slung on their backs.

These people belonged to a village which lay within Verhaeren's district. The tax laid on this village was three hundred cakes of cassava to be delivered at Yandjali every eight days.

The people of this village were a lazy lot, and if you have ever collected taxes in England, you can fancy the trouble of making such people—savages living in a tropical forest, who have no count of time and scarcely an idea of numbers—pay up.

Especially when one takes into consideration the fact that to produce three hundred cakes of cassava every eight days, the whole village must work literally like a beehive, the men gathering and the women grinding the stuff from dawn till dark.

Only by the heaviest penalties could such a desirable state of things be brought about, and the heavier and sharper the punishments inflicted at any one time, the easier was it for Verhaeren to work these people.

Adams watched the cassava bearers as they passed at a trot. They went by like automatic figures, without raising their eyes from the ground. There were some old women amongst them who looked more like shrivelled monkeys than human beings; extraordinary anatomical specimens, whose muscles, working as they ran, were as visible as though no skin covered them. There were young women, young children, and women far advanced in pregnancy; and they all went by like automatic figures, clockwork marionettes.

It was a pitiable spectacle enough, these laden creatures, mute looking as dumb beasts; but there was nothing especially to shock the eye of the

European, for it is the long-prepared treason against this people, devised and carried out by nature, that their black mask covers a multitude of other people's sins and their own untold sufferings.

Had they been white, the despairing look, the sunken eyes, the hundred signs that tell of suffering and slavery would have been visible, would have appealed to the heart; but the black mass could not express these things fully. They were niggers, uglier looking and more depressed looking than other niggers—that was all.

And so Adams passed on, without knowing what he had seen and the only impression the sight made on his mind was one of disgust.

One fact his professional eye noticed as the crowd passed by. Four of the women had lost their left hands.

The hands had been amputated just above the wrist in three cases, and one woman had suffered amputation at the middle of the forearm.

He spoke of this to Berselius, who did not seem to hear his remark.

At noon they halted for a three hours' rest, and then pushed on, camping for the night, after a twenty-five miles' journey, in a break of the forest.

CHAPTER IX
BIG GAME

Just as going along the coast by Pondoland one sees English park scenery running down to the very sea edge, so the Congo has its surprises in strips of country that might, as far as appearance goes, have been cut out of Europe and planted here.

This glade which Félix had chosen for a camping place was strewn with rough grass and studded here and there with what at first sight seemed apple trees: they were in reality thorns.

The camp was pitched and the fires lit on the edge of the forest, and then Berselius proceeded to take tale of his people and found one missing. One of the cook boys had dropped behind and vanished. He had been lame shortly after the start. The soldiers had not seen him drop behind, but the porters had.

"How many miles away was it?" asked Berselius of the collected porters.

"Nkoto, nkoto (Very many, very many)," the answer came in a chorus, for a group of savages, if they have the same idea in common, will all shout together in response to an answer, like one man.

"Why had they not told?"

"We did not know," came the irrelevant answer in chorus.

Berselius knew quite well that they had not told simply from heedlessness and want of initiative. He would have flogged the whole lot soundly, but he wanted them fresh for the morrow's work. Cutting down their rations would but weaken them, and as for threatening to dock their pay, such a threat has no effect on a savage.

"Look!" said Berselius.

He had just dismissed the porters with a reprimand when his keen eye caught sight of something far up the glade. It wanted an hour of sunset.

Adams, following the direction in which Berselius was gazing, saw, a great distance off, to judge by the diminishing size of the thorn trees, a form that made his heart to leap in him.

Massive and motionless, a great creature stood humped in the level light; the twin horns back-curving and silhouetted against the sky told him at once what it was.

"Bull rhinoceros," said Berselius. "Been lying up in the thick stuff all day; come out to feed." He made a sign to Félix who, knowing exactly what was wanted, dived into the tent and came back with a .400 cordite rifle and Adams's elephant gun.

"Come," said Berselius, "the brute is evidently thinking. They stay like that for an hour sometimes. If we have any luck, we may get a shot sideways before he moves. There's not a breath of wind."

They started, Félix following with the guns.

"I would not bother about him," said Berselius, "only the meat will be useful, and it will be an experience for you. You will take first shot, and, if he charges, aim just behind the shoulder—that's the spot for a rhino if you can reach it; for other animals aim at the neck, no matter what animal it is, or whether it is a lion or a buck; the neck shot is the knock-out blow. I have seen a lion shot through the heart travel fifty yards and kill a man; had he been struck in the neck he would have fallen in his tracks."

"Cow," said Félix from behind.

Out of the thick stuff on the edge of the forest another form had broken. She was scarcely smaller than the bull, but the horns were shorter; she was paler in colour, too, and showed up not nearly so well. Then she vanished into the thick stuff, but the bull remained standing, immovable as though he were made of cast iron, and the two awful horns, now more distinct, cut the background like scimitars.

The rhinoceros, like the aboriginal native of the Congo, has come straight down from pre-Adamite days almost without change. He is half blind now; he can scarcely see twenty yards, he is still moving in the night of the ancient world, and the smell of a man excites the wildest apprehension in his vestige of a mind. He scents you, flings his heavy head from side to side, and then to all appearances he charges you.

Nothing could appear more wicked, ferocious, and full of deadly intent than this charge; yet, in reality, the unfortunate brute is not seeking you at all, but running away from you; for the rhino when running away always runs in the direction from which the wind is blowing. You are in that direction, else your scent could not reach him; as your scent grows stronger and stronger, the more alarmed does he become and the quicker he runs. Now he sights you, or you fire. If you miss, God help you, for he charges the flash with all his fright suddenly changed to fury.

They had got within four hundred yards from the brute when a faint puff of wind stirred the grass, and instantly the rhino shifted his position.

"He's got our scent," said Berselius, taking the cordite rifle from Félix, who handed his gun also to Adams. "He's got it strong. We will wait for him here."

The rhino, after a few uneasy movements, began to "run about." One could see that the brute was ill at ease; he went in a half-circle, and then, the wind increasing, and bringing the scent strong, he headed straight for Berselius and his companions, and charged.

The sound of him coming was like the sound of a great drum beaten by a lunatic.

"Don't fire till I give the word," cried Berselius, "and aim just behind the shoulder."

Adams, who was to the left of the charging beast, raised the rifle and looked down the sights. He knew that if he missed, the brute would charge the flash and be on him perhaps before he could give it the second barrel.

It was exactly like standing before an advancing express engine. An engine, moreover, that had the power of leaving the metals to chase you should you not derail it.

Would Berselius never speak! Berselius all the time was glancing from the rhino to Adams.

"Fire!"

The ear-blasting report of the elephant gun echoed from the forest, and the rhino, just as if he had been tripped by an invisible wire fence, fell, tearing up the ground and squealing like a pig.

"Good," said Berselius.

Adams wiped the sweat from his forehead with the back of his hand. He had never gone through a moment of more deadly nerve tension.

He was moving toward his quarry, now stretched stiff and stark, when he was arrested by Félix.

"Cow," said Félix again.

The cow had broken cover at the report of the gun and had got their wind.

Just as two automatic figures of the same make will, when wound up, and touched off, perform the same actions, the cow did exactly what the bull had done—ran about in a fierce and distressed manner and then charged right in the eye of the wind.

"Mine," said Berselius, and he went forward twenty paces to meet her.

Berselius, chilling and aloof to the point of mysteriousness, had, since the very starting of the expedition, shown little of his true character to his companion. What he had shown up to this had not lowered Adams's respect for him.

Self-restraint seemed the mainspring of that commanding force which this strange man exercised. His reprimand to the porters for the loss of the boy, expressed in a few quiet words, had sent them shivering to their places, cowed and dumb. Animal instinct seemed to tell them of a terrible animal which the self-restraint of that quiet-looking little man, with the pointed beard, alone prevented from breaking upon them.

Berselius had allowed the bull to approach to a little over a hundred yards before letting Adams fire. He had gauged the American's nerve to a nicety and his power of self-restraint, and he knew that beyond the hundred-yard limit he dared not trust them; for no man born of woman who has not had a good experience of big game can stand up to a charging rhinoceros and take certain aim when the hundred-yard limit has been passed.

The thunderous drumming of the oncoming brute echoed from the forest. Had its head been a feather-pillow the impact of the three tons of solid flesh moving behind it would have been certain death; but the head was an instrument of destruction, devised when the megatherium walked the world, and the long raking horn would have ripped up an elephant as easily as a sharp penknife rips up a rabbit.

Before this thing, and to the right of it, rifle in hand, stood Berselius. He did not even lift the gun to his shoulder till the hundred-yard limit was passed, and then he hung on his aim so horribly that Adams felt the sweat-drops running on his face like ants, and even Félix swallowed like a man who is trying to choke down something nauseous. It was a magnificent exhibition of daring and self-restraint and cool assurance.

At twenty-five yards or a little under, the cordite rang out. The brute seemed to trip, just as the other had done, over some invisible taut-stretched wire, and skidding with its own impetus, squealing, striking out and tearing up the grass, it came right up to Berselius's feet before stiffening in death. Like the great automaton it was, it had scented the human beings just as the bull had scented them, "fussed" just as he had fussed, charged as he had charged, and died as he had died.

And now from the camp rose a great outcry, "Nyama, nyama! (Meat, meat!)." From the soldiers, from the gun-bearers, from the porters it came. There were no longer soldiers, or gun-bearers, or porters; every distinction was forgotten; they were all savages, voicing the eternal cry of the jungle, "Nyama, nyama! (Meat, meat!)."

In the last rays of the sunset the two gigantic forms lay stretched forever in death. They lay as they had composed themselves after that long stiff stretch which every animal takes before settling itself for eternal sleep; and Adams stood looking at the great grinning masks tipped with the murderous horns, whilst Berselius, with his gun butt resting on his boot, stood watching with a brooding eye as the porters and gun-bearers swarmed like ants around the slain animals and proceeded, under his direction, to cut them up. Then the meat was brought into camp. The tails and the best parts of the carcasses, including the kidneys, were reserved for the white men, and the rations from the rest of the meat were served out; but a dozen porters who had been last in the line, and who were accountable for letting the boy drop behind, got nothing.

It was pitiable to see their faces. But they deserved their punishment, notwithstanding the fact that in the middle of the meat distribution the missing boy limped into camp. He had a thorn half an inch long in his foot, which Adams extracted. Then the camp went to bed.

Adams in his tent under the mosquito net slept soundly and heard and knew nothing of the incidents of the night. Berselius was also sleeping soundly when, at about one o'clock in the morning, Félix aroused him.

One of the porters had been caught stealing some of the meat left over from the distribution of the night before.

The extraordinary thing was that he had fed well, not being one of the proscribed. He had stolen from pure greed.

He was an undersized man, a weakling, and likely to break down and give trouble anyway. His crime was great.

Berselius sent Félix to his tent for a Mauser pistol. Then the body was flung into the forest where the roaring, rasping cry of a leopard was splitting the dark.

CHAPTER X
M'BASSA

Seven days' march took them one hundred and twenty miles east of Yandjali and into the heart of the great rubber district of M'Bonga.

Twenty miles a day ought to have been covered on an average, but they had delayed here and there to shoot, and the extra porters, whose duty it was to carry the trophies, were already in requisition.

It had been forest most of the way, but forest broken by open spaces; they had crossed two great swards of park-like country where the antelope herds moved like clouds, marvellous natural preserves that might have been English but for the tropic haze and heat and the great n'sambya trees with their yellow bell-like blossoms, the m'binas with their bursts of scarlet bloom, the tall feather-palms, and the wild papaws of the adjoining woods.

But in the last two days of the march the forest had thickened and taken a more sombre note; nothing they had come upon heretofore had been quite so wild as this, so luxuriant and tropical. It was the haunt of the rubber vine, that mysterious plant which requires a glass-house atmosphere and a soil especially rich. The great rubber forest of M'Bonga, thousands of square miles in extent, is really composed of two forests joined by an isthmus of woods. Dimly, it is shaped like an hourglass; south of the constriction where the two forests join lies the elephant country for which Berselius was making, and Félix had led them so craftily and well, that they struck into the rubber district only fifty miles from the constriction.

In the forest, thirty miles from the elephant ground, lies the Belgian fort M'Bassa. They were making for this place now, which was to be the base from which they would start on the great hunt.

The fort of M'Bassa is not used to-day as a fort, only as a collecting-place for rubber. In the early days it was a very necessary entrenchment for the Belgians, as a tribe almost as warlike as the Zappo Zaps terrorized the districts; but the people of this tribe have long been brought under the blue flag with the white star. They are now "soldiers," and their savagery, like a keen tool, has been turned to good account by the Government.

In the great forest of M'Bonga the rubber vines are not equally distributed. Large areas occur in which they are not found; only in the most desolate places do they grow. You cannot tame and prune and bring the rubber vine into subjection; it will have nothing to do with the vineyard and the field; it chooses to grow alone.

Everything else comes to its harvest with a joyous face, but the rubber vine, like a dark green snake, fearful of death, has to be hunted for.

Even in the areas of the forest which it frequents, it is only to be found in patches, so the harvesters cannot go in a body, as men do to the harvesting of the corn, or the cotton, or the grape; they have to break up into small parties and these again subdivide, leaving a single individual here and there where the vines are thickest. He, entirely alone, at the mercy of the evil spirits that are in his imagination and the beasts that are in the forest, makes a rude shelter out of boughs and leaves, and sets to work making incisions in the vine and draining them drop by drop of their viscous sap.

Sometimes he sings over this monotonous work, and in the long rains between the intervals of the shower-bath roarings you can hear the ululations of these folk through the drip of the leaves, and at night the spark-like glimmer of their fires dots the reeking gloom.

These are the conditions of the rubber collector's task, and it is not a task that ever can be finished; year in, year out, it never ceases.

These woods through which Félix led them were to the woods near Yandjali what the music of Beethoven is to the music of Mozart.

Immense and gloomy symphonies. The trees were huge, and groaned beneath the weight of lianas cable-thick. At times they had to burst their way through the veils of leaves and vines, the porters losing themselves and calling one to the other, and the head of the expedition halting till the stragglers were collected; at times the ground they trod on was like grease from the cast-down fruit of the plantains that grew here enormous, and sodden, and dismal, showering their fruit in such quantities that the bush-pigs, devour as they might, could never dispose of it all.

On some of the trees, like huge withered leaves, hung bats, and from some of the trees the beard-moss hung yards long, and of a spectral gray; the very weeds trodden underfoot were sappy, and the smell of their squirting juice mixed itself with the smell of decay.

It was not even ground, either; the whole forest would dip down into an unseen valley; you felt yourself going down hill, down, down, and then you knew you were at the bottom of a sub-arboreal valley by the deeper stagnation of the air. Open spaces, when they came, showed little sky, and they were less open spaces than rooms in the surrounding prison.

Félix was not leading them through the uttermost depths of this place; he was following the vague indications of a road by which the rubber from M'Bassa was carted to the river.

They were travelling along a highway, in fact, and the dimmest indication of a track where other men have been before is a thing which robs the wilderness of much of its terror.

The loneliness of the forest beyond track or way, in those vast depths where the rubber collectors have to go alone, I leave you to imagine.

At last, at noon, on the third day of their journey to this place they struck rising ground where the trees fell away till no trees were left, and the blue sky of heaven lay above their heads, and before them on the highest point of the rise, Fort M'Bassa burning in the sun.

CHAPTER XI
ANDREAS MEEUS

The Parthenon in all its glory could not have looked more beautiful to the returning Greek than this half-ruined fort in the eyes of Adams.

A thing built by the hands of white men and shone on by the sun—what could be more acceptable to the eye after the long, long tramp through the heart-breaking forest!

The fort of M'Bassa was quite small; the surrounding walls had gone to decay, but the "guest house" and the office, and the great go-down where the rubber was stored, were in good repair and well thatched.

Outside the walls were a number of wretched hovels inhabited by the "soldiers" and their wives, and one of these soldiers, a tall black, with the eternal red fez on his head and a rifle slung on his back, was the first to sight the coming expedition, and to notify its approach with a yell that brought a dozen like him from the sun-baked hovels and, a moment later from the office, a white man in a pith helmet, who stood for a moment looking across the half-ruined wall at the newcomers, and then advanced to meet them.

He was a middle-sized man, with a melancholy face that showed very white under the shadow of the helmet; he was dressed in dingy white drill, and he had a cigarette between his lips.

He looked like a man who had never in his life smiled, yet his face was not an unpleasant face altogether, though there was much in it to give the observer pause.

His voice was not an unpleasant voice, altogether, yet there was that in it, as he greeted Berselius, which struck Adams sharply and strangely; for the voice of Andreas Meeus, *Chef de Poste* at M'Bassa, was the voice of a man who for two years had been condemned to talk the language of the natives. It had curious inflections, hesitancies, and a dulness that expressed the condition of a brain condemned for two years to think the thoughts of the natives in their own language.

Just as the voice of a violin expresses the condition of the violin, so does the voice of a man express the condition of his mind. And that is the fact that will strike you most if you travel in the wilds of the Congo State and talk to the men of your own colour who are condemned to live amongst the people.

One might have compared Meeus's voice to the voice of a violin—a violin that had been attacked by some strange fungoid growth that had filled its interior and dulled the sounding board.

He had been apprised a month before of the coming of Berselius's expedition, and one might imagine the servility which this man would show to the all-powerful Berselius, whose hunting expeditions were red-carpeted, who was hail-fellow-well-met with Leopold, who, by lifting his finger, could cause Andreas Meeus to be dismissed from his post, and by crooking his finger cause him to be raised to a Commissionership.

Yet he showed no servility at all. He had left servility behind him, just as he had left pride, just as he had left ambition, patriotism, country, and that divine something which blossoms into love of wife and child.

When he had shaken hands with Berselius and Adams, he led the way into the fort, or rather into the enclosure surrounded by the ruinous mud walls, an enclosure of about a hundred yards square.

On the right of the quadrangle stood the go-down, where the rubber and a small quantity of ivory was stored.

In the centre stood the misnamed guest house, a large mud and wattle building, with a veranda gone to decay.

The blinding sun shone on it all, showing up with its fierce light the true and appalling desolation of the place. There was not one thing in the enclosure upon which the eye could rest with thankfulness.

Turning from the enclosure and looking across the fort wall to the distance, one saw a world as far from civilization as the world that Romulus looked at when he gazed across the wall outlining the first dim sketch of Rome.

To the north, forest; to the south, forest; to the east, forest; and to the west, eternal and illimitable forest. Blazing sun, everlasting haze that in the rainy season would become mist and silence.

In the storms and under the rains the great rubber forest of M'Bonga would roar like a reef-tormented sea, but on a day like this, when, gazing from the high ground of the fort, the eye travelled across the swelling domes and heat-stricken valleys of foliage, the pale green of the feather-palms, the sombre green of the n'sambyas, to the haze that veiled all things beyond, on a day like this, silence gazed at one Sphinx-like, and from the distance of a million years. Silence that had brooded upon Africa before Africa had a name, before Pharaoh was born, before Thebes was built.

Meeus led the way into the guest house, which contained only two rooms—rooms spacious enough, but bare of everything except the ordinary necessities of life. In the living room there was a table of white deal-like wood and three or four chairs evidently made by natives from a European design. A leopard skin, badly dried and shrivelling at the edges, hung on one wall, presumably as an ornament; on another wall some Congo bows and arrows—bows with enormously thick strings and arrows poisoned so skilfully that a scratch from one would kill you, though they had been hanging there for many years. They were trophies of the early days when Fort M'Bassa was really a fort, and from those woods down there clouds of soot-black devils, with filed teeth, raided the place, only to be swept away by rifle fire.

There was no picture torn from an illustrated paper adorning the place, as in Verhaeren's abode, but on a rudely constructed shelf there lay just the same stack of "official letters," some of these two years old, some of last month, all dealing with trade.

Meeus brought out cigarettes and gin, but Berselius, safe now at his base of operations, to make a little festival of the occasion sent to the stores, which his porters had deposited in the go-down, for a magnum of champagne. It was Cliquot, and as Meeus felt the glow of the wine in his veins, a flush came into his hollow cheeks and a brightness into his dull eyes; forgotten things stirred again in his memory, with the shadows of people he had known—the glitter of lamplit streets in Brussels, the glare of the *Café de Couronne*—all the past, such as it was, lay in the wine.

Meeus was one of the "unfortunate men." He had held a small clerkship under the Belgian Government, from which he had been dismissed through a fault of his own.

This was five years ago. Up to his dismissal he had led the peddling and sordid life that a small government clerk on the Continent leads if he has nothing to save him from himself and from his fellows: the dry rot of official life had left him useless for anything but official life. A sensualist in a small way, he enlarged his sphere on the day of his dismissal, when he found himself cut off from work and adrift in the world, with five hundred francs in his pocket. In one glorious debauch, which lasted a week, he spent the five hundred francs, and then he settled down to live on a maiden aunt.

He called it looking for work.

She lasted for a year and nine months, and then she died, and her annuity died with her. He felt her loss deeply, for not only had her money helped to support him, but she was his only real friend, and he had a heart in those days that seemed so far distant from him now.

Then it was that Poverty took him by the hand and explained patiently and with diagrams the hardness of the world, the atrocious position of the *déclassé*, who has never studied the art of roguery so as to make a living by it, and the utter uselessness as friends of those good fellows who sat in the *cafés* and walked the boulevards and ogled the women.

He tramped the streets of Brussels, at first in seedy clothes and at last in filth and horrible rags. A relative came to his assistance with two hundred francs; he bought himself clothes and made himself respectable, but, in a fortnight, found himself relapsing again, sinking like a swimmer whose momentary support has gone to pieces.

Just as the waves were again about to close over his benighted head, an acquaintance got him a post under Government. Not under the Belgian but the Congo Government.

Andreas Meeus was exactly the type of man this Government required, and still requires, and still uses and must continue to use as long as the infernal machine which it has invented for the extraction of gold from niggers continues to work. A man, that is to say, who has eaten orange-peel picked up in the market-place; a man who has worn out his friends—and his clothes. A man without hope.

One would think for the work in hand they would choose the greatest blackguards possible: convicts convicted of the worst crimes of violence. Not at all. These men would be for one thing too intractable; for another thing, too unstable, and for another thing (strange to say), possessed of too much heart. The Congo Government knows its work far too well for that. It does not take the murderer or the violent criminal from the penitentiary to do its work; it takes from the streets the man without hope. The educated man who has fallen, the man who can still think.

Meeus went to Africa just as a man goes to prison. He hated the idea of going, but he had to go, or stay and starve. He was stationed three months at Boma and then he was moved to a post on the Upper Congo, a small and easily worked post, where he found out the full conditions of his new servitude.

This post had to do with what they call in the jargon of the Congo administration, Forest Exploitation. Gum copal and wax was the stuff he had to extract from the people round about.

Here he found himself morally in the clutches of that famous and infamous proclamation issued from Brussels on the twentieth of June, 1892, by Secretary of State Van Estvelde.

The Bonus Proclamation.

According to the terms of this proclamation, Meeus found that besides his pay he could get a bonus on every kilo of wax and copal he could extract from the natives, and that the cheaper he could get the stuff the more his bonus would be.

Thus, for every kilo of wax or copal screwed out of the natives at a cost of five centimes or less, he received into his pocket a bonus of fifteen centimes, that is to say the bonus to Meeus was three times what the natives got; if by any laxity or sense of justice, the cost of the wax or copal rose to six centimes a kilo, Meeus only got ten centimes bonus, and so on.

The cheaper he got the stuff the more he was paid for it. And those were the terms on which he had to trade with the natives.

Then there were the taxes. The natives had to bring in huge quantities of wax and copal for nothing, just as a tax owing to the State, a tax to the Government that was plundering and exploiting them.

Meeus, who had a spice of the tradesman in him, fell into this state of things as easily as a billiard ball falls into a pocket when skilfully directed.

The unfortunate man was absolutely a billiard ball in the hands of a professional player; the stroke of the cue had been given in Belgium, he rolled to his appointed post, fell into it, and was damned.

His fingers became crooked and a dull hunger for money filled his soul. His success in working the niggers was so great that he was moved to a more difficult post at higher pay, and then right on to M'Bassa.

He was not naturally a cruel man. In his childhood he had been fond of animals, but Matabiche, the god-devil of the Congo, changed all that.

He saw nothing extortionate in his dealings, nothing wrong in them. When things were going well, then all was well; but when the natives resisted his charges and taxes, defrauding him of his bonus and lowering him in the eyes of his superiors, then Meeus became terrible.

And he was absolute master.

Away here in the lonely fort, in the midst of the great M'Bonga rubber forest that was now speechless as a Sphinx, now roaring at him like a sea in torment; here in the endless sunlight of the dry seasons and the endless misery of the rains, Meeus driven in upon himself, had time to think.

There is no prison so terrible as a limitless prison. Far better for a man to inhabit a cell in Dartmoor than a post in the desert of the forest. The walls are companionable things, but there is no companionship in distance.

Meeus knew what it was to look over the walls of the fort and watch another sun setting on another day, and another darkness heralding another night. He knew what it was to watch infinite freedom and to know it for his captor and jailer. He knew what it was to wake from his noonday siesta and see the same great awful splash of sunlight striking the same old space of arid yard, where the empty tomato tin lay by the rotten plantain cast over by some nigger child. He knew what it was to lie and hear the flies buzzing and wonder what tune of the devil it was they were trying to imitate. He knew what it was to think of death with the impotent craving of a sick child for some impossible toy.

Look into your own life and see all the tiny things that save you from *ennui* and devilment, and give you heart to continue the journey from hour to hour in this world where we live. Your morning paper, the new book from the library you have just got to read, the pipe you hope to smoke when you return from work, the very details of your work; a hundred and one petty things that make up the day of an ordinary man, breaking the monotony and breaking the prospect before him into short views.

Meeus had none of these. Without literature or love, without a woman to help him through, without a child to care for or a dog to care for him, there at Fort M'Bassa in the glaring sunshine he faced his fate and became what he was.

CHAPTER XII
NIGHT AT THE FORT

The night was hot and close and the paraffin lamp in the guest house mixed its smell with the tobacco smoke and with a faint, faint musky odour that came from the night outside. Every now and then a puff of hot wind blew through the open doorway, hot and damp as though a great panther were breathing into the room.

The nights in the forest were chill, but up here at Fort M'Bassa they were stewing in a heat wave.

Adams, with his coat off, pipe in mouth, was leaning back in a basket chair with his feet on a sugar box. Berselius, in another easy chair, was smoking a cigar, and Meeus, sitting with his elbows on the table, was talking of trade and its troubles. There is an evil spirit in rubber that gives a lot of trouble to those who deal with it. The getting of it is bad enough, but the tricks of the thing itself are worse. It is subject to all sorts of influences, climatic and other, and tends to deteriorate on its journey to the river and the coast of Europe.

It was marvellous to see the passion with which this man spoke of this inanimate thing.

"And then, ivory," said Meeus. "When I came here first, hundred-pound tusks were common; when you reach that district, M. le Capitaine, you will see for yourself, no doubt, that the elephants have decreased. What comes in now, even, is not of the same quality. Scrivelloes (small tusks), defective tusks, for which one gets almost nothing as a bonus. And with the decrease of the elephant comes the increased subterfuge of the natives. 'What are we to do?' they say. 'We cannot make elephants.' This is the worst six months for ivory I have had, and then, on top of this—for troubles always come together—I have this bother I told you of with these people down there by the Silent Pools."

A village ten miles to the east had, during the last few weeks, suspended rubber payments, gone arrear in taxes, the villagers running off into the forest and hiding from their hateful work.

"What caused the trouble?" asked Berselius.

"God knows," replied Meeus. "It may blow over—it may have blown over by this, for I have had no word for two days; anyhow, to-morrow I will walk over and see. If it hasn't blown over, I will give the people very clearly to understand that there will be trouble. I will stay there for a few days and see what persuasion can do. Would you like to come with me?"

"I don't mind," said Berselius. "A few days' rest will do the porters no harm. What do you say, Dr. Adams?"

"I'm with you," said Adams. "Anything better than to stay back here alone. How do you find it here, M. Meeus, when you are by yourself?"

"Oh, one lives," replied the *Chef de Poste,* looking at the cigarette between his fingers with a dreamy expression, and speaking as though he were addressing it. "One lives."

That, thought Adams, must be the worst part about it. But he did not speak the words. He was a silent man, slow of speech but ready with sympathy, and as he lounged comfortably in his chair, smoking his pipe, his pity for Meeus was profound. The man had been for two years in this benighted solitude; two years without seeing a white face, except on the rare occasion of a District Commissioner's visit.

He ought to have been mad by this, thought Adams; and he was a judge, for he had studied madness and its causes.

But Meeus was not mad in the least particular. He was coldly sane. Lust had saved his reason, the lust inspired by Matabiche.

Berselius's cook brought in some coffee, and when they had talked long enough about the Congo trade in its various branches, they went out and smoked their pipes, leaning or sitting on the low wall of the fort.

The first quarter of the moon, low in the sky and looking like a boat-shaped Japanese lantern, lay above the forest. The forest, spectral-pale and misty, lay beneath the moon; the heat was sweltering, and Adams could not keep the palms of his hands dry, rub them with his pocket handkerchief or on his knees as much as he would.

This is the heat that makes a man feel limp as a wet rag; the heat that liquefies morals and manners and temper and nerve force, so that they run with the sweat from the pores. Drink will not "bite" in this heat, and a stiff glass of brandy affects the head almost as little as a glass of water.

"It is over there," said Meeus, pointing to the southeast, "that we are going to-morrow to interview those beasts."

Adams started at the intensity of loathing expressed by Meeus in that sentence. He had spoken almost angrily at rubber and tusks, but his languid, complaining voice had held nothing like this before.

Those beasts! He hated them, and he would not have been human had he not hated them. They were his jailers in very truth, their work was his deliverance.

The revolt of this village would make him short of rubber; probably it would bring a reprimand from his superiors.

A great bat flitted by so close that the smell of it poisoned the air, and from the forest, far away to the west, came the ripping saw-like cry of a leopard on the prowl. Many fierce things were hunting in the forest that night, but nothing fiercer than Meeus, as he stood in the moonlight, cigarette in mouth, staring across the misty forest in the direction of the Silent Pools.

PART THREE

CHAPTER XIII
THE POOLS OF SILENCE

Next morning Berselius ordered Félix to have the tents taken from the go-down and enough stores for two days. Tents and stores would be carried by the "soldiers" of the fort, who were to accompany them on the expedition.

Adams noticed with surprise the childlike interest Meeus took in the belongings of Berselius; the green rot-proof tents, the latest invention of Europe, seemed to appeal to him especially; the Roorkee chairs, the folding baths, the mosquito nets of the latest pattern, the cooking utensils of pure aluminum, filled his simple mind with astonishment. His mind during his sojourn at Fort M'Bassa had, in fact, grown childlike in this particular; nothing but little things appealed to him.

Whilst the expedition was getting ready Adams strolled about outside the fort walls. The black "soldiers," who were to accompany them, were seated in the sun near their hovels, some of them cleaning their rifles, others smoking; but for their rifles and fez caps they might, with a view of Carthage in the distance, have been taken for the black legionaries of Hamilcar, ferocious mercenaries without country or God, fierce as the music of the leopard-skin drums that led them to battle.

Turning, he walked round the west wall till he came to the wall on the north, which was higher than the others. Here, against the north wall, was a sheltered cover like an immense sty, indescribably filthy and evil-smelling; about thirty rings were fastened to the wall, and from each ring depended a big rusty chain ending in a collar.

It was the Hostage House of Fort M'Bassa. It was empty now, but nearly always full, and it stood there like a horrible voiceless witness.

A great disgust filled the mind of Adams; disgust of the niggers who had evidently lately inhabited this place, and disgust of the Belgians who had herded them there. He felt there was something very wrong in the state of Congo. The Hostage House of Yandjali had started the impression; Meeus in some subtle way had deepened it; and now this.

But he fully recognized what difficult people to deal with niggers are. He felt that all this was slavery under a thin disguise, this so-called taxation and "trade," but it was not his affair.

All work is slavery more or less pleasant. The doctor is the slave of his patients, the shopkeeper of his clients. These niggers were, no doubt, slaves of the Belgians, but they were not bought and sold; they had to work, it is true, but all men have to work. Besides, Berselius had told him that the Belgians had stopped the liquor traffic and stopped the Arab raiders. There was good and bad on the side of the Belgians, and the niggers were niggers. So reasoned Adams, and with reason enough, though from insufficient data.

At eight o'clock in the blazing sunshine, that even then was oppressive, the expedition started. The white men leading, Félix coming immediately behind, and eleven of the soldiers, bearing the tents and stores for two days, following after.

They plunged into the forest, taking a dim track, which was the rubber track from the village of the Silent Pools and from half a dozen other villages to the west. The ground here was different from the ground they had traversed in coming to the fort. This was boggy; here and there the foot sank with a sough into the pulp of morass and rotten leaves; the lianas were thinner and more snaky, the greenery, if possible, greener, and the air close and moist as the air of a steam-bath.

The forest of M'Bonga has great tracts of this boggy, pestiferous land, dreadful sloughs of despond caverned with foliage, and by some curse the rubber vines entrench themselves with these. The naked rubber collectors, shivering over their fires, are attacked by the rheumatism and dysentery and fever that lie in these swamps; diseases almost merciful, for the aches and pains they cause draw the mind away from the wild beasts and devils and phantoms that haunt the imagination of the rubber slaves.

It took them three hours to do the ten miles, and then at last the forest cleared away and fairyland appeared.

Here in the very depths of the hopeless jungle, as if laid out and forgotten by some ancient god, lie the Silent Pools of Matabayo and the park-like lands that hold them. Like a beautiful song in some tragic and gloomy opera, a regret of the God who created the hopeless forest, sheltered by the great n'sambya trees, they lie; pools of shadowy and tranquil water, broken by reflections of branches and mirroring speargrass ten feet high and fanlike fern fronds.

All was motionless and silent as a stereoscopic picture; the rocketing palms bursting into sprays of emerald green, the n'sambyas with their trumpet-like yellow blossoms, the fern fronds reduplicating themselves in the water's glass, all and each lent their motionless beauty to the completion of the perfect picture.

In the old days, long ago, before the land was exploited and the forest turned into a hunting ground for rubber, the lovely head of the oryx would push aside the long green blades of the speargrass; then, bending her lips to the lips of the oryx gazing up at her from the water, she would drink, shattering the reflection into a thousand ripples. The water-buck came here in herds from the elephant country away south, beyond the hour-glass-like constriction which divided the great forest, and the tiny dik-dik, smallest of all antelopes, came also to take its sip. But all that is past. The rifle and the trap, at the instigation of the devouring Government that eats rubber and antelope, ivory and palm-oil, cassava and copal, has thinned out the herds and driven them away. The "soldier" must be fed. Even the humble bush pig of the forest knows that fact.

It was four years since Berselius had hunted in this country, and even in that short time he found enormous change. But he could not grumble. He was a shareholder in the company, and in twenty industries depending on it.

Close up to the forest, where the m'bina trees showed their balls of scarlet blossom, lay the village they had come to reason with. There were twenty-five or more low huts of wattle and mud, roofed with leaves and grass. No one was visible but an old woman, naked, all but for a slight covering about the loins. She was on all fours, grinding something between two stones, and as she sighted the party she looked backward over her shoulder at them like a frightened cat.

She cried out in a chattering voice, and from the huts six others, naked as herself, came, stared at the whites, and then, as if driven by the same impulse, and just like rabbits, darted into the forest.

But Meeus had counted on this, and had detached seven of his men to crawl round and post themselves at the back of the huts amidst the trees.

A great hullaballoo broke out, and almost immediately the soldiers appeared, driving the seven villagers before them with their rifle-butts.

They were not hurting them, just pushing them along, for this was, up to the present, not a punitive expedition but a fatherly visitation to point out the evils of laziness and insubordination, and to get, if possible, these poor wretches to communicate with the disaffected ones and make them return to their work.

Adams nearly laughed outright at the faces of the villagers; black countenances drawn into all the contortions of fright, but the contortions of their bodies were more laughable still, as they came forward like naughty children, driven by the soldiers, putting their hands out behind to evade the prods of the gun-butts.

Berselius had ordered the tents to be raised on the sunlit grass, for the edge of the forest, though shady, was infested by clouds of tiny black midges—midges whose bite was as bad, almost, as the bite of a mosquito.

Meeus spoke to the people in their own tongue, telling them not to be afraid, and when the tents were erected he and Berselius and Adams, sitting in the shelter of the biggest tent, faced the seven villagers, all drawn up in a row and backed by the eleven soldiers in their red fez caps.

The villagers, backed by the soldiers and fronted by Meeus, formed a picture which was the whole Congo administration in a nutshell. In a sentence, underscored by the line of blood-red fezzes.

These seven undersized, downtrodden, hideously frightened creatures, with eyeballs rolling and the marks of old chain scars on their necks, were the representatives of all the humble and meek tribes of the Congo, the people who for thousands of years had lived a lowly life, humble as the coneys of Scripture; people who had cultivated the art of agriculture and had carried civilization as far as their weak hands would carry it in that benighted land. Literally the salt of that dark earth. Very poor salt, it is true, but the best they could make of themselves.

These eleven red-tipped devils, gun-butting the others to make them stand erect and keep in line, were the representatives of the warlike tribes who for thousands of years had preyed on each other and made the land a hell. Cannibals most of them, ferocious all of them, heartless to a man.

Meeus was the white man who, urged by the black lust of money, had armed and drilled and brought under good pay all the warlike tribes of the Congo State and set them as task-masters over the humble tribes.

By extension, Berselius and Adams were the nations of Europe looking on, one fully knowing, the other not quite comprehending the tragedy enacted before their eyes.

I am not fond of parallels, but as these people have ranged themselves thus before my eyes, I cannot help pointing out the full meaning of the picture. A picture which is photographically true.

There was a little pot-bellied boy amongst the villagers, the old woman of the grindstone was holding him by the hand; he, of all the crowd, did not look in the least frightened. His eyeballs rolled, but they rolled in wonder.

The tent seemed to take his fancy immensely; then the big Adams struck his taste, and he examined him from tip to toe.

Adams, greatly taken with the blackamoor, puffed out his cheeks, closed one eye, and instantly, as if at the blow of a hatchet, the black face split, disclosing two white rows of teeth, and then hid itself, rubbing a snub nose against the old woman's thigh.

But a rolling white eyeball reappeared in a moment, only to vanish again as Adams, this time, sucked in his cheeks and worked his nose, making, under his sun hat, a picture to delight and terrify the heart of any child.

All this was quite unobserved by the rest, and all this time Meeus gravely and slowly was talking to the villagers in a quiet voice. They were to send one of their number into the forest to find the defaulters and urge them to return. Then all would be well. That was the gist of his discourse; and the wavering line of niggers rolled their eyes and answered, "We hear, we hear," all together and like one person speaking, and they were nearly tumbling down with fright, for they knew that all would not be well, and that what the awful white man with the pale, grave face said to them was lies, lies, lies—all lies.

Besides the old woman and the child there were two young girls, an old man, a boy of fifteen or so, with only one foot, and a pregnant woman very near her time.

Adams had almost forgotten the nigger child when a white eyeball gazing at him from between the old woman's legs recalled its existence.

He thought he had never seen a jollier animal of the human tribe than that. The creature was so absolutely human and full of fun that it was difficult to believe it the progeny of these downtrodden, frightened looking folk. And the strange thing was, it had all the tricks of an English or American child.

The hiding and peeping business, the ready laugh followed by bashfulness and self-effacement, the old unalterable impudence, which is not least amidst the *prima mobilia* of the childish mind. In another moment, he felt, the thing would forget its respect and return his grimaces, so he ignored it and fixed his attention on Meeus and the trembling wretches he was addressing.

When the lecture was over they were dismissed, and the boy with the amputated foot was sent off to the forest to find the delinquents and bring them back. Till sunrise on the following day was the term given him.

If the others did not begin to return by that time there would be trouble.

CHAPTER XIV
BEHIND THE MASK

The Silent Pools and the woods around were the haunts of innumerable birds. Rose-coloured flamingoes and gorgeous ducks, birds arrayed in all the jewellery of the tropics, birds not much bigger than dragon-flies, and birds that looked like flying beetles.

When they had dined, Adams, leaving the others to smoke and take their siesta, went off by the water's edge on a tour of the pools. They were three in number; sheets of water blue and tranquil and well-named, for surely in all the world nowhere else could such perfect peace be found. Perhaps it was the shelter of the forest protecting these windless sheets of water; perhaps it was the nature of the foliage, so triumphantly alive yet so motionless; perhaps beyond these some more recondite reason influenced the mind and stirred the imagination. Who knows? The spirit of the scene was there. The spirit of deep and unalterable peace. The peace of shadowy lagoons, the peace of the cedar groves where the sheltering trees shaded the loveliness of Merope, the peace of the heart which passes all understanding and which men have named the Peace of God.

It was the first time since leaving Yandjali that Adams had found himself alone and out of sight of his companions. He breathed deeply, as if breathing in the air of freedom, and as he strode along, tramping through the long grass, his mind, whilst losing no detail of the scene around him, was travelling far away, even to Paris, and beyond.

Suddenly, twenty yards ahead, bounding and beautiful in its freedom and grace, a small antelope passed with the swiftness of an arrow; after it, almost touching it, came another form, yellow and fierce and flashing through the grass and vanishing, like the antelope, amidst the high grasses on the edge of the pool.

The antelope had rushed to the water for protection, and the leopard had followed, carried forward by its impetus and ferocity, for Adams could hear its splash following the splash of the quarry; then a roar split the silence, echoed from the trees, and sent innumerable birds fluttering and crying from the edge of the forest and the edge of the pool.

Adams burst through the long speargrass to see what was happening, and, standing on the boggy margin, holding the grasses aside, gazed.

The antelope had vanished as if it had never been, and a few yards from the shore, in the midst of a lather of water that seemed beaten up with a great swizzle-stick, the leopard's head, mouth open, roaring, horrified his eyes for a moment and then was jerked under the surface.

The water closed, eddied, and became still, and Silence resumed her sway over the Silent Pools.

Something beneath the water had devoured the antelope; something beneath the water had dragged the leopard to its doom, and swish! a huge flail tore the speargrass to ribbons and sent Adams flying backward with the wind of its passage.

Another foot and the crocodile's tail would have swept him to the fate of the antelope and leopard.

The place was alive with ferocity and horror, and it seemed to Adams that the Silent Pools had suddenly slipped the mask of silence and beauty and shown to him the face of hideous death.

He wiped the sweat from his brow. He was unarmed, and it seemed that a man, to walk in safety through this Garden of Eden, ought to be armed to the teeth. He turned back to the camp, walking slowly and seeing nothing of the beauties around him, nothing but the picture of the leopard's face, the paws frantically beating the water, and a more horrible picture still, the water resuming its calmness and its peace.

When he reached the camp, he found Berselius and Meeus absent. After their siesta they had gone for a stroll by the water's edge in the opposite direction to that which he had taken. The soldiers were on duty, keeping a watchful eye on the villagers; all were seated, the villagers in front of their huts and the soldiers in the shade, with their rifles handy; all, that is to say, except the nigger child, who was trotting about here and there, and who seemed quite destitute of fear or concern.

When this creature saw the gigantic Adams who looked even more gigantic in his white drill clothes, it laughed and ran away, with hands outspread and head half slewed round. Then it hid behind a tree. There is nothing more charming than the flight of a child when it wishes to be pursued. It is the instinct of women and children to run away, so as to lead you on, and it is the instinct of a rightly constituted man to follow. Adams came toward the tree, and the villagers seated before their huts and the soldiers seated in the shade all turned their heads like automata to watch.

"Hi there, you ink-bottle!" cried Adams. "Hullo there, you black dogaroo! Out you come, Uncle Remus!" Then he whistled.

He stood still, knowing that to approach closer would drive the dogaroo to flight or to tree climbing.

There was nothing visible but two small black hands clutching the tree bole; then the gollywog face, absolutely split in two with a grin, appeared and vanished.

Adams sat down.

The old, old village woman who was, in fact, the child's grandmother, had been looking on nervously, but when the big man sat down she knew he was only playing with the child, and she called out something in the native, evidently meant to reassure it. But she might have saved her breath, for the black bundle behind the tree suddenly left cover and stood with hands folded, looking at the seated man.

He drew his watch from his pocket and held it up. It approached. He whistled, and it approached nearer. Two yards away it stopped dead.

"Tick-tick," said Adams, holding up the watch.

"Papeete N'quong," replied the other, or words to that effect.

It spoke in a hoarse, crowing voice not at all unpleasant. If you listen to English children playing in the street you will often hear this croaking sort of voice, like the voice of a young rook.

Papeete struck Adams as a good name for the animal and, calling him by it, he held out the watch as a bait.

The lured one approached closer, held out a black claw, and next moment was seized by the foot.

It rolled on the ground like a dog, laughing and kicking, and Adams tickled it; and the grim soldiers laughed, showing their sharp white teeth, and the old grandmother beat her hands together, palm to palm, as if pleased, and the other villagers looked on without the ghost of an expression on their black faces.

Then he jumped it on its feet and sent it back to its people with a slap on its behind, and returned to his tent to smoke till Berselius and Meeus returned.

But he had worked his own undoing, for, till they broke camp, Papeete haunted him like a buzz-fly, peeping at him, sometimes from under the tent, trotting after him like a dog, watching him from a distance, till he began to think of "haunts" and "sendings" and spooks.

When Berselius and his companion returned, the three men sat and smoked till supper time.

At dark the villagers were driven into their huts and at the door of each hut lay a sentry.

A big fire was lit, and by its light two more sentries kept watch over the others and their prisoners. Then the moon rose, spreading silver over the silence of the pools and the limitless foliage of the forest.

CHAPTER XV
THE PUNISHMENT

The sun rose, bringing with it a breeze. Above the stir and bustle of the birds you could hear the gentle wind in the tree-tops like the sound of a sea on a low-tide beach.

The camp was still in gloom, but the whole arc of sky above the pools was thrilled and filled with living light. Sapphire blue, dazzling and pale, but deep with infinite distance, it had an intrinsic brilliancy as though filled with sunbeams brayed to dust.

The palm tops had caught the morning splendour and then, rapidly, as though the armies of light were moving to imperious trumpet-calls, charging with golden spears, legion on legion, a hurricane of brightness, Day broke upon the pools.

We call it Day, but what is it, this splendour that comes from nowhere, and vanishes to nowhere, that strikes our lives rhythmically like the golden wing of a vast and flying bird, bearing us along with it in the wind of its flight?

The rotation of the earth? But in the desert, on the sea, in the spaces of the forest you will see in the dawn a vision divorced from time, a recurring glance of a beauty that is eternal, a ray as if from the bright world toward which the great bird Time is flying, caught and reflected to our eyes by every lift of the wing.

The dawn had not brought the truants back from the forest.

This point Meeus carefully verified. Even the boy who had been sent to communicate with them had not returned.

"No news?" said Berselius, as he stepped from his tent-door and glanced around him.

"None," replied Meeus.

Adams now appeared, and the servants who had been preparing breakfast laid it on the grass. The smell of coffee filled the air; nothing could be more pleasant than this out-of-doors breakfast in the bright and lovely morning, the air fresh with the breeze and the voices of birds.

The villagers were all seated in a group, huddled together at the extreme left of the row of huts. They were no longer free, but tied together ankle to ankle by strips of *n'goji*. Only Papeete was at liberty, but he kept at a distance. He was seated near the old woman, and he was exploring the interior of an empty tomato tin flung away by the cook.

"I will give them two hours more," said Meeus, as he sipped his coffee.

"And then?" said Adams.

Meeus was about to reply when he caught a glance from Berselius.

"Then," he said, "I will knock those mud houses of theirs to pieces. They require a lesson."

"Poor devils!" said Adams.

Meeus during the meal did not display a trace of irritation. From his appearance one might have judged that the niggers had returned to their work, and that everything was going well. At times he appeared absent-minded, and at times he wore a gloomy but triumphant look, as though some business which had unpleasant memories attached to it had at last been settled to his satisfaction.

After breakfast he drew Berselius aside, and the two men walked away in the direction of the pools, leaving Adams to smoke his pipe in the shade of the tent.

They came back in about half an hour, and Berselius, after speaking a few words to Félix, turned to Adams.

"I must ask you to return to Fort M'Bassa and get everything in readiness for our departure. Félix will accompany you. I will follow in a couple of hours with M. Meeus. I am afraid we will have to pull these people's houses down. It's a painful duty, but it has to be performed. You will save yourself the sight of it."

"Thanks," said Adams. Not for a good deal of money would he have remained to see those wretched hovels knocked to pieces. He could perceive plainly enough that the thing had to be done. Conciliation had been tried, and it was of no avail. He was quite on the side of Meeus; indeed, he had admired the self-restraint of this very much tried *Chef de Poste*. Not a hard word, not a blow, scarcely a threat had been used. The people had been spoken to in a fatherly manner, a messenger had been sent to the truants, and the messenger had joined them. At all events he had not returned. Then, certainly, pull their houses down. But he did not wish to see the sight. He had nothing to do with the affair, so filling and lighting another pipe, and leaving all his belongings to be brought on by Berselius, he turned with Félix and, saying good-bye to his companions, started.

They had nearly reached the edge of the forest when shouts from behind caused Adams to turn his head.

The soldiers were shouting to Papeete to come back.

The thing had trotted after Adams like a black dog. It was within a few yards of him.

"Go back," shouted Adams.

"Tick-tick," replied Papeete. It was the only English the creature knew.

It stood frying in the sun, grinning and glistening, till Adams, with an assumption of ferocity, made for it, then back it went, and Adams, laughing, plunged under the veil of leaves.

Berselius, seated at his tent door, looked at his watch. Meeus, seated beside Berselius, was smoking cigarettes.

"Give him an hour," said Berselius. "He will be far away enough by that. Besides, the wind is blowing from there."

"True," said Meeus. "An hour." And he continued to smoke. But his hand was shaking, and he was biting the cigarette, and his lips were dry so that he had to be continually licking them.

Berselius was quite calm, but his face was pale, and he seemed contemplating something at a distance.

When half an hour had passed, Meeus rose suddenly to his feet and began to walk about, up and down, in front of the tent, up and down, up and down, as a man walks when he is in distress of mind.

The black soldiers also seemed uneasy, and the villagers huddled closer together like sheep. Papeete alone seemed undisturbed. He was playing now with the old tomato tin, out of which he had scraped and licked every vestige of the contents.

Suddenly Meeus began crying out to the soldiers in a hard, sharp voice like the yelping of a dog.

The time was up, and the soldiers knew. They ranged up, chattering and laughing, and all at once, as if produced from nowhere, two rhinoceros hide whips appeared in the hands of two of the tallest of the blacks. Rhinoceros hide is more than an inch thick; it is clear and almost translucent when properly prepared. In the form of a whip it is less an instrument of punishment than a weapon. These whips were not the smoothly prepared whips used for light punishment; they had angles that cut like sword edges. One wonders what those sentimental people would say—those sentimental people who cry out if a burly ruffian is ordered twenty strokes with the cat—could they see a hundred *chicotte* administered with a whip that is flexible as india-rubber, hard as steel.

Two soldiers at the yelping orders of Meeus cut the old woman apart from her fellows and flung her on the ground.

The two soldiers armed with whips came to her, and she did not speak a word, nor cry out, but lay grinning at the sun.

Papeete, seeing his old grandmother treated like this, dropped his tomato tin and screamed, till a soldier put a foot on his chest and held him down.

"Two hundred *chicotte,*" cried Meeus, and like the echo of his words came the first dull, coughing blow.

The villagers shrieked and cried altogether at each blow, but the victim, after the shriek which followed the first blow, was dumb.

Free as a top which is being whipped by a boy, she gyrated, making frantic efforts to escape, and like boys whipping a top, the two soldiers with their whips pursued her, blow following blow.

A semicircle of blood on the ground marked her gyrations. Once she almost gained her feet, but a blow in the face sent her down again. She put her hands to her poor face, and the rhinoceros whips caught her on the hands, breaking them. She flung herself on her back and they beat her on the stomach, cutting through the walls of the abdomen till the intestines protruded. She flung herself on her face and they cut into her back with the whips till her ribs were bare and the fat bulged through the long slashes in the skin.

Verily it was a beating to the bitter end, and Meeus, pale, dripping with sweat, his eyes dilated to a rim, ran about laughing, shouting—

"Two hundred chicotte. Two hundred chicotte."

He cried the words like a parrot, not knowing what he said.

And Berselius?

Berselius, also dripping with sweat, his eyes also dilated to a rim, tottering like a drunken man, gazed, drinking, drinking the sight in.

Down, away down in the heart of man there is a trapdoor. Beyond the instincts of murder and assassination, beyond the instincts that make a Count Cajus or a Marquis de Sade, it lies, and it leads directly into the last and nethermost depths of hell, where sits in eternal damnation Eccelin de Romano.

Cruelty for cruelty's sake: the mad pleasure of watching suffering in its most odious form: that is the passion which hides demon-like beneath this door, and that was the passion that held Berselius now in its grip.

He had drunk of all things, this man, but never of such a potent draught as this demon held now to his lips—and not for the first time. The draught would have been nothing but for the bitterness of it, the horror of it, the mad delight of knowing the fiendishness of it, and drinking, drinking, drinking, till reason, self-respect, and soul, were overthrown.

The thing that had been a black woman and, now, seemed like nothing earthly except a bundle of red rags, gave up the miserable soul it contained and, stiffening in the clutches of tetanus, became a hoop.

What happened then to the remaining villagers could be heard echoing for miles through the forest in the shrieks and wails of the tortured ones.

One cannot write of unnamable things, unprintable deeds. The screams lasted till noon.

At one o'clock the punitive expedition had departed, leaving the Silent Pools to their silence. The houses of the village had been destroyed and trampled out. The sward lay covered with shapeless remains, and scarcely had the last of the expedition departed, staggering and half drunk with the delirium of their deeds, than from the blue above, like a stone, dropped a vulture.

A vulture drops like a stone, with wings closed till it reaches within a few yards of the ground; then it spreads its wings and, with wide-opened talons, lights on its prey.

Then, a marabout with fore-slanting legs and domed-out wings, came sailing silently down to the feast, and another vulture, and yet another.

CHAPTER XVI
DUE SOUTH

When Berselius and Meeus returned to Fort M'Bassa Adams, who met them, came to the conclusion that Berselius had been drinking. The man's face looked stiff and bloated, just as a man's face looks after a terrible debauch. Meeus looked cold and hard and old, but his eyes were bright and he was seemingly quite himself.

"To-morrow I shall start," said Berselius. "Not to-day. I am tired and wish to sleep." He went off to the room where his bed was, and cast himself on it and fell instantly into a deep and dreamless sleep.

The innocent may wonder how such a man would dare to sleep—dare to enter that dark country so close to the frontier of death. But what should the innocent know of a Berselius, who was yet a living man and walked the earth but a few years ago, and whose prototype is alive to-day. Alive and powerful and lustful, great in mind, body, and estate.

Before sunrise next morning the expedition was marshalled in the courtyard for the start.

A great fire burned in the space just before the house, and by its light the stores and tents were taken from the go-down. The red light of the fire lit up the black glistening skins of the porters as they loaded themselves with the chop boxes and tents and guns; lit up the red fez caps of the onlooking "soldiers," their glittering white teeth, their white eyeballs, and the barrels of their rifles.

Beyond and below the fort the forest stretched in the living starlight like an infinite white sea. The tree-tops were roofed with a faint mist, no breath of wind disturbed it, and in contrast to the deathly stillness of all that dead-white world the sky, filled with leaping stars, seemed alive and vocal.

It was chill up here just before dawn. Hence the fire. Food had been served out to the porters, and they ate it whilst getting things ready and loading up. Berselius and his companions were breakfasting in the guest house and the light of the paraffin lamp lay on the veranda yellow as topaz in contrast with the red light of the fire in the yard.

Everything was ready for the start. They were waiting now for the sun.

Then, away to the east, as though a vague azure wind had blown up under the canopy of darkness, the sky, right down to the roof of the forest, became translucent and filled with distance.

A reef of cloud like a vermilion pencil-line materialized itself, became a rose-red feather tipped with dazzling gold, and dissolved as if washed away by the rising sea of light.

A great bustle spread through the courtyard. The remaining stores were loaded up, and under the direction of Félix, the porters formed in a long line, their loads on their heads.

As the expedition left the compound it was already day. The edge of the sun had leaped over the edge of the forest, the world was filled with light, and the sky was a sparkling blue.

What a scene that was! The limitless sea of snow-white mist rippled over by the sea of light, the mist billowed and spiralled by the dawn wind, great palm tops bursting through the haze, glittering effulgent with dew, birds breaking to the sky in coloured flocks, snow, and light, and the green of tremendous vegetation, and over all, new-built and beautiful, the blue, tranquil dome of sky.

It was song materialized in colour and form, the song of the primeval forests breaking from the mists of chaos, tremendous, triumphant, joyous, finding day at last, and greeting him with the glory of the palms, with the rustle of the n'sambyas tossing their golden bugles to the light, the drip and sigh of the euphorbia trees, the broad-leaved plantains and the thousand others whose forms hold the gloom of the forest in the mesh of their leaves.

"I have awakened, O God! I have awakened. Behold me, O Lord! I am Thine!"

Thus to the splendour of the sun and led by the trumpet of the wind sang the forest. A hundred million trees lent their voices to the song. A hundred million trees—acacia and palm, m'bina and cottonwood, thorn and mimosa; in gloom, in shine, in valley and on rise, mist-strewn and sun-stricken, all bending under the deep sweet billows of the wind.

At the edge of the forest Berselius and Adams took leave of Meeus. Neither Berselius nor Meeus showed any sign of the past day. They had "slept it off." As for Adams, he knew nothing, except that the villagers had been punished and their houses destroyed.

The way lay due south. They were now treading that isthmus of woods which connects the two great forests which, united thus, make the forest of M'Bonga. The trees in this vast connecting wood are different from the trees in the main forests. You find here enormous acacias, monkey-bread trees, raphia palms and baobabs; less gloom, and fewer creeping and hanging plants.

Berselius, as a rule, brought with him a taxidermist, but this expedition was purely for sport. The tusks of whatever elephants were slain would be brought back, but no skins; unless, indeed, they were fortunate enough to find some rare or unknown species.

CHAPTER XVII
SUN-WASHED SPACES

A two days' march brought them clear of the woods and into a broken country, vast, sunstrewn and silent; a beautiful desolation where the tall grass waved in the wind, and ridge and hollow, plain and mimosa tree, led the eye beyond, and beyond, to everlasting space.

Standing here alone, and listening, the only sound from all that great sunlit country was the sound of the wind in the grasses near by.

Truly this place was at the very back of the world, the hinterland of the primeval forests. Strike eastward far enough and you would sight the snow-capped crest of Kilimanjaro, King of African mountains, sitting snow-crowned above the vast territory to which he has given his name, and which stretches from Lake Eyasi to the Pare Mountains. The hunters of Kilimanjaro, which once was the home of elephants, have thinned the herds and driven them to wander. Elephants that a hundred years ago, even fifty years ago, were almost fearless of man, have altered their habits from the bitter lessons they have received, and now are only to be found in the most inaccessible places. Should they cling to more inhabited districts, they come out of the sheltered places only by night. A man may spend years in an elephant district without once seeing an elephant. Driven by the necessity of food and the fear of man, the great herds wander in their wonderful and mysterious journeys for hundreds and hundreds of miles. Never lying down, sleeping as they stand, always on guard, dim of sight yet keen of smell, they pass where there are trees, feeding as they go, stripping branches of leaves. Alarmed, or seeking a new feeding place, a herd moves in the rainy season, when the ground is soft, with the silence and swiftness of a cloud shadow; in the dry season when the ground is hard, the sound of them stampeding is like the drums of an army.

"Elephants," said Berselius, pointing to some bundles of dried stuff lying near a vangueria bush. "That stuff is a bundle of bowstring hemp. They chew it and drop it. Oh, that has been dropped a long time ago; see, there you have elephants again."

A tree standing alone showed half its bark ripped off, tusked off by some old bull elephant, and above the tusk marks, some fifteen feet up, could be seen the rubbing mark where great shoulders had scratched themselves.

As they marched, making due south, Berselius in that cold manner which never left him, and which made comradeship with the man impossible and reduced companionship to the thinnest bond, talked to Adams about the game they were after, telling in a few graphic sentences and not without feeling the wonderful story of the moving herds, to whom distance is nothing, to whom mountains are nothing, to whom the thickest jungle is nothing. The poem of the children of the mammoth who have walked the earth with the mastodon, who have stripped the trees wherein dwelt arboreal man, who have wandered under the stars and suns of a million years, seen rivers change their courses and hills arise where plains had been, and yet remain, far strewn and thinned out, it is true, but living still. At noon they halted and the tents were pitched for a four hours' rest.

Adams, whilst dinner was preparing, walked away by himself till the camp was hidden by a ridge, then he stood and looked around him.

Alone, like this, the spirit of the scene appeared before him: the sun, and wind, and sky; the vast, vast spaces of waving grass, broken by the beds of dried-up streams, strewn here and there with mimosas and thorns, here dim with the growth of vangueria bushes, here sharp and gray-green with cactus; this giant land, infinite, sunlit, and silent, spoke to him in a new language.

It seemed to Adams that he had never known freedom before.

A shadow swept by him on the grass. He looked up and watched the great bird that had cast the shadow sailing away on the wind, dwindling to a point, and vanishing in the dazzling blue.

CHAPTER XVIII
FAR INTO ELEPHANT LAND

They sighted a small herd of giraffe two days later, but so far off as to be beyond pursuit; but before evening, just as they were about to camp by some pools, they came across rhino.

Berselius's quick eye spotted the beasts, a bull and a cow. They were in the open, under shelter of some thick grass; the bull was half sitting up, and his head and horn in the evening light might have been taken for the stump of a broken tree. The cow was not visible at first, but almost immediately after they sighted the bull, she heaved herself up and stood a silhouette against the sky.

The wind was blowing from the beasts, so it was quite possible to get close up to them. The meat would be useful, so Berselius and his companion started, with Félix carrying the guns.

As they drew close Adams noticed that the back of the great cow seemed alive and in motion. Half a dozen rhinoceros birds, in fact, were upon it, and almost immediately, sighting the hunters, they rose chattering and fluttering in the air.

These birds are the guardians of the half-blind rhinoceros. They live on the parasites that infest his skin. It is a partnership. The birds warn the rhinoceros of danger, and he, vicariously, feeds the birds. Scarcely had the birds given warning than the bull heaved himself up. Berselius's rifle rang out, but the light was uncertain, and the brute wounded, but not mortally, charged forward took a half circle, swung his head from side to side in search of his assailant, and sighted the cow. Instantly, horn down and squealing, he charged her. She met him horn to horn, and the smash could be heard at the camp where the porters and the soldiers stood gazing open-mouthed at the battle between the two great brutes charging each other in the low evening light, fighting with the ferocity of tigers and the agility of cats.

Adams, close up as he was, had a better view, and unless he had seen with his own eyes, he could not have believed that two animals so heavy and unwieldy could display such nimbleness and such quickness of ferocity.

It was the wickedest sight, and it was brought to an end at last by the rifle of Berselius.

Curiously enough, neither brute had injured the other very much. The horns which, had they been of ivory, must have been shivered, were intact, for the horn of a rhinoceros is flexible; it is built up of a conglomeration of hairs, and though, perhaps, the most unbreakable thing in the universe, it bends up to a certain point just as a rapier does.

Next morning, two hours after daybreak, Félix, who was scouting just ahead of the column, came running back with news he had struck elephant spoor. Every tooth in his head told the tale. Not only spoor, but the spoor of a vast herd cutting right across the line of march.

Berselius came forward to examine, and Adams came with him.

The dry ground and wire grass was not the best medium for taking the track of the beasts, but to the experienced eyes of Berselius and the Zappo Zap everything was clear. A herd of elephant had passed not long ago, and they were undisturbed and unsuspicious. When elephants are suspicious they march in lines, single file, one stepping in the tracks of another. This herd was spread wide and going easy of mind, but at what pace it would be impossible to say.

The long boat-shaped back feet of the bulls leave a print unmistakable in the rainy season when the ground is soft, but still discernible to the trained eye in the dry season. Félix declared that there were at least twenty bulls in the herd, and some of huge size.

"How long is it since they passed here?" asked Berselius.

Félix held up the fingers of one hand. From certain indications he came to the conclusion they had passed late in the night, three hours or so before daybreak. They numbered forty or fifty, leaving aside the calves that might be with them. He delivered these opinions, speaking in the native, and Berselius instantly gave the order, "Left wheel!" to the crowd of porters; and at the word the long column turned at right angles to the line of march and struck due west, treading the track of the herd.

Nothing is more exciting than this following in the track of a mammoth army whose tactics you cannot foresee. This herd might be simply moving a few miles in search of a new feeding ground, or it might be making one of those great sweeping marches covering hundreds of miles that the mysterious elephant people make at the dictates of their mysterious instinct. It might be moving at a gentle pace, or swifter than a man could run. A mile on the new route they came on a broken tree, a great tree broken down as if by a storm; the fractures were quite recent. The elephant folk had done this.

They came across another tree whose sides, facing north and south, had been clearly barked, and the pieces of the bark, farther on, that had been chewed and flung away.

With one stroke of a tusk passing a tree, and without stopping, an elephant will tear off a strip of bark; and it was curious to see how the bark of this tree to east and west was intact. The moving herd had not stopped. Just in passing, an elephant on either side of the tree had taken his slice of bark, chewed it and flung it away. There were also small trees trodden down mercilessly under foot. Thus the great track of the herd lay before the hunters, but not a sign in all the sunlit, silent country before them of the herd itself.

It was Berselius's aim to crowd up his men as quickly as a forced march could do it, camp and then pursue the herd with a few swift followers, the barest possible amount of stores and one tent.

The calabashes and the water bottles had been filled at the last halt, but it was desirable to find water for the evening's camping place.

It was now that Berselius showed his capacity as a driver and his own enormous store of energy.

He took the tail of the column, and woe to the porters who lagged behind! Félix was with him, and Adams, who was heading the column, could hear the shouts of the Zappo Zap. The men with their loads went at a quick walk, sometimes breaking into a trot, urged forward by the gun-butt of Félix.

The heat was sweltering, but there was no rest. On, on, on, ever on through a country that changed not at all; the same breaks and ridges, the same limitless plains of waving grass, the same scant trees, the same heat-shaken horizon toward which the elephant road led straight, unwavering, endless.

The brain reeled with the heat and the dazzle, but the column halted not nor stayed. The energy of Berselius drove it forward as the energy of steam drives an engine. His voice, his very presence, put life into flagging legs and sight into dazzled eyes. He spared neither himself nor others; the game was ahead, the spoor was hot, and the panther in his soul drove him forward.

Toward noon they halted for two hours where some bushes spread their shade. The porters lay down on their bellies, with arms outspread, having taken a draught of water and a bite of food; they lay in absolute and profound slumber. Adams, nearly as exhausted, lay on his back. Even Félix showed signs of the journey, but Berselius sat right back into the bushes, with his knees drawn up and, with eyes fixed on the eastern distance, brooded.

He was always like this on a great hunt, when the game was near. Silent and brooding, and morose to the point of savagery.

One might almost have fancied that in far distant days this man had been a tiger, and that the tiger still lived slumbering in his soul, triumphant over death, driving him forth at intervals from civilization to wander in the wild places of the earth and slay.

Two hours past noon they resumed their journey: on, on, on, treading the elephant track which still went due east straight as an arrow to the blue horizon. The frightful tiredness they had felt before the noonday halt had passed, giving place to a dull, dreamy feeling, such as comes after taking opium. The column marched mechanically and without thought, knowing only two things, the feel of the hard ground and grass beneath their feet, and the smiting of the sun on their backs.

Thus the galley slaves of old laboured at their oars and the builders of the pyramids beneath their loads, all moving like one man. But here was no tune of flutes to set the pace, or monotonous song to help the lifting; only the voice of Berselius like a whip-lash, and the gun-butt of Félix drumming on the ribs of laggards.

A light, hot wind was blowing in their faces. Adams, still at the head of the column, had suffered severely during the morning march, and the re-start after the noon rest was painful to him as a beating; but the reserve forces of a powerful constitution that had never been tampered with were now coming into play, and, after a time, he felt little discomfort. His body, like a wound-up mechanism, did all the work; his mind became divorced from it; he experienced a curious exaltation, like that which comes from drink, only finer far and more ethereal. The column seemed marching far swifter than it was marching in reality, the vast sunlit land seemed vaster even than it was; the wind-blown grass, the far distant trees, the circling skyline, all spoke of freedom unknown to man: the freedom of the herd they were pursuing; the freedom of the bird flying overhead; the freedom of the wind blowing in the grass; the freedom of the limitless, endless, sunlit country. Meridians of silence, and light, and plains, and trees, and mountains, and forests. Parallels of virgin land.

He was feeling what the bird knows and feels when it beats up the mountains or glides down the vales of air; what the elephant herd knows and feels when it moves over mountains and across plains; what the antelopes know when distance calls them.

A shout from Félix, and the Zappo Zap came running up the line; his head was flung up and he was sniffing the air. Then, walking beside Adams, he stared ahead right away over the country before them to the far skyline.

"Elephant smell," he replied, when Adams asked him what was the matter; then, turning, he shouted some words in the native back to Berselius, and tramped on beside Adams, his nose raised to the wind, of which each puff brought the scent stronger.

Adams could smell nothing, but the savage could tell that right ahead there were elephants; close up, too, yet not a sign of them could be seen.

This puzzled him, and what puzzles a savage frightens him.

His nose told him that here were elephants in sight of his eyes; his eyes told him that there were none.

All at once the column came to a dead halt. Porters flung down their loads and cried out in fright. Even Berselius stood stock-still in astonishment.

From the air, blown on the wind from no visible source, came the shrill trumpeting of an elephant.

There, in broad daylight, close up to them, the sound came with the shock of the supernatural. Nothing stirred in all the land but the grass bending to the wind. There was not even a bird in the air; yet close to them an elephant was trumpeting shrilly and fiercely as elephants trumpet when they charge.

Again came the sound, and once again, but this time it broke lamentably to a complaint that died away to silence.

Instantly the Zappo Zap came to himself. He knew that sound. An elephant was dying somewhere near by, caught in a trap possibly. He rushed down the line, gun-butting the porters back to their places, shouting to Berselius, helping loads up on the heads of the men who had dropped them, so that in a minute the column was in motion again and going swiftly to make up for lost time.

Five minutes brought them to a slight rise in the ground, beyond which, deep-cut, rock-strewn and skeleton-dry, lay the bed of a river.

In the rains this would be scarcely fordable, but now not even a trickle of water could be seen. On the floor of this river-bed, like a huge dark rock, lay the body of an elephant.

An African elephant is the biggest creature on earth, far bigger than his Indian cousin, and far more formidable looking. Adams could scarcely believe that the thing before him was the body of an animal, as he contrasted its size with Félix, who had raced down the slope and was examining the carcass.

"Dead!" cried Félix, and the porters, taking heart, descended, but not without groaning and lamentations, for it is well-known to the natives that whoever comes across an elephant lying down must die, speedily and by violent means; and this elephant was lying down in very truth, his tusks humbly lowered to the ground, his great ears motionless, just as death had left him.

It was a bull and surely, from his size, the father of the herd. Berselius considered the beast to be of great age. One tusk was decayed badly and the other was chipped and broken, and on the skin of the side were several of those circular sores one almost always finds on the body of a rhinoceros, "dundos," as the natives call them; old scars and wounds told their tale of old battles and the wanderings of many years.

It might have been eighty or a hundred years since the creature had first seen the light and started on its wonderful journey over mountains and plains through jungle and forest, lying down maybe only twenty times in all those years, wandering hither and thither, and knowing not that every step of its journey was a step closer to here.

Just this little piece of ground on which it lay had been plotted out for it a hundred years ago, and it had come to it by a million mazy paths, but not less surely than had it followed the leading of a faultlessly directed arrow.

The herd had left it here to die. Berselius, examining the body closely, could find no wound. He concluded that it had come to its end just as old men come to their end at last—the mechanism had failed, hindered, perhaps, by some internal disease, and it had lain down to wait for death.

The tusks were not worth taking, and the party pursued its way up the eastern bank of the river, where the herd had also evidently pursued its way, and then on, on, across the country due east, in the track they had followed since morning.

As they left the river-bed a tiny dot in the sky above, which they had not noticed, enlarged, and like a stone from the blue fell a vulture. It lit on the carcass; then came a kite slanting down to the feast, and then from the blue, like stones dropped from the careless hand of a giant, vulture after vulture.

CHAPTER XIX
THE GREAT HERD

Félix kept his place beside Adams at the head of the column. The black seemed morose, and at the same time, excited.

Two things had disturbed him: the bad luck of meeting a lying-down elephant and the fact that a giraffe was with the herd. He had spotted giraffe spoor in the river-bed where the ground was sandy and showed up the impression well.

Now, the giraffe has the keen eyesight of a bird, and when he throws in his lot with the elephant folk who, though half-blind, have the keen scent of hounds, the combination is bad for the hunter.

An hour before sundown they struck some pools beside which grew a tree, the biggest they had yet come across, and here Berselius gave the order, halt and camp.

To half of the porters it was an order to fall down flat, their loads beside them, their arms outspread absolutely broken with the weariness of the march, broken, and speechless, and motionless, and plunged into such a depth of slumber that had you kicked them they would not have moved.

Berselius, himself, was nearly exhausted. He sat with his back against the tree and gave his orders in a languid voice, and it was very curious to see the tents going up, wielded by men who seemed working in their sleep, slowly and with fumbling fingers, tripping over each other, pausing, hesitating, yet working all the same, and all in the still level light of evening that lent unreality to the scene.

Luck was against Berselius. It was quite within the bounds of probability that the herd might have halted here by the water for the night; but they had not. They had drunk here, for the pool was all trodden up and still muddy, and then gone on.

They were evidently making one of their great marches, and it was probable now that they would never be caught up with. Under these circumstances, Berselius determined to halt for the night.

Some small trees and bushes were cut to make a camp fire, and when they had finished supper Berselius, still with his back to the tree, sat talking to Adams by the light of the crackling branches.

He did not seem in the least put out with his failure.

"The rains will be on us in a week or two," said he. "Then you will see elephants all over this place. They lie up in the inaccessible places in the dry season, but when the wet weather comes the herds spread over the plains. Not such herds as the one we have been following—it is rarely one comes across one like that. However, to-morrow we may have better luck with them. Félix tells me that forty miles beyond there, where they have gone, there are a lot of trees. They may stop and feed, and if they do, we will have them. To-morrow I shall start light. Leave the main camp here. You and I and Félix, and four of the best of those men, and the smallest tent, enough stores for three or four days. Yes, to-morrow——" The man dozed off, sleep-stricken, the pipe between his teeth.

"To-morrow!" Portentous word!

They retired to their tents. Two sentries were posted to keep the fire going and to keep watch. The porters lay about, looking just like men who had fallen in battle, and after awhile the sentries, having piled the fire with wood, sat down, and the moon rose, flooding the whole wide land with light.

She had scarcely lifted her own diameter above the horizon when the sentries, flat on their backs, with arms extended, were sleeping as soundly as the others. Brilliant almost as daylight, still and peaceful as death, the light of the great moon flooded the land, paling the stars and casting the shadows of the tents across the sleepers, and the wind, which was now blowing from the west, shook the twigs of the tree, like skeleton fingers, over the flicker of the red burning camp-fire.

Now, the great herd of elephants had been making, as Berselius imagined possible, for the forest that lay forty miles to the east.

They had reached it before sundown, and had begun to feed, stripping branches of their leaves, the enormous trunks reaching up like snakes and whirling the leaves Catherine-wheellike down enormous throats; the purring and grumbling of their cavernous bellies, the rubbing of rough shoulders against the bark, the stamping of feet crushing the undergrowth, resounded in echoes amongst the trees. The big bull giraffe that had cast its lot in with the herd was busy, too, tearing and snapping down twigs and leaves, feeding like the others, who were all feeding like one, even to the eighteen-month-old calves busy at the teats of their enormous dams.

The sunlight, level and low, struck the wonderful picture. Half the herd were in the wood, and you could see the tree branches bending and shaking to the reaching trunks. Half the herd were grazing on the wood's edge, the giraffe amidst them, its clouded body burning in the sunset against the green of the trees.

The wind was blowing steadily along the edge of the wood and against a band of hunters of the Congo State, blacks armed with rifles, who were worming their way along from tree bole to tree bole, till within shooting distance of the bull elephant nearest to them.

The creatures feeding knew nothing of their danger till three shots, that sounded like one, rang out, and the bull, struck in the neck, the shoulder, and between the ear and eye, fell, literally all of a heap, as though some giant's scimitar had swept its legs away from under it.

At this moment the sun's lower edge had just touched the horizon. The whole visible herd on the edge of the wood, at the sound of the shots and the crash of the falling bull, wheeled, trumpeted wildly, and with trunks swung up, ears spread wide, swept away toward the sunset, following the track by which they had come; whilst, bursting from the woods, leaf-strewn, with green branches tangled in their tusks, furious and mad with fright, came the remainder, following in the same track, sweeping after the others, and filling the air with the thunder of their stampede.

Shot after shot rang out, but not an elephant was touched, and in two great clouds, which coalesced, the broken herd with the sound of a storm passed away along the road they had come by, the night closing on them as the sun vanished from the sky.

Berselius had not reckoned on this. No man can reckon on what the wilderness will do. The oldest hunter is the man who knows most surely the dramatic surprises of the hunt, but the oldest hunter would never have taken this into his calculations.

Here, back along the road they had travelled all day, was coming, not a peacefully moving herd, but a storm of elephants. Elephants who had been disturbed in feeding, shot at, and shot after, filled with the dull fury that dwells in an elephant's brain for days, and with the instinct for safety that would carry them perhaps a hundred miles before dawn.

And right in the track of this terrible army of destruction lay the sleeping camp, the camp fire smouldering and fluttering its flames on the wind.

And the wind had shifted!

With the dark, as though the scene had been skilfully prepared by some infernal dramatist, just as the cover of night shut down tight and sealed, and suddenly, like a box-lid that had been upheld by the last rays of the setting sun, just as the great stars burst out above as if at the touch of an electric button, the wind shifted right round and blew due east.

This change of wind would dull the sound of the oncoming host to the people at the camp; at the same time it would bring the scent of the human beings to the elephants.

The effect of this might be to make them swerve away from the line they were taking, but it would be impossible to tell for certain. The only sure thing was, that if they continued in their course till within eyeshot of the camp fire, they would charge it and destroy everything round about it in their fury.

A camp fire to an angry elephant is the equivalent of a red rag to a bull.

Thus the dramatic element of uncertainty was introduced into the tragedy unfolding on the plains, and the great stars seemed to leap like expectant hearts of fire till the moon broke over the horizon, casting the flying shadows of the great beasts before them.

The first furious stampede had settled into a rapid trot, to a sound like the sound of a hundred muffled drums beating a rataplan.

Instinct told the herd that immediate danger was past, also that for safety they would have to cover an immense space of country; so they settled to the pace most suitable for the journey. And what a pace it was, and what a sight!

Drifting across the country before the great white moon, fantastic beasts and more fantastic shadows, in three divisions line ahead, with the lanes of moonlight ruled between each line; calves by the cows, bulls in the van, they went, keeping to the scent of the track they had come by as unswervingly as a train keeps to the metals.

The giraffe was still with them. He and his shadow, gliding with compass-like strides a hundred yards away from the southward column; and just as the scent of the camp came to his mammoth friends, the sight of the camp fire, like a red spark, struck his keen eyes.

With a rasping note of warning he swerved to the south.

Now was the critical moment. Everything lay with the decision of the bulls leading the van, who, with trunks flung up and crooked forward, were holding the scent as a man holds a line. They had only a moment of time, but he who knows the elephant folk knows well the rapidity with which their minds can reason, and from their action it would seem that the arbiters of Berselius's fate reasoned thus: "The enemy were behind; they are now in front. So be it. Let us charge."

And they charged, with a blast of trumpeting that shook the sky; with trunks flung up and forward-driving tusks, ears spread like great sails, and a sound like the thunder of artillery, they charged the scent, the body of the herd following the leaders, as the body of a battering-ram follows the head.

Adams, when he had flung himself down in his tent, fell asleep instantly. This sleep, which was profound and dreamless, lasted but half an hour, and was succeeded by a slumber in which, as in a darkened room where a magic-lantern is being operated, vivid and fantastic pictures arose before him. He was on the march with the column through a country infinite as is space; the road they were taking, like the road to the tombs of the Chinese kings, was lined on either side with animals done in stone. At first these were tigers, and then, as though some veil of illusion had been withdrawn, he discovered them to be creatures far larger and more cruel, remorseless, and fearful than tigers; they were elephants—great stone elephants that had been standing there under the sun from everlasting, and they dwindled in perspective from giants to pigmies and from pigmies to grains of sand, for they were the guardians of a road whose end was infinity.

Then these vanished, but the elephant country under the burning sun remained. There was nothing to be seen but the sun-washed spaces of wind-blown grass, and broken ground, and scattered trees, till across the sky in long procession, one following the other, passed shadow elephants. Shadows each thrice the height of the highest mountain, and these things called forth in the mind of the sleeper such a horror and depth of dread that he started awake with the sweat running down his face.

Sleep was shattered, and in the excitement and nerve-tension of over-tiredness he lay tossing on his back. The long march of the day before, in which men had matched themselves against moving mountains, the obsession of the things they had been pursuing, had combined to shatter sleep.

He came out in the open for a breath of air.

The camp was plunged in slumber. The two sentries ordered by Berselius to keep watch and to feed the fire lay like the others, with arms outspread; the fire was burning low, as though drowned out by the flood of moonlight, and Adams was on the point of going to the pile of fuel for some sticks to feed it, when he saw a sight which was one of the strangest, perhaps, that he would ever see.

The sentry lying on the right of the fire sat up, rose to his feet, went to the wood pile, took an armful of fuel and flung it on the embers.

The fire roared up and crackled, and the sleep-walker, who had performed this act with wide-staring eyes that saw nothing, returned to his place and lay down.

It was as if the order of Berselius still rang in his ears and the vision of Berselius still dominated his mind.

Adams, thinking of this strange thing, stood with the wind fanning his face, looking over the country to the west, the country they had traversed that day in tribulation under the burning sun. There was nothing to tell now of the weary march, the pursuit of phantoms, the long, long miles of labour; all was peaceful and coldly beautiful, moonlit and silent.

He was about to return to his tent when a faint sound struck his ear. A faint, booming sound, just like that which troubles us when the eardrum vibrates on its own account from exhaustion or the effect of drugs.

He stopped his ears and the sound ceased.

Then he knew that the sound was a real sound borne on the air.

He thought it was coming to him on the wind, which was now blowing steadily in his face, and he strained his eyes to see the cause; but he saw nothing. There was no cloud in the sky or storm on the horizon, yet the sound was increasing. Boom, boom, becoming deeper and more sonorous, now like the long roll of muffled drums, now like the sea bursting in the sea-caves of a distant coast, or the drums of the cyclone when they beat the charge for the rushing winds. But the heart-searching feature of this strange booming in the night was a rhythm, a pulsation that spoke of life. This was no dull shifting of matter, as in an earthquake, or of air as in a storm; this sound was alive.

Adams sprang to the tent where Berselius was sleeping, and dragged him out by the arm, crying, "Listen!"

He would have cried, "See!" but the words withered on his lips at the sight which was now before him as he faced east.

An acre of rollicking and tossing blackness storming straight for the camp across the plain under the thunder that was filling the night. A thing inconceivable and paralyzing, till the iron grip of Berselius seized his arm, driving him against the tree, and the voice of Berselius cried, "Elephants."

In a moment Adams was in the lower branches of the great tree, and scarcely had he gained his position than the sky split with the trumpeting of the charge and, as a man dying sees his whole life with one glance, he saw the whole camp of awakened sleepers fly like wind-blown leaves from before the oncoming storm, leaving only two figures remaining, the figures of Berselius and Félix.

The Zappo Zap had gone apart from the camp to sleep. He had drugged himself by smoking hemp, and he was lying half a hundred yards away, face down on the ground, dead to everything in earth and heaven.

Berselius had spied him.

What Adams saw then was, perhaps, the most heroic act ever recorded of man. The soul-shattering terror of the advancing storm, the thunder and the trumpeting that never ceased, had no effect on the iron heart of Berselius.

He made the instantaneous calculation that it was just possible to kick the man awake (for sound has no effect on the hemp-drugged one) and get him to the tree and a chance of safety. And he made the attempt.

And he would have succeeded but that he fell.

The root of a dead tree, whose trunk had long vanished, caught his foot when he had made half the distance, and brought him down flat on his face.

It was as though God had said, "Not so."

Adams, in an agony, sweat pouring from him, watched Berselius rise to his feet. He rose slowly as if with deliberation, and then he stood fronting the oncoming storm. Whether he was dazed, or whether he knew that he had miscalculated his chances, who knows? But there he stood, as if disdaining to fly, face fronting the enemy. And it seemed to the watcher that the figure of that man was the figure of a god, till the storm closed on him, and seized and swung aloft by a trunk, he was flung away like a stone from a catapult somewhere into the night.

Just as a man clings to a mast in a hurricane, deaf, blind, all his life and energy in his arms, Adams clung to the tree bole above the branch upon which he was.

The storm below, the smashing of great bodies against the tree, the trumpeting whose prolonged scream never ceased—all were nothing. His mind was cast out—he had flung it away just as the elephant had flung Berselius away. To him the universe was the tree to which he was clinging, just that part which his arms encircled.

The herd had attacked in three columns, keeping the very same formation as they had kept from the start. The northern column, consisting of cows with their calves, drove on as if to safety, the others, cows and bulls—the cows even more ferocious than the bulls—attacked the camps, the tents, and the fire. They stamped and trod the fire out, smashing tent poles and chop boxes, stores and cooking utensils, tusking one another in the tight-packed *mêlée,* and the scream of the trumpeting never ceased.

Then they drove on.

The porters, all except two, had, unhappily for themselves, fled in a body to the west, and now mixed with the trumpeting and thunder could be heard the screams of men trodden under foot or tusked to pieces. These sounds ceased, and the trumpeting died away, and nothing could be distinguished but the dull boom, boom of the herd sweeping away west, growing fainter and fainter, and dying away in the night.

CHAPTER XX
THE BROKEN CAMP

The whole thing had scarcely lasted twenty minutes. During the storming and trumpeting, Adams, clinging to the tree, had felt neither terror nor interest. His mind was cast out, all but a vestige of it; this remnant of mind recognized that it was lying in the open palm of Death, and it was not afraid. Not only that, but it felt lazily triumphant. It is only the reasoning mind that fears death, the mind that can still say to itself, "What will come after?" The intuitive mind, which does not reason, has no fear.

Had not the herd been so closely packed and so furious, Adams would have been smelt out, plucked from the tree and stamped to pieces without any manner of doubt. But the elephants, jammed together, tusking each other, and rooting the camp to pieces, had passed on, not knowing that they had left a living man behind them.

As the sound of the storm died away, he came to his senses as a man comes to his senses after the inhalation of ether, and the first thing that was borne in upon him was the fact that he was clinging to a tree, and that he could not let go. His arms encircled the rough bark like bands of iron; they had divorced themselves from his will power, they held him there despite himself, not from muscular rigidity or spasm, but just because they refused to let go. They were doing the business of clinging to safety on their own account, and he had to *think himself free*. There was no use in ordering them to release him, he had to reason with them. Then, little by little, they (fingers first) returned to discipline, and he slipped down and came to earth, literally, for his knees gave under him and he fell.

He was a very brave man and a very strong man, but now, just released from Death, now that all danger was over, he was very much afraid. He had seen and heard Life: Life whipped to fury, screaming and in maelstrom action, Life in its loudest and most appalling phase, and he felt as a man might feel to whom the gods had shown a near view of that tempest of fire we call the sun.

He sat up and looked around him on the pitiable ruins of the camp on which a tornado could not have wrought more destruction. Something lay glittering in the moonlight close to him. He picked it up. It was his shaving-glass, the most fragile thing in all their belongings, yet unbroken. Tent-poles had been smashed to matchwood, cooking utensils trodden flat, guns broken to pieces; yet this thing, useless and fragile, had been carefully preserved, watched over by some god of its own.

He was dropping it from his fingers when a cry from behind him made him turn his head.

A dark figure was approaching in the moonlight.

It was the Zappo Zap. The man whom Berselius, with splendid heroism, had tried to save. Like the looking-glass, and protected, perhaps, by some god of his own, the columns of destruction had passed him by. The column of cows with their calves had passed him on the other side. Old hunters say that elephants will not trouble with a dead man, and Félix, though awakened by the shaking of the earth, had lain like a dead man as the storm swept by.

He was very much alive, now, and seemingly unconcerned as he came toward Adams, stood beside him, and looked around.

"All gone dam," said Félix. And volumes would not have expressed the situation more graphically. Then the savage, having contemplated the scene for a moment, rushed forward to a heap of stuff—broken boxes and what not—dragged something from it and gave a shout.

It was the big elephant rifle, with its cartridge-bag attached. The stock was split, but the thing was practically intact. Félix waved it over his head and laughed and whooped.

"Gun!" yelled Félix.

Adams beckoned to him, and he came like a black devil in the moonlight—a black devil with filed teeth and flashing eyeballs—and Adams pointed to the tree and motioned him to leave the gun there and follow him. Félix obeyed, and Adams started in the direction in which he had seen Berselius flung.

It was not far to walk, and they had not far to search. A hundred yards took them to a break in the ground, and there in the moonlight, with arms extended, lay the body of the once powerful Berselius, the man who had driven them like sheep, the man whose will was law. The man of wealth and genius, great as Lucifer in evil, yet in courage and heroism tremendous. God-man or devil-man, or a combination of both, but great, incontestably great and compelling.

Adams knelt down beside the body, and the Zappo Zap stood by with incurious eyes looking on.

Berselius was not dead. He was breathing; breathing deeply and stertorously, as men breathe in apoplexy or after sunstroke or ruinous injury to the brain. Adams tore open the collar of the hunting shirt; then he examined the limbs.

Berselius, flung like a stone from a catapult, had, unfortunately for himself, not broken a limb. That might have saved him. His head was the injured part, and Adams, running his fingers through the hair, matted with blood, came on the mischief. The right parietal bone was dented very slightly for a space nearly as broad as a penny. The skin was broken, but the bone itself, though depressed slightly, was not destroyed. The inner table of the skull no doubt was splintered, hence the brain mischief.

There was only one thing to be done—trephine. And that as swiftly as possible.

Everything needful was in the instrument-case, but had it escaped destruction?

He raised Berselius by the shoulders. Félix took the feet, and between them they carried the body to the tree, where they laid it down.

Before starting to hunt for the instruments, Adams bled Berselius with his penknife. The effect was almost instantaneous. The breathing became less stertorous and laboured. Then he started to search hither and thither for the precious mahogany case which held the amputating knives, the tourniquets and the trephine. The Zappo Zap was no use, as he did not know anything about the stores, and had never even seen the instrument case, so Adams had to conduct the search alone, in a hurry, and over half an acre of ground. The case had almost to a certainty been smashed to pieces; still, there was a chance that the trephine had escaped injury. He remembered the shaving-glass, and how it had been miraculously preserved, and started to work. He came across a flat oblong disc of tin; it had been a box of sardines, it was now flattened out as though by a rolling mill. He came across a bottle of brandy sticking jauntily up from a hole in the ground, as if saying, "Have a drink." It was intact. He knocked the head off and, accepting the dumb invitation, put it back where he had found it, and went on.

He came across long strips of the green rot-proof stuff the tents had been made of. They looked as though they had been torn up like this for rib-roller bandages, for they were just of that width. He came across half a mosquito-net; the other half was sailing away north, streaming from the tusk of a bull in which it was tangled, and giving him, no doubt, a sufficiently bizarre appearance under the quiet light of the moon and stars.

There were several chop boxes of stores intact; and a cigar box without a crack in it, and also without a cigar. It looked as though it had been carefully opened, emptied, and laid down. There was no end to the surprises of this search: things brayed to pieces as if with a pestle and mortar, things easily smashable untouched.

He had been searching for two hours when he found the trephine. It lay near the brass lock of the amputating case, attached to which there were some pieces of mahogany from the case itself.

A trephine is just like a corkscrew, only in place of the screw you have a cup of steel. This steel cup has a serrated edge: it is, in fact, a small circular saw. Applying the saw edge to the bone, and working the handle with half turns of the wrist, you can remove a disc from the outer table of the skull just as a cook stamps cakes out of a sheet of dough with a "cutter."

Adams looked at the thing in his hands; the cup of chilled steel, thin as paper and brittle as glass, had been smashed to pieces, presumably; at all events, it was not there.

He flung the handle and the shaft away and came back to the tree beneath which the body of Berselius was lying. Berselius, still senseless, was breathing deeply and slowly, and Adams, having cut away the hair of the scalp round the wound with his penknife, went to the pool for water to bathe the wound; but the pool was trodden up into slush, and hours must elapse before the mud would settle. He remembered the bottle of brandy, fetched it, washed the wound with brandy, and with his handkerchief torn into three pieces bound it up.

There was nothing more to be done; and he sat down with his back to the tree to wait for dawn.

The bitterness of the thing was in his heart, the bitterness of being there with hands willing and able to help, yet helpless. A surgeon is as useless without his instruments as the cold, lifeless instruments are without a hand to guide them. It is not his fault that his hands are tied, but if he is a man of any feeling, that does not lessen the anguish of the situation.

Adams, listening to the breathing of the man he could not save, sat watching the moonlit desert where the grass waved in the wind. Félix, lying on his belly, had resumed his slumbers, and beside the sleeping savage lay the thing he worshipped more than his god, the big elephant rifle, across the stock of which his naked arm was flung.

CHAPTER XXI
THE FEAST OF THE VULTURES

Adams, who had fallen asleep, was awakened by a whoop from Félix.

It was full, blazing day, and the Zappo Zap, standing erect just as he had sprung from sleep, was staring with wrinkled eyes straight out across the land. Two black figures were approaching. They were the two porters who had fled westward, and who, with Félix, were all that remained of Berselius's savage train of followers. The rest were over there——

Over there to the west, where vultures and marabouts and kites were holding a clamorous meeting; over there, where the ground was black with birds.

The two wretches approaching the camping place rolled their eyes in terror, glancing over there. They had run for miles and hidden themselves in a donga. They had heard the tragedy from afar, the storming and trumpeting, and the shrieks of men being destroyed, torn to pieces, trampled to pulp; they had heard the thunder of the vanishing herd, and they had listened to the awful silence that followed, lying on their faces, clinging to the breast of their old, cold, cruel Mother Earth. With day, like homing pigeons, they had returned to the camp.

"Hi yi!" yelled Félix, and a response came like the cry of a seagull. They were shivering as dogs shiver when ill or frightened; their teeth were chattering, and they had a curious gray, dusky look; the very oil of their skins seemed to have dried up, and old chain scars on their necks and ankles showed white and leprous-looking in the bright morning sunshine.

But Adams had no time to attend to them. Having glanced in their direction, he turned to Berselius, bent over him, and started back in surprise.

Berselius's eyes were open; he was breathing regularly and slowly, and he looked like a man who, just awakened from sleep, was yet too lazy to move.

Adams touched him upon the shoulder, and Berselius, raising his right hand, drew it over his face as if to chase away sleep. Then his head dropped, and he lay looking up at the sky. Then he yawned twice, deeply, and turning

Under the presidency of these three spirits the land was ever changing; the country of the morning was not the country of the noon, nor was the country of the noon the country of the evening.

The morning was loud. I can express it in no other terms. Dawn came like a blast of trumpets, driving the flocks of the red flamingoes before it, tremendous, and shattering the night of stars at the first fanfare. A moment later, and, changing the image, imagination could hear the sea of light bursting against the far edge of the horizon, even as you watched the spindrift of it surging up to heaven and the waves of it breaking over ridge and tree and plain of waving grass.

Noon was the hour of silence. Under the pyramid of light the land lay speechless, without a shadow except the shadow of the flying bird, or a sound except the sigh of the grass, touched and bent by the wind, if it blew.

Evening brought with it a new country. There was no dusk here, no beauties of twilight, but the level light of sunset brought a beauty of its own. Distance stood over the land, casting trees farther away, and spreading the prairies of grass with her magic.

The country, now, had a new population. The shadows. Nowhere else, perhaps, do shadows grow and live as here, where the atmosphere and the level light of evening combine to form the quaintest shadows on earth. The giraffe has for his counterpart a set of shadow legs ten yards long, and the elephant in his shadow state goes on stilts. A man is followed by a pair of black compasses, and a squat tent flings to the east the shadow of a sword.

Adams was sitting looking at the two porters whom he had set to hunt for firewood; he was watching their grotesque figures, and more than grotesque shadows, when a movement of the sick man under the tent-cloth caused him to turn.

Berselius had awakened. More than that, he was sitting up, and before Adams could put up a hand, the tent-cloth was flung back, and the head and shoulders of the sick man appeared.

His face was pale, his hair in disorder; but his consciousness had fully returned. He recognized Adams with a glance, and then, without speaking, struggled to free himself of the tent-cloth and get on his feet.

Adams helped him.

Berselius, leaning on the arm of his companion, looked around him, and then stood looking at the setting sun.

The glorious day was very near its end. The sun huge and half-shorn of his beams, was sinking slowly, inevitably; scarce two diameters divided his lower edge from the horizon that was thirsting for him as the grave thirsts for man. Thus fades, shorn of its dazzle and splendour, the intellect so triumphant at noon, the personality, the compelling will; the man himself when night has touched him.

"Are you better?" asked Adams.

Berselius made no reply.

Like a child, held by some glittering bauble, he seemed fascinated by the sun. The western sky was marked by a thin reef of cloud; dull gold, it momentarily brightened to burnished gold, and then to fire.

The sun touched the horizon. Ere one could say "Look!" he was half gone. The blazing arc of his upper limb hung for a moment palpitating, then it dwindled to a point, vanished, and a wave of twilight, like the shadow of a wing, passed over the land.

As Berselius, leaning on the arm of his companion, turned, it was already night.

The camp fire which the porters had lit was crackling, and Berselius, helped by his friend, sat down with his back to the tree and his face toward the fire.

"Are you better?" asked Adams, as he took a seat beside him and proceeded to light a pipe.

"My head," said Berselius. As he spoke he put his hand to his head as a person puts his hand to his forehead when he is dazed.

"Have you any pain?"

"No, no pain, but there is a mist."

"You can see all right?"

"Yes, yes, I can see. It is not my sight, but there is a mist—in my head."

Adams guessed what he meant. The man's mind had been literally shaken up. He knew, too, that thought and mental excitement were the worst things for him.

"Don't think about it," said he. "It will pass. You have had a knock on the head. Just lean back against the tree, for I want to dress the wound."

He undid the bandage, fetched some water from the pool, which was now clear, and set to work. The wound was healthy and seemed much less severe than it had seemed the night before. The dent in the bone seemed quite inconsiderable. The inner table of the skull might, after all, be not injured. One thing was certain: whatever mischief the cortex of the brain had suffered, the prime centres had escaped. Speech and movement were perfect and thought was rational.

"There," said Adams, when he had finished his dressings and taken his seat, "you are all right now. But don't talk or do any thinking. The mist, as you call it, in your head will pass away."

"I can see," said Berselius; then he stopped, hesitated, and went on—"I can see last night—I can see us all here by the camp fire, but beyond that I cannot see, for a great white mist hides everything. And still"—he burst out—"I seem to know everything hidden by that mist, but I can't see, I can't see. What is this thing that has happened to me?"

"You know your name?"

"Yes, my name is Berselius, just as your name is Adams. My mind is clear, my memory is clear, but I have lost the sight of memory. Beyond the camp fire of last night, everything is a thick mist—I am afraid!"

He took Adams's big hand, and the big man gulped suddenly at the words and the action.

The great Berselius afraid! The man who had faced the elephants, the man who cared not a halfpenny for death, the man who was so far above the stature of other men, sitting there beside him and holding his hand like a little child, and saying, "I am afraid!"

And the voice of Berselius was not the voice of the Berselius of yesterday. It had lost the decision and commanding tone that made it so different from the voices of common men.

"It will pass," said Adams. "It is only a shake-up of the brain. Why, I have seen a man after a blow on the head with his memory clean wiped out. He had to learn his alphabet again."

Berselius did not reply. His head was nodding forward in sleep. He had slept all day, but sleep had taken him again suddenly, just as it takes a child, and Adams placed him under the improvised tent with the coat for a pillow under his head, and then sat by the fire.

Memory of all things in this wonderful world is surely the most wonderful. It is there now, and the next moment it is not. You leave your house in London, and you are next found in Brighton, sane to all intents and purposes, but your memory is gone. A dense fog hides everything you have ever done, dreamed or spoken. You may have committed crimes in your past life, or you may have been a saint. It is all the same, for the moment, until the mist breaks up and your past reappears.

Berselius's case was a phase of this condition. He knew his name—everything lay before his mind up to a certain point. Beyond that, he knew all sorts of things were lying, but he could not see them. To use his own eloquent expression, he had lost the sight of memory.

If you recall your past, it comes in pictures. You have to ransack a great photographic gallery. Before you can think, you must see.

Beyond a certain point Berselius had lost the sight of memory, In other words, he had lost his past.

CHAPTER XXIII
BEYOND THE SKYLINE

Adams, wearied to death with the events of the past day and night, slept by the camp fire the deep dreamless sleep of utter exhaustion. He had piled the fire with wood, using broken boxes, slow-burning vangueria brushwood, and the remains of a ruined mimosa tree that lay a hundred yards from the camp, and he lay by it now as soundly asleep as the two porters and Berselius. The fire stood guard; crackling and flickering beneath the stars, it showed a burning spark that made the camping place determinable many miles away.

Now the Zappo Zap, when he had fled from Adams, put ten miles of country behind him, going almost with the swiftness of an antelope, taking low bush and broken ground in his stride, and halting only when instinct brought him to a stand, saying, "You are safe."

He knew the country well, and the thirty miles that separated him from the eastern forest, where he could obtain food and shelter, were nothing to him. He could have run nearly the whole distance and reached there in a few hours' time.

But time was also nothing to him. He had fed well, and could last two days without food. It was not his intention to desert the camp yet; for at the camp, under that tree away to the west, lay a thing that he lusted after as men lust for drink or love: the desire of his dark soul—the elephant gun.

Before Adams drove him away from the camp he had made up his mind to steal it. Sneak off with it in the night and vanish with it into his own country away to the northeast, leaving B'selius and his broken camp to fend for themselves. This determination was still unshaken; the thing held him like a charm, and he sat down, squatting in the grass with his knees drawn up to his chin and his eyes fixed westward, waiting for evening.

An hour before sunset he made for the camp, reaching within a mile of it as the light left the sky. He watched the camp fire burning, and made for it. Toward midnight, crawling on his belly, soundless as a snake, he crept right up beside Adams, seized the gun and the cartridge bag, and with them in his hands stood erect.

He had no fear now. He knew he could outrun anyone there. He held the gun by the barrels. Adams's white face, as he lay with mouth open, snoring and deep in slumber, presented an irresistible mark for the heavy gun-butt, and all would have been over with that sleeper in this world, had not the attention of the savage been drawn to an object that suddenly appeared from beneath the folds of the improvised tent.

It was the hand of Berselius.

Berselius, moving uneasily in his sleep, had flung out his arm; the clenched fist, like the emblem of power, struck the eye of the Zappo Zap, and quelled him as the sight of the whip quells a dog.

B'selius was alive and able to clench his fist. That fact was enough for Félix, and next moment he was gone, and the moonlight cast his black shadow as he ran, making northeast, a darkness let loose on life and on the land.

Adams awoke at sun-up to find the gun and the cartridge bag gone. The porters knew nothing. He had picked up enough of their language to interrogate them, but they could only shake their heads, and he was debating in his own mind whether he ought to kick them on principle, when Berselius made his appearance from the tent.

His strength had come back to him. The dazed look of the day before had left his face, but the expression of the face was altered. The half smile which had been such a peculiar feature of his countenance was no longer there. The level eye that raised to no man and lowered before no man, the aspect of command and the ease of perfect control and power—where were they?

Adams, as he looked at his companion, felt a pang such as we feel when we see a human being suddenly and terribly mutilated.

Who has not known a friend who, from an accident in the hunting field, the shock of a railway collision, or some great grief, has suddenly changed; of whom people say, "Ah, yes, since the accident he has never been the same man"?

A friend who yesterday was hale and hearty, full of will power and brain, and who to-day is a different person with drooping under-lip, lack-lustre eye, and bearing in every movement the indecision which marks the inferior mind.

Berselius's under-lip did not droop, nor did his manner lack the ordinary decision of a healthy man; the change in him was slight, but it was startlingly evident. So high had Nature placed him above other men, that a crack in the pedestal was noticeable; as to the injury to the statue itself, the ladder of time would be required before that could be fully discovered.

So far from being downcast this morning, Berselius was mildly cheerful. He washed and had his wound dressed, and then sat down to a miserable breakfast of cold tinned meat and cassava cakes, with water fetched from the pool in a cracked calabash.

He said nothing about the mist in his head, and Adams carefully avoided touching on the question.

"Sleep has put him all right," said Adams to himself. "All the same, he's not the man he was. He's a dozen times more human and like other men. Wonder how long it will last. Just as long as he's feeling sick, I expect."

He rose to fetch his pipe when Berselius, who had finished eating and had also risen to his feet, beckoned him to come close.

"That is the road we came by?" said Berselius, pointing over the country toward the west.

"Yes," said Adams, "that is the road."

"Do you see the skyline?" said Berselius.

"Yes, I see the skyline."

"Well, my memory carries me to the skyline, but not beyond."

"Oh, Lord!" said Adams to himself, "here he is beginning it all over again!"

"I can remember," said Berselius, "everything that happened as far as my eye carries me. For instance, by that tree a mile away a porter fell down. He was very exhausted. And when we had passed that ridge near the skyline we saw two birds fighting; two bald-headed vultures——"

"That is so," said Adams.

"But beyond the skyline," said Berselius, suddenly becoming excited and clutching his companion's arm, "I see nothing. I know nothing. All is mist—all is mist."

"Yes, yes," said the surgeon. "It's only memory blindness. It will come back."

"Ah, but will it? If I can get to the skyline and see the country beyond, and if I remember that, and if I go on and on, the way we came, and if I remember as I go, then, then, I will be saved. But if I get to that skyline and if I find that the mist stops me from seeing beyond, then I pray you kill me, for the agony of this thing is not to be borne." Suddenly he ceased, and then, as if to some unseen person, he cried out—

"I have left my memory on that road."

Adams, frightened at the man's agitation, tried to soothe him, but Berselius, in the grip of this awful desire to pierce back beyond that mist and find himself, would not be soothed. Nothing would satisfy him but to strike camp and return along the road they had come by. Some instinct told him that the sight of the things he had seen would wake up memory, and that bit by bit, as he went, the mist would retreat before him, and perhaps vanish at last. Some instinct told him this, but reason, who is ever a doubter, tortured him with doubts.

The only course was to go back and see. Adams, who doubted if his patient was physically fit for a march, at last gave in; the man's agony of mind was more dangerous to him than the exhaustion of physical exercise could prove. He gave orders to the porters to strike camp, and then turned to himself, and helped them. They only carried what was barely needful, and was even less than needful, to take them to Fort M'Bassa, ten days, journey in Berselius's condition. Four water bottles that had been left intact they filled with water; they took the tent, and the pole that Félix had spliced. Cassava cakes and tinned meat and a few pounds of chocolate made up the provisions. There were no guns to carry, no trophies of the chase. Of all the army of porters only two were left. Berselius was broken down, Félix had fled, they had no guide, and the crowning horror of the thing was that they had struck off in pursuit of the herd at right angles to the straight path they had taken from the forest, and Adams did not know in the least the point where they had struck off. The porters were absolutely no use as guides, and unless God sent a guide from heaven or chance interposed to lead them in the right way, they were lost; for they had no guns or ammunition with which to get food.

Truly the omen of the elephant lying down had not spoken in vain.

When all was loaded up, and Adams was loaded even like the porters, they turned their backs on the tree and the pools, and leaving them there to burn in the sun forever struck straight west in the direction from which they had come.

Berselius had come in pursuit of a terrible thing and a merciless thing; he was returning in search of a more terrible and a more merciless thing—Memory.

It was four hours after sun-up when they left the camp; and two hours' march brought them to that ridge which Berselius had indicated from the camp as being near the skyline.

When they reached the ridge, and not before, Berselius halted and stared over the country in front of him, his face filled with triumph and hope.

He seized Adams's hand and pointed away to the west. The ridge gave a big view of the country.

"I can remember all that," said he, "keenly, right up to the skyline."

"And at the skyline?"

"Stands the mist," replied Berselius. "But it will lift before me as I go on. Now I know it is only the sight of the things I have seen that is needful to recall the memory of them and of myself in connection with them."

Adams said nothing. It struck him with an eerie feeling that this man beside him was actually walking back into his past. As veil after veil of distance was raised, so would the past come back, bit by bit.

But he was yet to learn what a terrible journey that would be.

One thing struck him as strange. Berselius had never tried to pierce the mist by questions. The man seemed entirely obsessed by the curtain of mist, and by the necessity of piercing it by physical movement, of putting tree to tree and mile to mile.

Berselius had not asked questions because, no doubt, he was under the dominion of a profound instinct, telling him that the past he had lost could only be recalled by the actual picture of the things he had seen.

CHAPTER XXIV
THE SENTENCE OF THE DESERT

Berselius had not asked a single question as to the catastrophe. His own misfortune had banished for him, doubtless, all interest in everything else.

Adams had said to him nothing of Félix, his horrible deeds or his theft of the rifle. Félix, though he had vanished from Adams's life completely and forever, had not vanished from the face of the earth. He was very much alive and doing, and his deeds and his fate are worth a word, for they formed a tragedy well fitting the stage of this merciless land.

The Zappo Zap, having secured the gun and its ammunition, revelling in the joy of possession and power, went skipping on his road, which lay to the northeast. Six miles from the camp he flung himself down by a bush, and, with the gun covered by his arm, slept, and hunted in his sleep, like a hound, till dawn.

Then he rose and pursued his way, still travelling northeast, his bird-like eyes skimming the land and horizon. He sang as he pursued his way, and his song fitted his filed teeth to a charm. If a poisoned arrow could sing or a stabbing spear, it would sing what Félix sang as he went, his long morning shadow stalking behind him; he as soulless and as heartless as it.

What motive of attachment had driven him to follow Verhaeren to Yandjali from the Bena Pianga country heaven knows, for the man was quite beyond the human pale. The elephants were far, far above him in power of love and kindness; one had to descend straight to the alligators to match him, and even then one found oneself at fault.

He was not. Those three words alone describe this figure of india-rubber that could still walk and talk and live and lust, and to whom slaying and torture were amongst the æsthetics of life.

An hour before noon, beyond and above a clump of trees, he sighted a moving object. It was the head of a giraffe.

It was the very same bull giraffe that had fled with the elephant herd and then wheeled away south from it. It was wandering devious now, feeding by itself, and the instant Félix saw the tell-tale head, he dropped flat to the ground as if he had been shot. The giraffe had not seen him, for the head, having vanished for a moment, reappeared; it was feeding, plucking down small branches of leaves, and Félix, lying on his side, opened the breech of the rifle, drew the empty cartridge case, inserted a cartridge in each barrel, and closed the breech. Now, unknown to Adams, when he had fired the gun the day before, there was a plug of clay in the left-hand barrel about two inches from the muzzle; just an inconsiderable wad of clay about as thick as a gun wad; the elephant folk had done this when they had mishandled the gun, and, though the thing could have been removed with a twig, Puck himself could not have conceived a more mischievous obstruction. He certainly never would have conceived so devilish a one.

Adams had, fortunately for himself, fired the right-hand barrel; the concussion had not broken up the plug, for it was still moist, being clay from the trodden-up edge of the pool. It was moist still, for the night dew had found it.

The Zappo Zap knew nothing of the plug. He knew nothing, either, of the tricks of these big, old-fashioned elephant guns, for he kept both barrels full cock, and it is almost three to two that if you fire one of these rifles with both barrels full cock, both barrels will go off simultaneously, or nearly so, from the concussion.

With the gun trailing after him—another foolish trick—the savage crawled on his belly through the long grass to within firing distance of the tree clump.

Then he lay and waited.

He had not long to wait.

The giraffe, hungry and feeding, was straying along the edge of the clump of trees, picking down the youngest and freshest leaves, just as a *gourmet* picks the best bits out of a salad.

In a few minutes his body was in view, the endless neck flung up, the absurd head and little, stumpy, useless horns prying amidst the leaves, and every now and then slewing round and sweeping the country in search of danger.

Félix lay motionless as a log; then, during a moment when the giraffe's head was hidden in the leaves, he flung himself into position and took aim.

A tremendous report rang out, the giraffe fell, squealing, and roaring and kicking, and Félix, flung on his back, lay stretched out, a cloud of gauzy blue smoke in the air above him.

The breech of the rifle had blown out. He had fired the right-hand barrel, but the concussion had sprung the left-hand cock as well.

It seemed to the savage that a great black hand struck him in the face and flung him backward. He lay for a moment, half-stunned; then he sat up, and, behold! the sun had gone out and he was in perfect blackness.

He was blind, for his eyes were gone, and where his nose had been was now a cavity. He looked as though he had put on a red velvet domino, and he sat there in the sun with the last vestige of the blue smoke dissolving above him in the air, not knowing in the least what had happened to him.

He knew nothing of blindness; he knew little of pain. An Englishman in his wounded state would have been screaming in agony; to Félix the pain was sharp, but it was nothing to the fact that the sun had "gone down."

He put his hand to the pain and felt his ruined face, but that did not tell him anything.

This sudden black dark was not the darkness which came from shutting one's eyes; it was something else, and he scrambled on his feet to find out.

He could feel the darkness now, and he advanced a few steps to see if he could walk through it; then he sprang into the air to see if it was lighter above, and dived on his hands and knees to see if he could slip under it, and shouted and whooped to see if he could drive it away.

But it was a great darkness, not to be out-jumped, jumped he as high as the sun, or slipped under, were he as thin as a knife, or whooped away, though he whooped to everlasting.

He walked rapidly, and then he began to run. He ran rapidly, and he seemed to possess some instinct in his feet which told him of broken ground. The burst gun lay where he had left it in the grass, and the dead giraffe lay where it had fallen by the trees; the wind blew, and the grass waved, the sun spread his pyramid of light from horizon to horizon, and in the sparkle above a black dot hung trembling above the stricken beast at the edge of the wood.

The black figure of the man continued its headlong course. It was running in a circle of many miles, impelled through the nothingness of night by the dark soul raging in it.

Hours passed, and *then* it fell, and lay face to the sky and arms outspread. You might have thought it dead. But it was a thing almost indestructible. It lay motionless, but it was alive with hunger.

During all its gyrations it had been followed and watched closely. It had not lain for a minute when a vulture dropped like a stone from the sky and lit on it with wings outspread.

Next moment the vulture was seized, screeching, torn limb from limb, and in the act of being devoured!

But the sentence of the desert on the blind is death, trap vultures as cunningly as you will, and devour them as ferociously. The eye is everything in the battle of the strong against the weak. And so it came about that two days later a pair of leopards from the woods to the northeast fought with the figure, which fought with teeth and hands and feet, whilst the yellow-eyed kites looked on at a battle that would have turned with horror the heart of Flamininus.

CHAPTER XXV
TOWARD THE SUNSET

When Berselius, standing on the ridge, had looked long enough at the country before him, taking in its every detail with delight, they started again on their march, Berselius leading.

They had no guide. The only plan in Adams's head was to march straight west toward the sunset for a distance roughly equivalent to the forced march they had made in pursuit of the herd, and then to strike at right angles due north and try to strike the wood isthmus of the two great forests making up the forest of M'Bonga.

But the sunset is a wide mark and only appears at sunset. They had no compass; the elephant folk had made away with all the instruments of the expedition. They must inevitably stray from the true direction, striking into that infernal circle which imprisons all things blind and all things compassless. Even should they, by a miracle, strike the isthmus of woods, the forest would take them, confuse them, hand them from tree to tree and glade to glade, and lose them at last and for ever in one of the million pockets which a forest holds open for the lost.

The stout heart of the big man had not quailed before this prospect. He had a fighting chance; that was enough for him. But now at the re-start, as Berselius stepped forward and took the lead, a hope sprang up in his breast. A tremendous and joyful idea occurred to him. Was it possible that Berselius would guide them back?

The memory that the man possessed was so keen, his anxiety to pierce the veil before him was so overpowering, was it possible that like a hound hunting by sight instead of smell, he would lead them straight?

Only by following the exact track they had come by, could Berselius pierce back into that past he craved to see. Only by putting tree to tree and ridge to ridge, memory to memory, could he collect what he had lost.

Could he do this?

The life of the whole party depended upon the answer to that question.

The track they ought to follow was the track by which the herd had led them. Adams could not tell whether they were following that track—even Félix could scarcely have told—for the dew and the wind had made the faint traces of the elephants quite indiscernible now to civilized eyes; and Berselius never once looked at the ground under his feet, he was led entirely by the configuration of the land. That to the eyes of Adams was hopeless. For the great elephant country is all alike, and one ridge is the counterpart of another ridge, and one grassy plain of another grassy plain, and the scattered trees tell you nothing when you are lost, except that you are lost.

The heat of the day was now strong on the land; the porters sweated under their loads, and Adams, loaded like them, knew for once in his life what it was to be a slave and a beast of burden.

Berselius, who carried nothing, did not seem to feel the heat; weak though he must have been from his injury and the blood-letting. He marched on, ever on, apparently satisfied and well pleased as horizon lifted, giving place to new horizon, and plain of waving grass succeeded ridge of broken ground.

But Adams, as hour followed hour, felt the hope dying out in his breast, and the remorseless certainty stole upon him that they were out of their track. This land seemed somehow different from any he had seen before; he could have sworn that this country around them was not the country through which they had pursued the herd. His hope had been built on a false foundation. How could a man whose memory was almost entirely obscured lead them right? This was not the case of the blind leading the blind, but the case of the blind leading men with sight.

Berselius was deceiving himself. Hope was leading him, not memory.

And still Berselius led on, assured and triumphant, calling out, "See! do you remember that tree? We passed it at just this distance when we were coming." Or, now, "Look at that patch of blue grass. We halted for a minute here."

Adams, after a while, made no reply. The assurance and delight of Berselius as these fancied memories came to him shocked the heart. There was a horrible and sardonic humour in the whole business, a bathos that insulted the soul.

The dead leading the living, the blind leading the man with sight, lunacy leading sanity to death.

Yet there was nothing to be done but follow. As well take Berselius's road as any other. Sunset would tell them whether they were facing the sunset; but he wished that Berselius would cease.

The situation was bad enough to bear without those triumphant calls.

It was past noon now; the light wind that had been blowing in their faces had died away; there was the faintest stirring of the air, and on this, suddenly, to Adams's nostrils came stealing a smell of corruption, such as he had never experienced before.

It grew stronger as they went.

There was a slight rise in the ground before them just here, and as they took it the stench became almost insupportable, and Adams was turning aside to spit when a cry from Berselius, who was a few yards in advance, brought him forward to his side.

The rise in the ground had hidden from them a dried-up river-bed, and there before them in the sandy trough, huge amidst the boulders, lay the body of an elephant.

A crowd of birds busy about the carcass rose clamouring in the air and flew away.

"Do you remember?" cried Berselius.

"Good God!" said Adams. "Do I remember!"

It was the body of the great beast they had passed when in pursuit of the herd.

Yes, there was no doubt now that Berselius was guiding them aright. He had followed the track they had come by without deviating a hundred yards.

The great animal was lying just as they had left it, but the work of the birds was evident; horribly so, and it was not a sight to linger over.

They descended into the river bed, passed up the other bank, and went on, Berselius leading and Adams walking by his side.

"Do you know," said Adams, "I was beginning to think you were out of the track."

Berselius smiled.

Adams, who was glancing at his face, thought that he had never seen an expression like that on the man's face before. The smile of the lips that had marked and marred his countenance through life, the smile that was half a sneer, was not there; this came about the eyes.

"He was in exactly the same position, too," said Adams. "But the birds will have him down before long. Well, he has served one purpose in his life; he has shown us we are on the right road, and he has given you back another bit of memory."

"Poor brute," said Berselius.

These words, coming from the once iron-hearted Berselius, struck Adams strangely; there was a trace of pity in their tone.

CHAPTER XXVI
THE FADING MIST

They camped two hours before sundown. One of the few mercies of this country is the number of dead trees and the bushes from which one can always scrape the materials for a fire.

Adams, with his hunting knife and a small hatchet which was all steel and so had been uninjured in the catastrophe, cut wood enough for the fire. They had nothing to cook with, but fortunately the food they had with them did not require cooking.

The tent was practicable, for the pole, so well had it been spliced, was as good as new. They set it up, and having eaten their supper, crept under it, leaving the porters to keep watch or not as they chose.

Berselius, who had marched so well all day, had broken down at the finish. He seemed half dead with weariness, and scarcely spoke a word, eating mechanically and falling to sleep immediately on lying down.

But he was happy. Happy as the man who suddenly finds that he can outwalk the paralysis threatening him, or the man who finds the fog of blindness lifting before him, showing him again bit by bit the world he had deemed forever lost. Whilst this man sleeps in the tent beside his companion and the waning moon breaks up over the horizon and mixes her light with the red flicker of the fire, a word about that past of which he was in search may not be out of place.

Berselius was of mixed nationality. His father of Swedish descent, his mother of French.

Armand Berselius the elder was what is termed a lucky man. In other words, he had that keenness of intellect which enables the possessor to seize opportunities and to foresee events.

This art of looking into the future is the key to Aladdin's Palace and to the Temple of Power. To know what will appreciate in value and what will depreciate, that is the art of success in life, and that was the art which made Armand Berselius a millionaire.

Berselius the younger grew up in an atmosphere of money. His mother died when he was quite young. He had neither brothers nor sisters; his father, a chilly-hearted sensualist, had a dislike to the boy; for some obscure reason, without any foundation in fact, he fancied that he was some other man's son.

The basis of an evil mind is distrust. Beware of the man who is always fearful of being swindled. Who cannot trust, cannot be trusted.

Berselius treated his son like a brute, and the boy, with great power for love in his heart, conceived a hatred for the man who misused him that was hellish in intensity.

But not a sign of it did he show. That power of will and restraint so remarkable in the grown-up man was not less remarkable in the boy. He bound his hate with iron bands and prisoned it, and he did this from pride. When his father thrashed him for the slightest offence, he showed not a sign of pain or passion; when the old man committed that last outrage one can commit against the mind of a child, and sneered at him before grown-up people, young Berselius neither flushed nor moved an eyelid. He handed the insult to the beast feeding at his heart, and it devoured it and grew.

The spring was poisoned at its source.

That education of the heart which only love can give was utterly cut off from the boy and supplanted by the education of hate.

And the mind tainted thus from the beginning was an extraordinary mind, a spacious intellect, great for evil or great for good, never little, and fed by an unfailing flood of energy.

The elder Berselius, as if bent on the utter damnation of his son, kept him well supplied with money. He did this from pride.

The young man took his graduate degree in vice, with higher marks from the devil than any other young man of his time. He passed through the college of St. Cyr and into the cavalry, leaving it at the death of his father and when he had obtained his captaincy.

He now found himself free, without a profession and with forty million francs to squander, or save, or do what he liked with.

He at once took his place as a man of affairs with one hand in politics and the other in finance. There are a dozen men like Berselius on the Continent of Europe. Politicians and financiers under the guise of Boulevardiers. Men of leisure apparently, but, in reality, men of intellect, who work their political and financial works quite unobtrusively and yet have a considerable hand in the making of events.

Berselius was one of these, varying the monotony of social life with periodic returns to the wilderness.

With the foundation of the Congo State by King Leopold, Berselius saw huge chances of profit. He knew the country, for he had hunted there. He knew the ivory, the copal, and the palm oil resources of the place, and in the rubber vines he guessed an untapped source of boundless wealth. He saw the great difficulty in the way of making this territory a paying concern; that is to say, he saw the labour question. Europeans would not do the work; the blacks would not, unless paid, and even then inefficiently.

To keep up a large force of European police to make the blacks work on European terms, was out of the question. The expense would run away with half the profits; the troops would die, and, worst of all, other nations would say, "What are you doing with that huge army of men?" The word "slavery" had to be eliminated from the proceedings, else the conscience of Europe would be touched. He foresaw this, and he was lost in admiration at the native police idea. The stroke of genius that collected all the Félixes of the Congo basin into an army of darkness, and collected all the weak and defenceless into a herd of slaves, was a stroke after his own heart.

Of the greatest murder syndicate the world has ever seen, Berselius became a member. He was not invited to the bloody banquet—he invited himself.

He had struck the Congo in a hunting expedition; he had seen and observed; later on, during a second expedition, he had seen the germination of Leopold's idea. He dropped his gun and came back to Europe.

He was quite big enough to have smashed the whole infernal machinery then and there. America had not yet, hoodwinked, signed the licence to kill, which she handed to Leopold on the 22d of April, 1884. Germany had not been roped in. England and France were still aloof, and Berselius, arriving at the psychological moment, did not mince matters.

The result was two million pounds to his credit during the next ten years.

So much for Berselius and his past.

An hour after dawn next day they started. The morning was windless, warm, and silent, and the sun shining broad on the land cast their shadows before them as they went, the porters with their loads piled on their heads, Adams carrying the tent-pole and tent, Berselius leading.

He had recovered from his weakness of the night before. He had almost recovered his strength, and he felt that newness of being which the convalescent feels—that feeling of new birth into the old world which pays one, almost, for the pains of the past sickness.

Never since his boyhood had Berselius felt that keen pleasure in the sun and the blue sky and the grass under his feet; but it called up no memories of boyhood, for the mist was still there, hiding boyhood and manhood and *everything* up to the skyline.

But the mist did not frighten him now. He had found a means of dispelling it; the photographic plates were all there unbroken, waiting only to be collected and put together, and he felt instinctively that after a time, when he had collected a certain number, the brain would gain strength, and all at once the mist would vanish for ever, and he would be himself again.

Three hours after the start they passed a broken-down tree.

Adams recognized it at once as the tree they had passed on the hunt, shortly after turning from their path to follow the herd of elephants.

Berselius was still leading them straight, and soon they would come to the crucial point—the spot where they had turned at right angles to follow the elephants.

Would Berselius remember and turn, or would he get confused and go on in a straight line?

The question was answered in another twenty minutes by Berselius himself.

He stopped dead and waved his arm with a sweeping motion to include all the country to the north.

"We came from there," he said, indicating the north. "We struck the elephant spoor just here, and turned due west."

"How on earth do you know?" asked Adams. "I can't see any indication, and for the life of me I couldn't tell where we turned or whether we came from there," indicating the north, "or there," pointing to the south. "How do you know?"

"How do I know?" replied Berselius. "Why, this place and everything we reach and pass is as vivid to me as if I had passed it only two minutes ago. *It hits me with such vividness that it blinds me.* It is that which I believe makes the mist. The things I can see are so extraordinarily vivid that they hide everything else. My brain seems new born—every memory that comes back to it comes back glorious in strength. If there were gods, they would see as I see."

A wind had arisen and it blew from the northwest. Berselius inhaled it triumphantly.

Adams stood watching him. This piece-by-piece return of memory, this rebuilding of the past foot by foot, mile by mile, and horizon by horizon, was certainly the strangest phenomenon of the brain that he had ever come across.

This thing occurs in civilized life, but then it is far less striking, for the past comes to a man from a hundred close points—a thousand familiar things in his house or surroundings call to him when he is brought back to them; but here in the great, lone elephant land, the only familiar thing was the track they had followed and the country around it. If Berselius had been taken off that track and placed a few miles away, he would have been as lost as Adams.

They wheeled to the north, following in their leader's footsteps.

That afternoon, late, they camped by the same pool near which Berselius had shot the rhinos.

Adams, to make sure, walked away to where the great bull had fought the cow before being laid low by the rifle of the hunter.

The bones were there, picked clean and bleached, exemplifying the eternal hunger of the desert, which is one of the most horrible facts in life. These two great brutes had been left nearly whole a few days ago; tons of flesh had vanished like snow in sunshine, mist in morning.

But Adams, as he gazed at the colossal bones, was not thinking of that; the marvel of their return filled his mind as he looked from the skeletons to where, against the evening blue, a thin wreath of smoke rose up from the camp fire which the porters had lighted.

Far away south, so far away as to be scarcely discernible, a bird was sailing along, sliding on the wind without a motion of the wings. It passed from sight and left the sky stainless, and the land lay around silent with the tremendous silence of evening, and lifeless as the bones bleaching at his feet.

CHAPTER XXVII
I AM THE FOREST

The day after the next, two hours before noon, they passed an object which Adams remembered well.

It was the big tree which Berselius had pointed out to him as having been tusked by an elephant; and an hour after they had started from the mid-day rest, the horizon to the north changed and grew dark.

It was the forest.

The sky immediately above the dark line, from contrast, was extraordinarily bright and pale, and, as they marched, the line lifted and the trees grew.

"Look!" said Berselius.

"I see," replied Adams.

A question was troubling his mind. Would Berselius be able to guide them amidst the trees? Here in the open he had a hundred tiny indications on either side of him, but amidst the trees how could he find his way? Was it possible that memory could lead him through that labyrinth once it grew dense?

It will be remembered that it was a two days' march from Fort M'Bassa through the isthmus of woods to the elephant country. At the edge of the forest the trees were very thinly set, but for the rest, and a day's march from the fort, it was jungle.

Would Berselius be able to penetrate that jungle? Time would tell. Berselius knew nothing about it; he only knew what lay before his sight.

Toward evening the trees came out to meet them, baobab and monkey-bread, set widely apart; and they camped by a pool and lit their fire, and slept as men sleep in the pure air of the woods and the desert.

Next morning they pursued their journey, Berselius still confident. At noon, however, he began to exhibit slight signs of agitation and anxiety. The trees were thickening around them; he still knew the way, but the view before him was getting shorter and shorter as the trees thickened; that is to say, the mist was coming closer and closer. He knew nothing of the dense jungle before them; he only knew that the clear road in front of him was shortening up rapidly and horribly, and that if it continued to do so it would inevitably vanish.

The joy that had filled his heart became transformed to the grief which the man condemned to blindness feels when he sees the bright world fading from his sight, slowly but surely as the expiring flame of a lamp.

He walked more rapidly, and the more rapidly he went the shorter did the road before him grow.

All at once the forest—which had been playing, up to this, with Berselius as a cat plays with a mouse—all at once the forest, like a great green Sphinx, put down its great green paw and spoke from its cavernous heart—

"I am the Forest."

They had passed almost at a step into the labyrinths. Plantain leaves hit them insolently in the face, lianas hung across their path like green ropes placed to bar them out, weeds tangled the foot.

Berselius, like an animal that finds itself trapped, plunged madly forward. Adams following closely behind heard him catching back his breath with a sob. They plunged on for a few yards, and then Berselius stood still.

The forest was very silent, and seemed listening. The evening light and the shade of the leaves cast gloom around them. Adams could hear his own heart thumping and the breathing of the porters behind him. If Berselius had lost his way, then they were lost indeed.

After a moment Berselius spoke, as a man speaks whose every hope in life is shattered.

"The path is gone."

Adams's only reply was a deep intake of the breath.

"There is nothing before me. I am lost."

"Shall we try back?" said Adams, speaking in that hard tone which comes when a man is commanding his voice.

"Back? Of what use? I cannot go back; I must go forward. But here there is nothing."

The unhappy man's voice was terrible to hear. He had marched so triumphantly all day, drawing nearer at each step to himself, to that self which memory had hidden from him and which memory was disclosing bit by bit. And now the march was interrupted as if by a wall set across his path.

But Adams was of a type of man to whom despondency may be known, but never despair.

They had marched all day; they were lost, it is true, but they were not far, now, from Fort M'Bassa. The immediate necessity was rest and food.

There was a little clearing amidst the trees just here, and with his own hands he raised the tent. They had no fire, but the moon when she rose, though in her last quarter, lit up the forest around them with a green glow-worm glimmer. One could see the lianas and the trees, the broad leaves shining with dew, some bright, some sketched in dimly, and all bathed in gauze green light; and they could hear the drip and patter of dew on leaf and branch.

This is a mournful sound—the most mournful of all the sounds that fill the great forests of the Congo. It is so casual, so tearful. One might fancy it the sound of the forest weeping to itself in the silence of the night.

CHAPTER XXVIII
GOD SENDS A GUIDE

To be lost in the desert or in a land like the elephant country is bad, but to be lost in the dense parts of the tropical forest is far worse.

You are in a horrible labyrinth, a maze, not of intricate paths but of blinding curtains. I am speaking now of that arrogant jungle, moist and hot, where life is in full ferment, and where the rubber vine grows and thrives; where you go knee-deep in slush and catch at a tree-bole to prevent yourself going farther, cling, sweating at every pore and shivering like a dog, feeling for firmer ground and finding it, only to be led on to another quagmire. The bush pig avoids this place, the leopard shuns it; it is bad in the dry season when the sun gives some light by day, and the moon a gauzy green glimmer by night, but in the rains it is terrific. Night, then, is black as the inside of a trunk, and day is so feeble that your hand, held before your face at arm's length, is just a shadow. The westward part of the forest of M'Bonga projects a spur of the pestiferous rubber-bearing land into the isthmus of healthy woods. It was just at the tip of this spur that Berselius and his party were entangled and lost.

The two porters were Yandjali men, they knew nothing of these woods, and were utterly useless as guides; they sat now amidst the leaves near the tent eating their food; dark shadows in the glow-worm light, the glistening black skin of a knee or shoulder showing up touched by the glimmer in which leaf and liana, tree trunk and branch, seemed like marine foliage bathed in the watery light of a sea-cave.

Adams had lit a pipe, and he sat beside Berselius at the opening of the tent, smoking. The glare of the match had shown him the face of Berselius for a moment. Berselius, since his first outcry on finding the path gone, had said little, and there was a patient and lost look on his face, sad but most curious to see. Most curious, for it said fully what a hundred little things had been hinting since their start from the scene of the catastrophe—that the old Berselius had vanished and a new Berselius had taken his place. Adams had at first put down the change in his companion to weakness, but the weakness had passed, the man's great vitality had reasserted itself, and the change was still there.

This was not the man who had engaged him in Paris; this person might have been a mild twin-brother of the redoubtable Captain of the Avenue Malakoff, of Matadi and Yandjali. When memory came fully back, would it bring with it the old Berselius, or would the new Berselius, mild, inoffensive, and kindly, suddenly find himself burdened with the tremendous past of the man he once had been?

Nothing is more true than that the human mind from accident, from grief, or from that mysterious excitement, during which in half an hour a blaspheming costermonger "gets religion" and becomes a saint of God—nothing is more certain than that the human mind can like this, at a flash, turn topsy-turvy; the good coming to the top, the bad going to the bottom. Mechanical pressure on the cortex of the brain can bring this state of things about, even as it can convert a saint of God into a devil incarnate.

Was Berselius under the influence of forced amendment of this sort?

Adams was not even considering the matter, he was lost in gloomy thoughts.

He was smoking slowly, holding his index and middle fingers over the pipe-bowl to prevent the tobacco burning too quickly, for he had only a couple of pipefuls left. He was thinking that to-morrow evening the pouch would be empty, when, from somewhere in the forest near by, there came a sound which brought him to his feet and the two porters up on hands and knees like listening dogs.

It was the sound of a human voice raised in a sort of chant, ghostly and mournful as the sound of the falling dew. As it came, rising and falling, monotonous and rhythmical, the very plain song of desolation, Adams felt his hair lift and his flesh crawl, till one of the porters, springing erect from his crouching position, sent his voice through the trees—

"Ahi ahee!"

The song ceased; and then, a moment later, faint and wavering, and like the voice of a seagull, came the reply—

"Ahi aheee!"

"Man," said the porter, turning white eyeballs and glinting teeth over his shoulder at Adams.

He called again, and again came the reply.

"Quick," said Adams, seizing the arm of Berselius, who had risen, "there's a native here somewhere about; he may guide us out of this infernal place; follow me, and for God's sake keep close."

Holding Berselius by the arm, and motioning the other native to follow, he seized the porter by the shoulder and pushed him forward. The man knew what was required and obeyed, advancing, calling, and listening by turns, till, at last, catching the true direction of the sound he went rapidly, Berselius and Adams following close behind. Sometimes they were half up to the knees in boggy patches, fighting their way through leaves that struck them like great wet hands; sometimes the call in the distance seemed farther away, and they held their pace, they held their breath, they clung to each other, listening, till, now, by some trick of the trees, though they had not moved and though there was no wind, the cry came nearer.

"Ahi, ahee!"

Then, at last, a dim red glow shone through the foliage before them and bursting their way through the leaves they broke into an open space where, alone, by a small fire of dry branches and brushwood, sat a native, stark naked, except for a scrap of dingy loincloth, and looking like a black gnome, a faun of this horrible place, and the very concretion of its desolation and death.

He was sitting when they caught their first glimpse of him, with his chin supported on his hand, but the instant he saw the faces of the white men he rose as if to escape, then the porter called out something that reassured him, and he sat down again and shivered.

He was one of the rubber collectors. He had reached this spot the day before, and had built himself a shelter of leaves and branches. He would be here for ten days or a fortnight, and his food, chiefly cassava, lay in a little pile in the shelter, covered over with leaves.

The porter continued speaking to the collector, who, now regaining the use of his limbs, stood up before the white men, hands folded in front of him, and his eyes rolling from Berselius to Adams.

"M'Bassa," said Adams, touching the porter, pointing to the collector, and then away into the forest in the direction he fancied Fort M'Bassa to be.

The porter understood. He said a few words to the collector, who nodded his head furiously and struck himself on the breast with his open hand.

Then the porter turned again to Adams.

"M'Bassa," said he, nodding his head, pointing to the collector, and then away into the forest.

That was all, but it meant that they were saved.

Adams gave a great whoop that echoed away through the trees, startling bats and birds in the branches and losing itself without an echo in the depths of the gloom. Then he struck himself a blow on the chest with his fist.

"My God!" said he, "the tent!"

They had only travelled an eighth of a mile or so from the camping place, but they had wandered this way and that before the porter had found the true direction of the call, and the tent, provisions, and everything else were lost as utterly and irrevocably as though they had been dropped in mid-ocean.

To step aside from a thing—even for a hundred yards—in this terrible place was to lose it; even the rubber collectors, from whom the forest holds few secrets have, in these thick places, to blaze a trail by breaking branches, tying lianas and marking tree trunks.

"True," said Berselius in a weary voice, "we have lost even that."

"No matter," said Adams, "we have got a guide. Cheer up, this man will take us to Fort M'Bassa and there you will find the road again."

"Are you sure?" said Berselius, a touch of hope in his voice.

"Sure? Certain. You've forgotten Fort M'Bassa. Well, when you see it, you will remember it, and it will lead you right away home. Cheer up, cheer up; we've got a fire and a bit of shelter for you to sleep under, and we'll start bright and early in the morning, and this black imp of Satan will lead you straight back to your road and your memory—hey! Uncle Joe!"

He patted the collector on the naked shoulder and a faint grin appeared on that individual's forlorn countenance; never had he come across a white man like this before. Then, bustling about, Adams piled up the fire with more sticks, got Berselius under the shelter of the collector's wretched hut, sat himself down close to the fire, produced his pipe, and proceeded, in one glorious debauch, to finish the last of his tobacco.

This rubber collector, the last and the humblest creature on earth, had given them fire and shelter; they were also to be beholden to him for food. His wretched cassava cakes and his calabash of water gave them their breakfast next morning, and then they started, the collector leading, walking before them through the dense growth of the trees as assuredly as a man following a well-known road. It was a terrible thing for him to leave his post, but the white men were from M'Bassa and wished to return to M'Bassa, and

M'Bassa was the head centre of his work and the terrible Mecca of his fears. White men from there and going to there must be obeyed.

This was the last phase of the great hunt. Berselius had been slowly stripped by the wilderness of everything now but the clothes he stood up in, his companion and two porters. Guns, equipment, tents, stores, the Zappo Zap, and the army of men under that ferocious lieutenant, had all "gone dam." He was mud to the knees, his clothing was torn, he was mud to the elbows from having tripped last night and fallen in a quagmire, his face was white and drawn and grimy as the face of a London cabrunner, his hair was grayer and dull, but his eyes were bright and he was happy. At M'Bassa he would be put upon the road again—the only road to the thing he craved for as burning Dives craved for water—himself.

But it was ordained that he should find that questionably desirous person before reaching M'Bassa.

They had been on the march for an hour when Adams, fussing like a person who is making his first journey by rail, stopped the guide to make sure he was leading them right.

"M'Bassa?" said Adams.

"M'Bassa," replied the other, nodding his head. Then with outspread hand he pointed before them and made a semicircular sweep to indicate that he was leading them for some reason by a circuitous route.

He was making, in fact, for open ground that would bring them in the direction of the fort by a longer but much easier road than a direct line through the jungle. He was making also for water, for his scant supply had been exhausted by his guests, and he knew the road he was taking would lead him to broad pools of water. Adams nodded his head to imply that he understood, and the man led on.

CHAPTER XXIX
THE VISION OF THE POOLS

Somewhere about noon they halted for a rest and some food. It was less boggy here, and the sunlight showed stronger through the dense roof of foliage. The cassava cakes were tainted with must, and they had no water, but the increasing light made them forget everything but the freedom that was opening before them.

Adams pointed to the empty calabash which their guide carried, and the collector nodded and pointed before them, as if to imply that soon they would come to water and that all would be well.

Now, as they resumed their way, the trees altered and drew farther apart, the ground was solid under foot, and through the foliage of the euphorbia and raphia palm came stray glimmers of sunshine, bits of blue sky, birds, voices, and the whisper of a breeze.

"This is better," said Berselius.

Adams flung up his head and expanded his nostrils.

"Better, my God!" said he; "this is heaven!"

It was heaven, indeed, after that hell of gloom; that bog roofed in with leaves, the very smell of which clings to one for ever like the memory of a fever dream.

All at once patches of sunlight appeared in front as well as above. They quickened their pace, the trees drew apart, and, suddenly, with theatrical effect, a park-like sward of land lay before them leading to a sheet of blue water reflecting tall feather-palms and waving speargrass, all domed over with blue, and burning in the bright, bright sunshine.

"The Silent Pools!" cried Adams. "The very place where I saw the leopard chasing the antelope! Great Scott!—Hi! hi! hi! you there!—where are you going?"

The collector had raced down to the water's edge; he knew the dangers of the place, for he divided the grass, filled his calabash with water, and dashed back before anything could seize him. Then, without drinking, he came running with the calabash to the white men.

Adams handed the calabash first to his companion.

Berselius drank and then wiped his forehead; he seemed disturbed in his mind and had a dazed look.

He had never come so far along the edge of the pools as this, but there was something in the configuration of the place that stirred his sleeping memory.

"What is it?" asked Adams.

"I don't know," replied Berselius. "I have dreamt—I have seen—I remember something—somewhere—"

Adams laughed.

"I know," said he; "you come along, and in a few minutes you will see something that will help your memory. Why, man, we camped near here, you and I and Meeus; when you see the spot you'll find yourself on your road again. Come, let's make a start."

The collector was standing with the half-full calabash in his hands.

He had not dared to drink. Adams nodded to him, motioning him to do so, but he handed it first to the porter. Then, when the porter had drunk, the collector finished the remains of the water and the last few drops he flung on the ground, an offering, perhaps, to some god or devil of his own. Then he led on, skirting the water's edge. The loveliness of the place had not lessened since Adams had seen it last; even the breeze that was blowing to-day did not disturb the spirit of sweet and profound peace which held in a charm this lost garden of the wilderness; the palms bent as if in sleep, the water dimpled to the breeze and seemed to smile, a flamingo, with rose-coloured wings, passed and flew before them and vanished beyond the rocking tops of the trees that still sheltered the camping place where once Berselius had raised his tent.

Again, with theatrical effect, as the pools had burst upon them on leaving the forest, the camping place unveiled itself.

"Now," said Adams in triumph, "do you remember that?"

Berselius did not reply. He was walking along with his eyes fixed straight before him. He did not stop, or hesitate, or make any exclamation to indicate whether he remembered or not.

"Do you remember?" cried Adams.

But Berselius did not speak. He was making noises as if strangling, and suddenly his hands flew up to the neck of his hunting shirt, and tore at it till he tore it open.

"Steady, man, steady," cried Adams catching the other's arm. "Hi, you'll be in a fit if you don't mind—steady, I *say*."

But Berselius heard nothing, knew nothing but the scene before him, and Adams, who was running now after the afflicted man, who had broken away and was making straight for the trees beneath which the village had once been, heard and knew nothing of what lay before and around Berselius.

Berselius had stepped out of the forest an innocent man, and behold! memory had suddenly fronted him with a hell in which he was the chief demon.

He had no time to accommodate himself to the situation, no time for sophistry. He was not equipped with the forty years of steadily growing callousness that had vanished; the fiend who had inspired him with the lust for torture had deserted him, and the sight and the knowledge of himself came as suddenly as a blow in the face.

Under that m'bina tree two soldiers, one with the haft of a blood-stained knife between his teeth, had mutilated horribly a living girl. Little Papeete had been decapitated just where his skull lay now; the shrieks and wails of the tortured tore the sky above Berselius; but Adams heard nothing and saw nothing but Berselius raving amidst the remains.

Bones lay here and bones lay there, clean picked by the vultures and white bleached by the sun; skulls, jawbones, femurs, broken or whole. The remains of the miserable huts faced the strewn and miserable bones, and the trees blew their golden trumpets over all.

As Adams looked from the man who with shrill cries was running about as a frantic woman runs about, to the bones on the ground, he guessed the tragedy of Berselius. But he was to hear it in words spoken with the torrid eloquence of madness.

PART FOUR

CHAPTER XXX
THE AVENGER

It was a hot night up at the fort, a night eloquent of the coming rains. The door of the guest house stood open and the light of the paraffin lamp lay upon the veranda and the ground of the yard, forming a parallelogram of topaz across which were flitting continually great moth shadows big as birds.

Andreas Meeus was seated at the white-wood table of the sitting room before a big blue sheet of paper. He held a pen in his hand, but he was not writing just at present; he was reading what he had written.

He was, in fact, making up his three-monthly report for headquarters, and he found it difficult, because the last three months had brought in little rubber and less ivory. A lot of things had conspired to make trade bad. Sickness had swept two villages entirely away; one village, as we know, had revolted; then, vines had died from some mysterious disease in two of the very best patches of the forest. All these explanations Meeus was now putting on paper for the edification of the Congo Government. He was devoting a special paragraph to the revolt of the village by the Silent Pools, and the punishment he had dealt out to the natives. Not a word was said of torture and slaughtering. "Drastic Measures" was the term he used, a term perfectly well understood by the people to whom he was writing.

On the wall behind him the leopard-skin still hung, looking now shrivelled at the edges in this extreme heat. On the wall in front of him the Congo bows and poisoned arrows looked more venomous and deadly than by the light of day. A scorpion twice the size of a penny was making a circuit of the walls just below the ceiling; you could hear a faint scratch from it as it travelled along, a scratch that seemed an echo of Meeus's pen as it travelled across the paper.

He held between his lips the everlasting cigarette.

Sitting thus, meditating, pen in hand, he heard sounds: the sound of the night wind, the sound of one of the soldiers singing as he cleaned his rifle—the men always sang over this business, as if to propitiate the gun god—the scratch of the scorpion and the "creak, creak" of a joist warping and twisting to the heat.

But the sound of the wind was the most arresting. It would come over the forest and up the slope and round the guest house with a long-drawn, sweeping "Ha-a-a-r," and sob once or twice, and then die away down the slope and over the forest and away and beyond to the east, where Kilimanjaro was waiting for it, crowned with snow on his throne beneath the stars.

But the wind was almost dead now—the heat of the night had stifled it. The faintest breathing of air took the place of the strong puffs that had sent the flame of the lamp half up the glass chimney. As Meeus listened, on this faint breath from the forest he heard a sound—

"Boom—boom"—very faint, and as if someone were striking a drum in a leisurely manner.

"Boom—boom."

A great man-ape haunted this part of the forest of M'Bonga like an evil spirit. He had wandered here, perhaps from the west coast forests. Driven away from his species—who knows?—for some crime. The natives of the fort had caught glimpses of him now and then; he was huge and old and gray, and now in the darkness of the forest was striking himself on the chest, standing there in the gloom of the leaves, trampling the plantains under foot, taller than the tallest man, smiting himself in the pride of his strength.

"Boom—boom."

It is a hair-lifting sound when you know the cause, but it left Meeus unmoved. His mind was too full of the business of writing his report to draw images or listen to imagination; all the same, this sinister drum-beat acted upon his subconscious self and, scarcely knowing why he did so, he got up from the table and came outside to the fort wall and looked over away into the dark.

There was not a star in the sky. A dense pall of cloud stretched from horizon to horizon, and the wind, as Meeus stepped from the veranda into the darkness, died away utterly.

He stood looking into the dark. He could make out the forest, a blackness humped and crouching in the surrounding blackness. There was not a ray of light from the sky, and now and again came the drum—

"Boom—boom."

Then it ceased, and a bat passed so close that the wind of it stirred his hair. He spat the taint of it from his mouth, and returning to the house, seated himself at the table and continued his work.

But the night was to be fateful in sounds and surprises. He had not been sitting five minutes when a voice from the blackness outside made him drop his pen and listen.

It was a European voice, shouting and raving and laughing, and Meeus, as he listened, clutched at the table, for the voice was known to him. It was the voice of Berselius!

Berselius, who was hundreds of miles away in the elephant country!

Meeus heard his own name. It came in to him out of the darkness, followed by a peal of laughter. Rapid steps sounded coming across the courtyard, and the sweat ran from Meeus's face and his stomach crawled as, with a bound across the veranda, a huge man framed himself in the doorway and stood motionless as a statue.

For the first moment Meeus did not recognize Adams. He was filthy and tattered, he wore no coat, and his hunting shirt was open at the neck, and the arms of it rolled up above the elbows.

Adams, for the space of ten seconds, stood staring at Meeus from under his pith helmet. The face under the helmet seemed cast from bronze.

Then he came in and shut the door behind him, walked to the table, took Meeus by the coat at the back of the neck, and lifted him up as a man lifts a dog by the scruff.

For a moment it seemed as if he were going to kill the wretched man without word or explanation, but he mastered himself with a supreme effort, put him down, took the vacant seat at the table and cried:

"Stand before me there."

Meeus stood. He held on to the table with his left hand and with his right he made pawing movements in the air.

The big man seated at the table did not notice. He sat for a few seconds with both hands clasped together, one making a cup for the other, just as a man might sit about to make a speech and carefully considering his opening words.

Then he spoke.

"Did you kill those people by the Silent Pools?"

Meeus made no reply, but drew a step back and put out his hand, as if fending the question off, as if asking for a moment in which to explain. He had so many things to say, so many reasons to give, but he could say nothing, for his tongue was paralyzed and his lips were dry.

"Did you kill those people by the Silent Pools?"

The awful man at the table was beginning to work himself up. He had risen at the second question, and at the third time of asking he seized Meeus by the shoulders. *"Did you kill those people——?"*

"Punishment," stuttered Meeus.

A cry like the cry of a woman and a crash that shook the plaster from the ceiling, followed the fatal word. Adams had swung the man aloft and dashed him against the wall with such force, that the wattling gave and the plaster fell in flakes.

Meeus lay still as death, staring at his executioner with a face expressionless and white as the plaster flakes around him.

"Get up," said Adams.

Meeus heard and moved his arms.

"Get up."

Again the arms moved and the body raised itself, but the legs did not move. "I cannot," said Meeus.

Adams came to him and bending down pinched his right thigh hard.

"Do you feel me touching you?"

"No."

Adams did the same to the other thigh.

"Do you feel that?"

"No."

"Lie there," said Adams.

He opened the door and went out into the night. A moment later he returned; after him came the two porters bearing Berselius between them.

Berselius was quiet now; the brain fever that had stricken him had passed into a muttering stage, and he let himself be carried, passive as a bag of meal, whilst Adams went before with the lamp leading the way into the bedroom. Here, on one of the beds, the porters laid their burden down. Then they came back, and under the directions of Adams lifted Meeus and carried him into the bedroom and placed him on the second bed.

Adams, with the lamp in his hand, stood for a moment looking at Meeus. His rage had spent itself; he had avenged the people at the Silent Pools. With his naked hands he had inflicted on the criminal before him an injury worse than the injury of fire or sword.

Meeus, frightened now by the pity in the face of the other, horribly frightened by the unknown thing that had happened to him, making him dead from the waist down, moved his lips, but made no sound.

"Your back is broken," replied Adams to the question in the other's eyes.

Then he turned to Berselius.

At midnight the rains broke with a crash of thunder that seemed to shake the universe.

Adams, worn out, was seated at the table in the living room smoking some tobacco he had found in a tin on the shelf, and listening to the rambling of Berselius, when the thunder-clap came, making the lamp shiver on the table.

Meeus, who had been silent since his death sentence had been read to him, cried out at the thunder, but Berselius did not heed—he was hunting elephants under a burning sun in a country even vaster than the elephant country.

Adams rose up and came to the door; not a drop of rain had fallen yet. He crossed the yard and stood at the fort wall looking into blackness. It was solid as ebony, and he could hear the soldiers, whose huts were outside the wall, calling to one another.

A great splash of light lit up the whole roof of the forest clear as day, and the darkness shut down again with a bang that hit the ear like a blow, and the echoes of it roared and rumbled and muttered, and died, and Silence wrapped herself again in her robe and sat to wait.

Now, there was a faint stirring of the air, increasing to a breeze, and far away a sound like the spinning of a top came on the breeze. It was the rain, miles away, coming over the forest in a solid sheet, the sound of it increasing on the great drum of the forest's roof to a roar.

Another flash lit the world, and Adams saw the rain.

He saw what it is given to very few men to see. From horizon to horizon, as if built by plumb, line and square, stretched a glittering wall, reaching from the forest to the sky. The base of this wall was lost in snow-white billows of spray and mist.

Never was there so tremendous a sight as this infinite wall and the Niagara clouds of spray, roaring, living, and lit by the great flash one second, drowned out by the darkness and the thunder the next.

Adams, terrified, ran back to the house, shut the door, and waited.

The house was solidly built and had withstood many rains, but there were times when it seemed to him that the whole place must be washed away bodily. Nothing could be heard but the rain, and the sound of such rain is far more terrifying than the sound of thunder or the rumble of the earthquake.

There were times when he said to himself, "This cannot last," yet it lasted. With the lamp in his hand he went into the sleeping room to see how Berselius and Meeus were doing. Berselius was still, to judge from the movements of his lips, delirious, and just the same. Meeus was lying with his hands on his breast. He might have been asleep, only for his eyes, wide open and bright, and following every movement of the man with the lamp.

Meeus, catching the other's eye, motioned to him to come near. Then he tried to speak, but the roar outside made it impossible to hear him. Adams pointed to the roof, as if to say, "Wait till it is over," then he came back to the sitting room, tore the leopard skin down from the wall, rolled it up for a pillow, and lay down with his head on it.

He had been through so much of late that he had grown callous and case-hardened; he did not care much whether the place was washed away or not—he wanted to sleep, and he slept.

Meeus, left alone, lay watching the glimmer of the lamp shining through the cracks of the door, and listening to the thunder of the rain.

This was the greatest rain he had experienced. He wondered if it would flood the go-down and get at the rubber stored there; he wondered if the soldiers had deserted their huts and taken refuge in the office. These thoughts were of not the slightest interest to him; they just came and strayed across his mind, which was still half-paralyzed by the great calamity that had befallen him.

For the last half-hour an iron hand seemed round his body just on a level with the diaphragm; this seemed growing tighter, and the tighter it grew the more difficult it was to breathe. The fracture had been very high up, but he knew nothing of this; he knew that his back was broken, and that men with broken backs die, but he did not fully realize that he was going to die till—all at once—his breathing stopped dead of its own accord, and then of its own accord went on rapidly and shallowly. Then he recognized that his breathing was entirely under the control of something over which *he* had no control.

This is the most terrible thing a man can know, for it is a thing that no man ever knows till he is in the hands of death.

It was daylight when Adams awoke, and the rain had ceased.

He went to the door and opened it. It was after sunrise, but the sun was not to be seen. The whole world was a vapour, but through which the forest was dimly visible. The soldiers were in the courtyard; they had just come out of the office where they had taken refuge during the night. Their huts had been washed away, but they did not seem to mind a bit; they showed their teeth in a grin, and shouted something when they saw the white man, and pointed to the rainswept yard and the sky.

Adams nodded, and then went back into the house and into the bedroom, where he found Meeus hanging head downward out of his bed.

Rubber would trouble Andreas Meeus no more; his soul had gone to join the great army of souls in the Beyond.

It is strange enough to look upon the body of a man you have killed. But Adams had no more pity or compunction in his mind than if Meeus had been a stoat.

He turned to Berselius, who was sleeping. The delirium had passed, and he was breathing evenly and well. There was hope for him yet—hope for his body if not for his mind.

CHAPTER XXXI
THE VOICE OF THE FOREST BY NIGHT

The first thing to be done was to bury Meeus. And now came the question, How would the soldiers take the death of the *Chef de Poste*? They knew nothing of it yet. Would they revolt, or would they seek to revenge him, guessing him to have been killed.

Adams did not know and he did not care. He half hoped there would be trouble. The Congo had burst upon his view, stripped of shams, in all its ferocity, just as the great scene of the killing had burst upon Berselius. All sorts of things—from the Hostage House of Yandjali to the Hostage House of M'Bassa, from Mass to Papeete's skull—connected themselves up and made a skeleton, from which he constructed that great and ferocious monster, the Congo State. The soldiers, with their filed teeth, were part of the monster, and, such was the depth of fury in his heart, he would have welcomed a fight, so that he might express with his arms what his tongue ached to say.

The original man loomed large in Adams. God had given him a character benign and just, a heart tempered to mercy and kindliness; all these qualities had been outraged and were now under arms. They had given a mandate to the original man to act. The death of Meeus was the first result.

He went to the shelf where Meeus had kept his official letters and took Meeus's Mauser pistol from it. It was in a holster attached to a belt. He strapped the belt round his waist, drew the pistol from the holster and examined it. It was loaded, and in an old cigar-box he found a dozen clips of cartridges. He put three of these in his pocket and with the pistol at his side came out into the courtyard.

Huge billows of white cloud filled the sky, broken here and there by a patch of watery blue. The whole earth was steaming and the forest was absolutely smoking. One could have sworn it was on fire in a dozen places when the spirals of mist rose and broke and vanished like the steam clouds from locomotive chimneys.

He crossed the courtyard to the go-down, undid the locking bar and found what he wanted. Half a dozen mattocks stood by the rubber bales—he had noticed them when the stores had been taken out for the expedition; they were still in the same place and, taking two of them, he went to the break in the wall that gave exit from the courtyard and called to the soldiers, who were busy at work rebuilding their huts.

They came running. He could not speak twenty words of their language, but he made them line up with a movement of his arm.

Then he addressed them in a perfectly unprintable speech. It was delivered in unshod American—a language he had not spoken for years. It took in each individual of the whole gang, it told them they were dogs and sons of dogs, killers of men, unmentionable carrion, cayotes, kites, and that he would have hanged them each and individually with his own hands (and I believe by some legerdemain of strength he would), but that they were without hearts, souls or intellect, not responsible creatures, tools of villains that he, Adams, would expose and get even with yet.

Furthermore, that if by a look or movement they disobeyed his orders, he would make them sweat tears and weep blood, so help him God. Amen.

They understood what he said. At least they understood the gist of it. They had found a new and angry master, and not an eye was raised when Adams stood silent; some looked at their toes and some at the ground, some looked this way, some that, but none at the big, ferocious man, with three weeks' growth of beard, standing before them and, literally, over them.

Then he chose two of them and motioned them to follow to the guest house. There he brought them into the sleeping room and pointed to the body of Meeus, motioning them to take it up and carry it out. The men rolled their eyes at the sight of the *Chef de Poste*, but they said no word; one took the head, the other the feet, and between them they carried the burden, led by their new commander, through the dwelling room, across the veranda and then across the yard.

The rest of the soldiers were in a group near the gate. When they saw the two men and their burden, they set up a chattering like a flock of magpies, which, however, instantly ceased at the approach of Adams.

He pointed to the two mattocks which he had placed against the wall. They understood what he meant; the last *Chef de Poste* had shot himself in the presence of the District Commissioner, and they had dug his grave.

"Here," said Adams, stopping and pointing to a spot at a convenient distance from the walls.

When the body was buried, Adams stood for a second looking at the mound of earth, wet and flattened down by blows of the spades.

He had no prayers to offer up. Meeus would have to go before his Maker just as he was, and explain things—explain all that business away there at the Silent Pools and other things as well. Prayers over his tomb or flowers on it would not help that explanation one little bit.

Then Adams turned away and the soldiers trooped after him.

He had looked into the office and seen the rifles and ammunition which they had placed there out of the wet. A weak man would have locked the office door and so have deprived the soldiers of their arms, but Adams was not a weak man.

He led his followers to the office, handed them their arms, carefully examining each rifle to see that it was clean and uninjured, drew them up on a line, addressed them in some more unprintable language but in a milder tone, dismissed them with a wave of his hand and returned to the house.

As he left them the wretched creatures all gave a shout—a shout of acclamation.

This was the man for them—very different from the pale-faced Meeus—this was a man they felt who would lead them to more unspeakable butchery than Meeus had ever done. Therefore they shouted, piled their arms in the office and returned to the rebuilding of their huts with verve.

They were not physiognomists, these gentlemen.

Berselius awoke from sleep at noon, but he was so weak that he could scarcely move his lips. Fortunately there were some goats at the fort, and Adams fed him with goats' milk from a spoon, just as one feeds an infant. Then the sick man fell asleep and the rain came down again—not in a thunder shower this time, but steadily, mournfully, playing a tattoo on the zinc roof of the veranda, filling the place with drizzling sounds, dreary beyond expression. With the rain came gloom so deep that Adams had to light the paraffin lamp. There were no books, no means of recreation, nothing to read but the old official letters and the half-written report which the dead man had left on the table before leaving earth to make his report elsewhere. Adams having glanced at this, tore it in pieces, then he sat smoking and thinking and listening to the rain.

Toward night a thunderstorm livened things up a little, and a howling wind came over the forest on the heels of the storm.

Adams came out on the veranda to listen.

He could have sworn that a great sea was roaring below in the darkness. He could hear the waves, the boom and burst of them, the suck-back of the billows tearing the shrieking shale to their hearts, the profound and sonorous roar of leagues of coast. Imagination could do anything with that sound except figure the reality of it or paint the tremendous forest bending to the wind in billows of foliage a hundred leagues long; the roar of the cotton-woods, the cry of the palm, the sigh of the withered euphorbias, the thunderous drumming of the great plantain leaves, all joining in one tremendous symphony led by the trumpets of the wind, broken by rainbursts from the rushing clouds overhead, and all in viewless darkness, black as the darkness of the pit.

This was a new phase of the forest, which since the day Adams entered it first, had steadily been explaining to him the endlessness of its mystery, its wonder, and its terror.

CHAPTER XXXII
MOONLIGHT ON THE POOLS

Now began for Adams a time of trial, enough to break the nerve of any ordinary man. Day followed day and week followed week, Berselius gaining strength so slowly that his companion began to despair at last, fancying that the main fountain and source of life had been injured, and that the stream would never flow again but in a trickle, to be stopped at the least shock or obstruction.

The man was too weak to talk, he could just say "Yes" and "No" in answer to a question, and it was always "Better" when he was asked how he felt, but he never spoke a word of his own volition.

Nearly every day it rained, and it rained in a hundred different ways—from the thunderous shower-bath rush of water that threatened to beat the roof in, to the light spitting shower shone through by the sun. Sometimes the clouds would divide, roll up in snow-white billows of appalling height, and over the fuming foliage a rainbow would form, and flocks of birds, as if released by some wizard, break from the reeking trees. Adams could hear their cries as he stood at the foot wall watching them circle in the air, and his heart went out to them, for they were the only living things in the world around him that spoke in a kindly tongue or hinted at the tenderness of God.

All else was vast and of tragic proportions. The very rainbow was titanic; it seemed primeval as the land over which it stretched and the people to whom it bore no promise.

But the forest was the thing which filled Adams's heart with a craving for freedom and escape that rose to a passion.

He had seen it silent in the dry season; he had seen it divided by the great rain-wall and answering the downpour with snow-white billows of mist and spray; he had heard it roaring in the dark; it had trapped him, beaten him with its wet, green hands, sucked him down in its quagmires, shown him its latent, slow, but unalterable ferocity, its gloom, its devilment.

The rubber collector who had helped to carry Berselius to the fort had gone back to his place and task—the forest had sucked him back. This gnome had explained without speaking what the gloom and the quagmire, and the rope-like lianas had hinted, what the Silent Pools had shouted, what the vulture and the kite had laid bare, what the heart had whispered: *There is no God in the forest of M'Bonga, no law but the law of the leopard, no mercy but the mercy of Death.*

The forest had become for Adams a living nightmare—his one desire in life now was to win free of it, and never did it look more sinister than when, rainbow-arched and silently fuming, it lay passive, sun-stricken, the palms bursting above the mist and the great clouds rolling away in billows, as if to expose fully the wonder of those primeval leagues of tree-tops sunlit, mist-strewn, where the feathery fingers of the palms made banners of the wrack and the baobabs held fog-banks in their foliage.

At the end of the third week Berselius showed signs of amendment. He could raise himself now in bed and speak. He said little, but it was evident that his memory had completely returned, and it was evident that he was still the changed man. The iron-hearted Berselius, the man of daring and nerve, was not here, he had been left behind in the elephant country in the immeasurable south.

The mist had departed entirely from his mind; his whole past was clear before him, and with his new mind he could reckon it up and see the bad and the good. The extraordinary fact was that in reviewing this past he did not feel terrified—it seemed a dead thing and almost as the past of some other man. All those acts seemed to Berselius to have been committed by a man who was now dead.

He could regret the acts of that man and he could seek to atone for them, but he felt no personal remorse. "He was not I," would have reasoned the mind of Berselius; "those acts were not my acts, because *now I could not commit them,*" so he would have reasoned had he reasoned on the matter at all. But he did not. In that wild outburst by the Silent Pools the ego had screamed aloud, raving against itself, raving against the trick that fate had played it, by making it the slave of two personalities, and then torturing it by showing it the acts of the old personality through the eyes of the new.

When the brain fever had passed, it awoke untroubled; the junction had been effected, the new Berselius was It, and all the acts of the old Berselius were foreign to it and far away.

It is thus the man who gets religion feels when the great change comes on his brain. After the brain-storm and the agony of new birth comes the peace and the feeling that he is "another man." He feels that all his sins are washed away; in other words, he has lost all sense of responsibility for the crimes he committed in the old life, he has cast them off like an old suit of clothes. The old man is dead. Ah, but is he? Can you atone for your vices by losing your smell and taste for vice, and slip out of your debt for crime by becoming another man?

Does the old man ever die?

The case of Berselius stirs one to ask the question, which is more especially interesting as it is prompted by a case not unique but almost typical.

The interesting point in Berselius's case lay in the question as to whether his change of mind was initiated by the injury received in the elephant country or by the shock at the Silent Pools. In other words, was it due to some mechanical pressure on the brain produced by the accident, or was it due to "repentance" on seeing suddenly unveiled the hideous drama in which he had taken part?

This remains to be seen.

At the end of the fourth week Berselius was able to leave his bed, and every day now marked a steady improvement in strength.

Not a word about the past did he say, not a question did he ask, and what surprised Adams especially, not a question did he put about Meeus, till one day in the middle of the fifth week.

Berselius was seated in one of the arm chairs of the sitting room when he suddenly raised his head.

"By the way," said he, "where is the *Chef de Poste*?"

"He is dead," replied Adams.

"Ah!" said Berselius; there was almost a note of relief in his voice. He said nothing more and Adams volunteered no explanation, for the affair was one entirely between Meeus, himself, and God.

A few minutes later, Berselius, who seemed deep in thought, raised his head again.

"We must get away from here. I am nearly strong enough to go now. It will be a rough journey in these rains, but it will be a much shorter road than the road we came by."

"How so?"

"We came from Yandjali right through the forest before striking south to here; we will now make straight for the river, along the rubber road. I think the post on the river which we will reach is called M'Bina, it is a hundred miles above Yandjali; we can get a boat from there to Leopoldsville. I have been thinking it all out this morning."

"How about a guide?"

"These soldiers here know the rubber track, for they often escort the loads."

"Good," said Adams. "I will have some sort of litter rigged up and we will carry you. I am not going to let you walk in your present condition."

Berselius bowed his head.

"I am very sensible," said he, "of the care and attention you have bestowed on me during the past weeks. I owe you a considerable debt, which I will endeavour to repay, at all events, by following your directions implicitly. Let the litter be made, and if you will send me in the corporal of those men, I will talk to him in his own language and explain what is to be done."

"Good," said Adams, and he went out and found the corporal and sent him in to Berselius.

"Good!" The word was not capacious enough to express what he felt. Freedom, Light, Humanity, the sight of a civilized face, for these he ached with a great longing, and they were all there at the end of the rubber road, only waiting to be met with.

He went to the fort wall and shook his fist at the forest.

"Another ten days," said Adams.

The forest, whose spirit counted time by tens of thousands of years, waved its branches to the wind.

A spit of rain from a passing cloud hit Adams's cheek, and in the "hush" of the trees there seemed a murmur of derision and the whisper of a threat.

"It is not well to shake your fist at the gods—in the open."

Adams went back to the house to begin preparations, and for the next week he was busy. From some spare canvas and bamboos in the go-down he made a litter strong enough to carry Berselius—he had to do nearly all the work himself, for the soldiers were utterly useless as workmen. Then stores had to be arranged and put together in a convenient form for carrying; clothes had to be mended and patched—even his boots had to be cobbled with twine—but at last all was ready, and on the day before they started the weather improved. The sun came out strong and the clouds drew away right to the horizon, where they lay piled in white banks like ranges of snow-covered mountains.

That afternoon, an hour before sunset, Adams announced his intention of going on a little expedition of his own.

"I shall only be a few hours away," said he, "five at most."

"Where are you going?" asked Berselius.

"Oh, just down into the woods," replied Adams. Then he left the room before his companion could ask any more questions and sought out the corporal.

He beckoned the savage to follow him, and struck down the slope in the direction of the Silent Pools. When they reached the forest edge he pointed before them and said, "Matabayo."

The man understood and led the way, which was not difficult, for the feet of the rubber collectors had beaten a permanent path. There was plenty of light, too, for the moon was already in the sky, only waiting for the sun to sink before blazing out.

When they were half-way on their journey heavy dusk fell on them suddenly, and deepened almost to dark; then, nearly as suddenly, all the forest around them glowed green to the light of the moon.

The Silent Pools and the woods, when they reached them, lay in mist and moonlight, making a picture unforgettable for ever.

It recalled to Adams that picture of Doré's, illustrating the scene from the "Idylls of the King," where Arthur labouring up the pass "all in a misty moonlight," had trodden on the skeleton of the once king, from whose head the crown rolled like a rivulet of light down to the tarn—the misty tarn, where imagination pictured Death waiting to receive it and hide it in his robe.

The skeleton of no king lay here, only the poor bones still unburied of the creatures that a far-off king had murdered. The rain had washed them about, and Adams had to search and search before he found what he had come to find.

At last he saw it. The skull of a child, looking like a white stone amidst the grass. He wrapped it in leaves torn from the trees near by, and the grim corporal stood watching him, and wondering, no doubt, for what fetish business the white man had come to find the thing.

Then Adams with the dreary bundle under his arm looked around him at the other remains and swore—swore by the God who had made him, by the mother who had borne him, and the manhood that lay in him, to rest not nor stay till he had laid before the face of Europe the skull of Papeete and the acts of the terrible scoundrel who for long years had systematically murdered for money.

Then, followed by the savage, he turned and retook his road. At the wood's edge he looked back at the silent scene, and it seemed to look at him with the muteness and sadness of a witness who cannot speak, of a woman who cannot tell her sorrow.

CHAPTER XXXIII
THE RIVER OF GOLD

Next morning they started.

The corporal, three of the soldiers, and the two porters made up the escort.

Berselius, who was strong enough to walk a little way, began the journey on foot, but they had not gone five miles on their road when he showed signs of fatigue, and Adams insisted on him taking to the litter.

It was the same road by which Félix had led them, but it was very different travelling; where the ground had been hard underfoot it was now soft, and where it had been elastic it was now boggy; it was more gloomy, and the forest was filled with watery voices; where it dipped down into valleys, you could hear the rushing and mourning of waters. Tiny trickles of water had become rivulets—rivulets streams.

Away in the elephant country it was the same, the dry river-bed where they had found the carcass of the elephant, was now the bed of rushing water. The elephant and antelope herds were wandering in clouds on the plains. A hundred thousand streams from Tanganyika to Yandjali were leaping to form rivers flowing for one destination, the Congo and the sea.

On the second day of their journey, an accident happened; one of the porters, released for a spell from bearing the litter, and loitering behind, was bitten by a snake.

He died despite all Adams's attempts to save him, and, leaving his body to be buried by the leopards, they passed on.

But the soldiers, especially the corporal, took the matter strangely. These bloodthirsty wretches, inured to death and thinking nothing of it, seemed cast down, and at the camping place they drew aside, chattered together for a few minutes, and then the corporal came to Berselius and began a harangue, his eyes rolling toward Adams now and then as he proceeded.

Berselius listened, spoke a few words, and then turned to Adams.

"He says you have brought something with you that is unlucky, and that unless you throw it away, we shall all die."

"I know what he means," replied Adams; "I have brought a relic from that village by the Silent Pools. I shall not throw it away. You can tell him so."

Berselius spoke to the man who still stood sullenly waiting, and who was opening his mouth to continue his complaints, when Adams seized him by the shoulders, turned him round, and with a kick, sent him back to his companions.

"You should not have done that," said Berselius; "these people are very difficult to deal with."

"Difficult!" said Adams. He stared at the soldiers who were grouped together, slapped the Mauser pistol at his side, and then pointed to the tent.

The men ceased muttering, and came as beaten dogs come at the call of their master, seized the tent and put it up.

But Berselius still shook his head. He knew these people, their treachery, and their unutterable heartlessness.

"How far are we from the river now?" asked Adams, that night, as they sat by the fire, for which the corporal by some miracle of savagery had found sufficient dry fuel in the reeking woods around them.

"Another two days' march," replied Berselius, "I trust that we shall reach it."

"Oh, we'll get there," said Adams, "and shall I tell you why? Well, we'll get there just because of that relic I am carrying. God has given me it to take to Europe. To take to Europe and show to men that they may see the devilment of this place, and the work of Satan that is being carried out here."

Berselius bowed his head.

"Perhaps you are right," said he, at last, slowly and thoughtfully.

Adams said no more. The great change in his companion stood as a barrier between him and the loathing he would have felt if Berselius had been still himself.

The great man had fallen, and was now very low. That vision of him in his madness by the Silent Pools had placed him forever on a plane above others. God had dealt with this man very visibly, and the hand of God was still upon him.

Next day they resumed their journey. The soldiers were cheerful and seemed to have forgotten all about their grievance, but Berselius felt more uneasy than ever. He knew these people, and that nothing could move them to mirth and joy that was not allied to devilment, or treachery, or death.

But he said nothing, for speech was useless.

Next morning when they woke they found the soldiers gone; they had taken the porter with them, and as much of the provisions as they could steal without disturbing the white men.

"I thought so," said Berselius.

Adams raged and stormed, but Berselius was perfectly calm.

"The thing I fear most," said he, "is that they have led us out of our road. Did you notice whether we were in the track for the last mile or so of our journey yesterday?"

"No," replied Adams, "I just followed on. Good God! if it is so we are lost."

Now, the rubber road was just a track so faint, that without keeping his eyes on the ground where years of travel had left just a slight indication of the way, a European would infallibly lose it. Savages, who have eyes in their feet, hold it all right, and go along with their burdens even in the dark.

Adams searched, but he could find no track.

"We must leave all these things behind us," said Berselius, pointing to the tent and litter. "I am strong enough to walk; we must strike through the forest and leave the rest to chance."

"Which way?" asked Adams.

"It does not matter. These men have purposely lost us, and we do not know in the least the direction of the river."

Adams's eyes fell on a bundle wrapped in cloth. It was the relic.

He knelt down beside it, and carefully removed the cloth without disturbing the position of the skull.

He noted the direction in which the eye-holes pointed.

"We will go in that direction," said he. "We have lost ourselves, but God has not lost us."

"Let it be so," replied Berselius.

Adams collected what provisions he could carry, tied the skull to his belt with a piece of rope taken from the tent, and led the way amidst the trees.

Two days later, at noon, still lost, unutterably weary, they saw through the trees before them a sight to slay all hope.

It was the tent and the litter just as they had left them.

Two days' heart-breaking labour had brought them to this by all sorts of paths.

They had not wandered in a circle. They had travelled in segments of circles, and against all mathematical probability, had struck the camp.

But the camp was not tenantless. Someone was there. A huge man-like form, a monstrous gorilla, the evil spirit that haunted the forest, bent and gray and old-looking, was picking the things about, sniffing at them, turning them over.

When they saw him first, he was holding the tent-cloth between both his hands just as a draper holds a piece of cloth, then he ripped it up with a rending sound, flung the pieces away, and began turning over the litter.

He heard the steps of the human beings, and sat up, looking around him, sniffing the air. He could not see them, for he was purblind.

The human beings passed on into the terrible nowhere of the forest.

When you are lost like this, you cannot rest. You must keep moving, even though you are all but hopeless of reaching freedom.

Two days later they were still lost, and now entirely hopeless.

To torment their hearts still more, faint sun-rays came through the leaves overhead.

The sun was shining overhead; the sun they would never see again. It was the very end of all things, for they had not eaten for twelve hours now.

The sun-rays danced, for a breeze had sprung up, and they could hear it passing free and happily in the leaves overhead.

Berselius cast himself down by a huge tree and leaned his head against the bark. Adams stood for a moment with his hand upon the tree-bole. He knew that when he had cast himself down he would never rise again. It was the full stop which would bring the story of his life to a close.

He was standing like this when, borne on the breeze above the tree-tops, came a sound, stroke after stroke, sonorous and clear. The bell of a steamboat!

It was the voice of the Congo telling of Life, Hope, Relief.

Berselius did not hear it. Sunk in a profound stupor, he would not even raise his head.

Adams seized his companion in his arms and came facing the direction of the breeze. He walked like a man in his sleep, threading the maze of the trees on, on, on, till before him the day broke in one tremendous splash of light, and the humble frame-roof of M'Bina seemed to him the roofs of some great city, beyond which the river flowed in sheets of burnished gold.

CHAPTER XXXIV THE SUBSTITUTE

District Commissioner De Wiart, chief at M'Bina, was a big man with a blond beard and a good-natured face. He worked the post at M'Bina with the assistance of a subordinate named Van Laer.

De Wiart was a man eminently fitted for his post. He had a genius for organization and overseeing. He would not have been worth a centime away up-country, for his heart was far too good to allow him to personally supervise the working of the niggers, but at M'Bina he was worth a good deal to the Government that employed him.

This man who would not hurt a fly—this man who would have made an excellent father of a family—was terrible to his subordinates when he took a pen in his hand. He knew the mechanism of every *Chef de Poste* in his district, and the sort of letter that would rouse him up, stimulate him to renewed action, and the slaves under him to renewed work.

Van Laer was of quite a different type. Van Laer had the appearance of a famished hound held back by a leash. He was tall and thin. He had been a schoolmaster dismissed from his school for a grave offence; he had been a billiard-marker; he had walked the streets of Brussels in a frock-coat and tall hat, a "guide" on the lookout for young foreigners who wished to enjoy the more dubious pleasures of the city. He had been many things, till, at the age of thirty-five, he became a servant of the crown.

The pale blue eyes of Van Laer held in them a shallowness and murderous cruelty, an expression of negation and coldness combined with mind such as one finds nowhere in the animal kingdom, save that branch of it which prides itself on its likeness to God. His thumbs were cruelly shaped and enormous. A man may disguise his soul, he may disguise his mind, he may disguise his face, but he cannot disguise his thumbs unless he wears gloves.

No one wears gloves on the Congo, so Van Laer's thumbs were openly displayed.

He had been six months now at M'Bina and he was sick of the place, accounts were of no interest to him. He was a man of action, and he wanted to be doing. He could make money up there in the forest at the heart of things; here, almost in touch with civilization, he was wasting his time. And he wanted money. The bonus-ache had seized him badly. When he saw the great tusks of green ivory in their jackets of matting, when he saw the bales of copal leafed round with aromatic unknown leaves, and speaking fervently of the wealth of the tropics and the riches of the primeval forests, when he saw the tons of rubber and remembered that this stuff, which in the baskets of the native collectors looks like fried potato chips, in Europe becomes, by the alchemy of trade, minted gold, a great hunger filled his hungry soul.

At M'Bina great riches were eternally flowing in and flowing out. Wealth in its original wrappings piled itself on the wharf in romantical packets and bales, piled itself on board steamers, floated away down the golden river, and was replaced by more wealth flowing in from the inexhaustible forests.

The sight of all this filled Van Laer with an actual physical hunger. He could have eaten that stuff that was wealth itself. He could have devoured those tusks. He was Gargantua as far as his appetite was concerned, and for the rest he was only Van Laer driving a quill in the office of De Wiart.

He did not know that he was here on probation; that the good-natured and seemingly lazy de Wiart was studying him and finding him satisfactory, that very soon his desires would be fulfilled, and that he would be let loose like a beast on the land of his longing, a living whip, an animated thumb-screw, a knife with a brain in its haft.

When the soldiers had lost Berselius and Adams, they struck at once for M'Bina, reaching it in a day's march.

Here they told their tale.

Chef de Poste Meeus was dead. They had escorted a sick white man and a big white man toward M'Bina. One night three leopards had prowled round the camp and the soldiers had gone in pursuit of them.

The leopards escaped, but the soldiers could not find the white men again.

De Wiart listened to this very fishy tale without believing a word of it, except in so far as it related to Meeus.

"Where did you lose the white men?" asked de Wiart.

The soldiers did not know. One does not know where one loses a thing; if one did, then the thing would not be lost.

"Just so," said De Wiart, agreeing to this very evident axiom, and more than ever convinced that the story was a lie. Meeus was dead and the men had come to report. They had delayed on the road to hold some jamboree of their own, and this lie about the white men was to account for their delay.

"Did anyone else come with you as well as the white men?" asked De Wiart.

"Yes, there was a porter, a Yandjali man. He had run away."

De Wiart pulled his blond beard meditatively, and looked at the river.

From the office where he was sitting the river, great with the rains and lit by the sun which had broken through the clouds, looked like a moving flood of gold. One might have fancied that all the wealth of the elephant country, all the teeming riches of the forest, flowing by a thousand streams and disdaining to wait for the alchemy of trade, had joined in one Pactolian flood flowing toward Leopoldsville and the sea.

De Wiart was not thinking this. He dismissed the soldiers and told them to hold themselves in readiness to return to M'Bassa on the morrow.

That evening he called Van Laer into the office.

"*Chef de Poste* Meeus of Fort M'Bassa is dead," said De Wiart; "you will go there and take command. You will start to-morrow."

Van Laer flushed.

"It is a difficult post," said De Wiart, "wild country, and the natives are the laziest to be found in the whole of the state. The man before Meeus did much harm; he had no power or control, he was a weak man, and the people frankly laughed at him. Actually rubber came in here one-third rubbish, the people were half their time in revolt, they cut the vines in two districts. I have a report of his saying, 'There is no ivory to be got. The herds are very scarce, and the people say they cannot make elephants.' Fancy writing nigger talk like that in a report. I replied in the same tone. I said, 'Tell the people they must make them: and make them in a hurry. Tell them that they need not trouble to make whole elephants, just the tusks will do—eighty-pound tusks, a hundred-pound if possible.' But sarcasm was quite thrown away on him. He listened to the natives. Once a man does that he is lost, for they lose all respect for him. They are just like children, these people; once let children get in the habit of making excuses and you lose control.

"Meeus was a stronger man, but he left much to be desired. He had too much whalebone in his composition, not enough steel, but he was improving.

"You will find yourself at first in a difficult position. It always is so when a *Chef de Poste* dies suddenly and even a few days elapse before he is replaced. The people get out of hand, thinking the white man is gone for ever. However, you will find yourself all right in a week or so, if you are firm."

"Thank you," said Van Laer. "I have no doubt at all that I will be able to bring these people into line. I do not boast. I only ask you to keep your eye on the returns."

Next day Van Laer, escorted by the soldiers, left M'Bina to take up the station at Fort M'Bassa left vacant by the death of *Chef de Poste* Andreas Meeus.

Three days later at noon De Wiart, drawn from his house by shouts from the sentinels on duty saw, coming toward him in the blazing sunshine, a great man who stumbled and seemed half-blinded by the sunlight, and who was bearing in his arms another man who seemed dead.

Both were filthy, ragged, torn and bleeding. The man erect had, tied to his waistbelt by a piece of liana, a skull.

Fit emblem of the forest he had passed through and the land that lay behind it.

CHAPTER XXXV
PARIS

One hot day in June Schaunard was seated in the little office just behind his shop. He was examining an improved telescopic sight which had just been put upon the market by an opponent, criticizing it as one poet criticizes the poem of another poet—that is to say, ferociously.

To him, thus meditating, from the Rue de la Paix suddenly came a gush of sound which as suddenly ceased.

The shop door had opened and closed again, and Schaunard leaving his office came out to see who the visitor might be.

He found himself face to face with Adams. He knew him by his size, but he would scarcely have recognized him by his face, so brown, so thin and so different in expression was it from the face of the man with whom he had parted but a few months ago.

"Good day," said Adams. "I have come to pay you for that gun."

"Ah, yes, the gun," said Schaunard with a little laugh, "this is a pleasant surprise. I had entered it amidst my bad debts. Come in, monsieur, come into my office, it is cooler there, and we can talk. The gun, ah, yes. I had entered that transaction in Ledger D. Come in, come in. There, take that armchair, I keep it for visitors. Well, and how did the expedition go off?"

"Badly," said Adams. "We are only back a week. You remember what you said to me when we parted? You said, 'Don't go.' I wish I had taken your advice."

"Why, since you are back sound and whole, it seems to me you have not done so badly—but perhaps you have got malaria?"

The old man's sharp eyes were investigating the face of the other. Schaunard's eyes had this peculiarity, that they were at once friendly to one and cruel, they matched the eternal little laugh which was ever springing to his lips—the laugh of the eternal mocker.

Schaunard made observations as well as telescopic sights and wind-gauges—he had been making observation for sixty years—he took almost as much interest in individual human beings as in rifles, and much more interest in Humanity than in God.

He was afflicted with the malady of the nineteenth and twentieth centuries—he did not believe in God, only instead of hiding his disease under a cloak of mechanical religion, or temporizing with it, he frankly declared himself to be what he was, an atheist.

This fact did not interfere with his trade—a godly gunmaker gets no more custom than an atheistical one; besides, Schaunard did not obtrude his religious opinions after the fashion of his class, he was a good deal of a gentleman, and he was accustomed to converse familiarly with emperors and kings.

"No, it is not malaria," replied Adams, following the old man who was leading the way into the office. "I never felt better in my life. It is just the Congo. The place leaves an impression on one's mind, M. Schaunard, a flavour that is not good."

He took the armchair which Schaunard kept for visitors. He was only a week back—all he had seen out there was fresh to him and very vivid, but he felt in Schaunard an antagonistic spirit, and he did not care to go deeper into his experiences.

Schaunard took down that grim joke, Ledger D, placed it on the table and opened it, but without turning the leaves.

"And how is Monsieur le Capitaine?" asked he.

"He has been very ill, but he is much better. I am staying with him in the Avenue Malakoff as his medical attendant. We only arrived at Marseilles a week ago."

"And Madame Berselius, how is she?"

"Madame Berselius is at Trouville."

"The best place this weather. *Ma foi,* you must find it warm here even after Africa—well, tell me how you found the gun to answer."

Adams laughed. "The gun went off—in the hands of a savage. All your beautiful guns, Monsieur Schaunard, are now matchwood and old iron, tents, everything went, smashed to pieces, pounded to pulp by elephants."

He told of the great herd they had pursued and how in the dark it had charged the camp. He told of how in the night, listening by the camp fire, he had heard the mysterious boom of its coming, and of the marvellous sight he had watched when Berselius, failing in his attempt to waken the Zappo Zap, had fronted the oncoming army of destruction.

Schaunard's eyes lit up as he listened.

"Ah," said he, "that is a man!"

The remark brought Adams to a halt.

He had become strangely bound up in Berselius; he had developed an affection for this man almost brotherly, and Schaunard's remark hit him and made him wince. For Schaunard employed the present tense.

"Yes," said Adams at last, "it was very grand." Then he went on to tell of Berselius's accident, but he said nothing of his brain injury, for a physician does not speak of his patient's condition to strangers, except in the vaguest and most general terms.

"And how did you like the Belgians?" asked the old man, when Adams had finished.

"The Belgians!" Adams, suddenly taken off his guard, exploded; he had said nothing as yet about the Congo to anyone. He could not help himself now; the horrors rushed to his mouth and escaped—the cry of the great mournful country—the cry that he had brought to Europe with him in his heart, found vent.

Schaunard sat amazed, not at the infamies pouring from Adams's mouth, for he was well acquainted with them, but at the man's vehemence and energy.

"I have come to Europe to expose him," finished Adams.

"Expose who?"

"Leopold, King of the Belgians."

"But, my dear Monsieur Adams, you have come to waste your time; he is already exposed. Expose Leopold, King of the Belgians! Say at once that you are going to expose the sun. He doesn't care. He exposes himself. His public and his private life are common property."

"You mean to say that everyone knows what I know?"

"Precisely, and perhaps even more, but everyone has not seen what you have seen, and that's all the difference."

"How so?"

"In this way, monsieur; let us suppose that you have just seen a child run over in the Rue de la Paix. You come in here and tell me of it; the horror of it is in your mind, but you cannot convey that horror to me, simply because I have not seen what you have seen. Still, you can convey a part of it, for I know the Rue de la Paix, it is close to me, outside my door, and I know French children.

"You come to me and tell me of hideous sights you have seen in Africa. That does not move me a tenth so much, for Africa is very far away—it is, in fact, for me a geographical expression; the people are niggers I have never seen, dwelling in a province I have never heard of. You come to seek sympathy for this people amongst the French public? Well, I tell you frankly you are like a man searching in a dark room for a black hat that is not there."

"Nevertheless I shall search."

"As monsieur wills, only don't knock yourself against the chairs and tables. Ah, monsieur, monsieur, you are young and a medical man. Remain so, and don't lose your years and your prospects fighting the impossible. Now listen to me, for it is old Schaunard of the Rue de la Paix who is speaking to you. The man you would expose, as you term it, is a king to begin with; to go on with, he is far and away the cleverest king in Christendom. That man has brains enough to run what you in America call a department store. Every little detail of his estate out there, even to the cap guns and rifles of the troops, he looks after himself; that's why it pays. It is a bad-smelling business, but it doesn't poison the nose of Europe, because it is so far away. Still, smells are brought over in samples by missionaries and men like you, and people say 'Faugh!' Do you think he did not take that into his consideration when he planned the affair and laid down the factory? If you think so, you would be vastly mistaken. He has agents everywhere—I have met them, apologists everywhere—in the Press, in Society, in the Church. The Roman Catholic Church is entirely his; he is triple-ringed with politicians, priests, publicists, and financiers, all holding their noses to keep out the stench and all singing the *Laus Leopold* at the top of their voices.

"Ah! you don't know Europe. I do, from the Ballplatz to Willhelmstrasse, from the Winter Palace to the Elysée, my trade has brought me everywhere, and if you could see with my eyes, you would see the great, smooth plain of ice you hope to warm with your poor breath in the name of Humanity."

"At all events I shall try," replied Adams, rising to go.

"Well, try, but don't get frozen in making the trial——"

"Oh, the gun—well, look here—you are starting on another hunting expedition, it seems to me, a more dangerous one, too, than the last, for there is no forest where one loses oneself more fatally than the forest of social reform—pay me when you come back."

"Very well," said Adams, laughing.

"Only if you are successful though."

"Very well."

"And, see here, in any event come and tell me the result. *Bon jour*, monsieur, and a word in your ear——"

The old man was opening the shop door.

"Yes?"

"Don't go."

Schaunard closed his door and retired to his office to chuckle over his joke, and Adams walked off down the Rue de la Paix.

Paris was wearing her summer dress; it was the end of the season, and the streets were thronged with foreigners—the Moor from Morocco, in his white burnous, elbowed the Slav from Moscow; the Eiffel Tower had become a veritable Tower of Babel; the theatres were packed, the *cafés* crowded. Austrian, Russian, English, and American gold was pouring into the city—pouring in ceaselessly from the four corners of the world and by every great express disgorging at the Gare du Nord, the Gare de l'Est, and the Gare de Lyons.

To Adams, fresh from the wilderness and the forest, fresh from those great, silent, sunlit plains of the elephant country and the tremendous cavern of the jungle, the city around him and the sights affected him with vividness and force.

Here, in the centre of the greatest civilization that the world has ever seen, he stood fresh from that primeval land.

He had seen civilization with her mask off, her hair in disorder, her foot on the body of a naked slave and the haft of a blood-stained knife between her teeth, he was watching her now with her mask on, her hair in powder, Caruso singing to her; sitting amidst her court of poets, philosophers, churchmen, placemen, politicians, and financiers.

It was a strange experience.

He took his way down the Rue de Rivoli and then to the Avenue Malakoff, and as he walked the face of the philosophic Schaunard faded from his mind and was replaced by the vision of Maxine Berselius. Opposites in the world of thought often awaken images one of the other, just because of the fact that they are opposites.

Maxine was not at Trouville. She had met them at the railway station on the day of their arrival.

La Joconde had been cabled for from Leopoldsville, and the great yacht had brought them to Marseilles. Nothing had been cabled as to Berselius's accident or illness, and Madame Berselius had departed for Trouville, quite unconscious of anything having happened to her husband.

Maxine was left to discover for herself the change in her father. She had done so at the very first sight of him, but as yet she had said no word.

CHAPTER XXXVI
DREAMS

When Adams arrived at the Avenue Malakoff he found Berselius in the library. He was seated in a big armchair, and M. Pinchon, his secretary, a man dry-looking as an account-book, bald, and wearing spectacles, was just leaving the room with some shorthand notes of business letters to be typed.

Berselius was much changed; his hair was quite gray, his eyes, once so calm, forceful, and intrinsically brilliant, had lost their lustre, his face wore the expression of a confirmed invalid.

Great discontent was the predominant feature of this expression.

It was only within the last few days that this had appeared. On recovering from the hardships of the forest and on the voyage home, though weak enough, he had been serene, mild, amiable and rather listless, but during the last few days something was visibly troubling him.

He had "gone off," to use an expressive phrase sometimes employed by physicians.

A strange thing had happened to Berselius. Ever since the recovery of his memory his new self had contemplated the past from the heights of new birth, calmly conscious of the fact that this past belonged to a man who was dead. The more he examined this past the more he loathed the man to whom it had belonged, but the difference between that man and himself was so profound that he felt, rightly, that he was not *He*.

Three mornings ago Berselius, who rarely dreamt, had awakened from a long night of hunting in Dreamland. In Dreamland he had cast off his new personality and became his old self, and then, in his hunting shirt and with a cordite rifle in his hand, accompanied by the Zappo Zap, he had tracked elephant herds across illimitable plains.

He had awakened to his new self again with the full recognition in his mind that only a few moments ago he had been thinking with that other man's brain, acting under his passions, living his life.

The Berselius of Dreamland had not the remotest connection with, or knowledge of, the Berselius of real life. Yet the Berselius of real life was very intimately connected with the Berselius of Dreamland, knew all his actions, knew all his sensations, and remembered them to the minutest detail.

The next night he did not dream at all—not so on the third night, when the scene of horror by the Silent Pools was reenacted, himself in the original *role*. The incidents were not quite the same, for scenes from real life are scarcely ever reproduced on the stage of Dreamland in their entirety; but they were ghastly enough in all conscience, and Berselius, awake and wiping the sweat from his brow, saw them clearly before him and remembered the callousness with which he had watched them but a few moments ago.

No man can command his dreams; the dreaming man lives in a world beyond law, and it came as a shock to Berselius that his old self should be alive in him like this, powerful, active, and beyond rebuke.

Physically, he was a wreck of his old self, but that was nothing to the fact which was now borne in on him—the fact that this new mentality was but a thin shell covering the old, as the thin shell of earth, with its flowers and pleasant landscapes, covers the burning hell which is the earth's core.

The thing was perfectly natural. A great and vivid personality, and forty years of exuberant and self-willed life had at a stroke been checked and changed. The crust of his mind had cooled; tempestuous passions had passed from the surface, giving place to kindlier emotions, but the furnace was there beneath the flower garden just as it is in the case of the earth.

Captain Berselius was still alive, though suppressed and living in secrecy. At night, touched by the magic wand of sleep, he became awake, and became supreme master of the tenement in the cellars of which he was condemned to sleep by day.

So far from having been touched by death, Captain Berselius was now secure from death or change; a thing not to be reasoned with or altered—beyond human control—yet vividly alive as the fabled monster that inhabits the cellars of Glamis Castle.

Between the dual personalities of the man complete fission had taken place, a terrible accident of the sort condemning the cast-off personality to live in darkness beyond the voice of mind or amendment.

"Well," said Adams, as he entered the room. "How are you to-day?"

"Oh, about the same, about the same. If I could sleep properly I would mend, but my sleep is broken."

"I must give you something to alter that."

Berselius laughed.

"Drugs?"

"Yes, drugs. We doctors cannot always command health, but we can command sleep. Do you feel yourself able to talk for a bit?"

"Oh, yes, I feel physically well. Sit down, you will find some cigars in that cabinet."

Adams lit a cigar and took his seat in an armchair close to his companion. All differences of rank and wealth were sunk between these two men who had gone through so much together. On their return, when Berselius had desired Adams to remain as his medical attendant, he had delegated M. Pinchon as intermediary to deal with Adams as to the financial side of the question.

Adams received a large salary paid monthly in advance by the secretary. Berselius did not have any hand in the matter, thus the feeling of employer and employed was reduced to vanishing point and the position rendered more equal.

"You know," said Adams, "I have always been glad to do anything I can for you, and I always shall be, but since I have come back to Paris I have been filled with unrest. You complain of sleeplessness—well, that is my disease."

"Yes?"

"It's that place over there; it has got into my blood. I declare to God that I am the last man in the world to sentimentalize, but that horror is killing me, and I must act—I must do something—even if I have to go into the middle of the Place de la Concorde and shout it aloud. I shall shout it aloud. I'm not made so that I can stand seeing a thing like that in silence."

Berselius sat with his eyes fixed on the carpet; he seemed abstracted and scarcely listening. He knew perfectly well that Adams was acquainted with the affair at the Silent Pools, but the subject had never been mentioned between them, nor was it now.

"That missionary I met on the return home at Leopoldsville," went on Adams, "he was a Baptist, a man, not a religion-machine. He gave me details from years of experience that turned my heart in me. With my own eyes I saw enough——"

Berselius held up his hand.

"Let us not speak of what we know," said he. "The thing is there—has been there for years—can you destroy the past?"

"No; but one can improve the future." Adams got up and paced the floor. "Now, now as I am talking to you, that villainy is going on; it is like knowing that a murder is slowly being committed in the next house and that one has no power to interfere. When I look at the streets full of people amusing themselves; when I see the *cafés* crammed, and the rich driving in their carriages; the churches filled with worshippers worshipping a God who serenely sits in heaven without stretching a hand to help His poor, benighted creatures—when I see all this and contrast it with what I have seen, I could worship *that*!"

He stopped, and pointed to the great gorilla shot years ago in German West Africa by Berselius. "That was a being at least sincere. Whatever brutalities he committed in his life, he did not talk sentiment and religion and humanitarianism as he pulled his victims to pieces, and he did not pull his victims to pieces for the sake of gold. He was an honest devil, a far higher thing than a dishonest man."

Again Berselius held up his hand.

"What would you do?"

"Do? I'd break that infernal machine which calls itself a State, and I'd guillotine the ruffian that invented it. I cannot do that, but I can at least protest."

Berselius, who had helped to make the machine, and who knew better than most men its strength, shook his head sadly.

"Do what you will," said he. "If you need money my funds are at your disposal, but you cannot destroy the past."

Adams, who knew nothing of Berselius's dream-obsession, could not understand the full meaning of these words.

But he had received permission to act, and the promise of that financial support without which individual action would be of no avail.

He determined to act; he determined to spare neither Berselius's money nor his own time.

But the determination of man is limited by circumstance, and circumstance was at that moment preparing and rehearsing the last act of the drama of Berselius.

CHAPTER XXXVII
BERSELIUS BEHOLDS HIS OTHER SELF

On the morning after Berselius's conversation with Adams, Berselius left the Avenue Malakoff, taking his way to the Avenue des Champs Elysées on foot.

The change in the man was apparent even in his walk. In the old days he was rapid in his movements, erect of head, keen of eye. The weight of fifteen years seemed to have suddenly fallen on his shoulders, bowing them and slowing his step. He was in reality carrying the most terrible burden that a man can carry—himself.

A self that was dead, yet with which he had to live. A past which broke continually up through his dreams.

He was filled with profound unrest, irritation and revolt; everything connected with that other one, even the money he had made and the house he had built for himself and the pursuits he had followed, increased this irritation and revolt. He had already formed plans for taking a new house in Paris, but to-day, as he walked along the streets, he recognized that Paris itself was a house, every corner of which belonged to that other one's past.

In the Avenue Champs Elysées, he hailed a *fiacre* and drove to the house of his lawyer, M. Cambon, which was situated in the Rue d'Artiles.

Cambon had practically retired from his business, which was carried on now by his son. But for a few old and powerful clients, such as Berselius, he still acted personally.

He was at home, and Berselius was shown into a drawing room, furnished heavily after the heart of the prosperous French *bourgeois*.

He had not to wait long for the appearance of the lawyer, a fat, pale-faced gentleman, wearing gold-rimmed spectacles, tightly buttoned up in a frock-coat, the buttonhole of which was adorned with the red rosette of the Legion of Honour.

Cambon had known Berselius for years. The two men were friends, and even more, for Cambon was the depository of Berselius's most confidential affairs.

"Well," said the lawyer, "you have returned. I saw a notice of your return in the *Echo de Paris*, and indeed, this very day I had promised myself the pleasure of calling on you. And how is Madame Berselius?"

"She is at Trouville."

"I had it in my mind that you proposed to remain away twelve months."

"Yes, but our expedition came to an end."

Berselius, in a few words, told how the camp had been broken up, without referring, however, to his accident; and the fat and placid Cambon listened, pleased as a child with the tale. He had never seen an elephant except at the Jardin d'Acclimatation. He would have run from a milch-cow. Terrible in the law courts, in life he was the mildest of creatures, and the tale had all the attraction that the strong has for the weak and the ferocious for the mild.

But even as he listened, sitting there in his armchair, he was examining his visitor with minute attention, trying to discover some clue to the meaning of the change in him.

"And now," said Berselius, when he had finished, "to business."

He had several matters to consult the lawyer about, and the most important was the shifting of his money from the securities in which they were placed.

Cambon, who was a large holder of rubber Industries, grew pale beneath his natural pallor when he discovered that Berselius was about to place his entire fortune elsewhere.

Instantly he put two and two together. Berselius's quick return, his changed appearance, the fact that suddenly and at one sweep he was selling his stock. All these pointed to one fact—disaster.

The elephant story was all a lie, so resolved Cambon, and, no sooner had he bowed his visitor out, than he rushed to the telephone, rang up his broker, and ordered him to sell out his rubber stock at any price.

Berselius, when he left the lawyer's house, drove to his club. The selling of his rubber industry shares had been prompted by no feeling of compunction; it was an act entirely dictated by the profound irritation he felt against the other one who had made his fortune out of those same rubber industries.

He wished to break every bond between himself and the infernal entity that dominated him by night. Surely it was enough to be that other one at night, without being perpetually haunted by that other one's traces by day.

In the Place de L'Opera, his *fiacre* paused in a crowd of vehicles. Berselius heard himself hailed. He turned his head. In a barouche drawn up beside his carriage, was seated a young and pretty woman. It was Sophia Melmotte, a flame from his past life, burning now for a space in the life of a Russian prince.

"*Ma foi*," said Sophia, as her carriage pushed up till it was quite level with Berselius. "So you are back from—where was it you went to? And how are the tigers? Why, heavens, how you are changed! How gloomy you look. One would think you had swallowed a hearse and had not digested the trappings——"

To all of which Berselius bowed.

"*You* are just the same as ever," said he.

The woman flushed under her rouge, for there was something in Berselius's tone that made the simple words an insult. Before she could reply, however, the block in the traffic ceased, and as the carriage drove on Berselius bowed again to her coldly, and as though she were a stranger with whom he had spoken for a moment, and whom he had never seen before.

At the club in the smoking room, where he went for an absinthe before luncheon, he met Colonel Tirard, the very man who had presided at the banquet given to him on the day of his leaving for Africa. This man, who had been his friend, this man, in whose society he had always felt pleasure, was now obnoxious to him. And after a while the weird fact was borne in on the mind of Berselius that Tirard was not talking to him. Tirard was talking to the man who was dead—the other Berselius. The new rifle for the army, which filled Tirard's conversation, would have been an interesting subject to the old Berselius; it was absolutely distasteful to the new.

Now, for the first time, he quite clearly recognized that all the friends, pursuits, and interests that had filled his life till this, were useless to him and dead as the cast-off self that had once dominated his being. Not only useless and dead, but distasteful in a high degree. He would have to re-create a world of interests for himself out of new media. He was living in a world where all the fruit and foliage and crops had been blighted by some wizard's wand; he would have to re-plant it over anew, and at the present moment he did not know where to cast about him for a single seed.

Yet he did not give in all at once. Like a person persisting in some disagreeable medicine, hoping to become accustomed to it, he continued his conversation with Tirard.

After luncheon, he sat down to a game of écarté in the card-room with an old acquaintance, but after half an hour's play he left the table on the plea of indisposition and left the club, taking his way homeward on foot.

Near the Madeleine occurred one of those incidents which, in tragic lives, appear less incidents than occurrences prepared by Fate, as though she would say, "Look and deny me if you dare."

Toward Berselius was approaching a victoria drawn by two magnificent horses, and in the victoria lolled a man. An old man with a gray beard, who lolled on the cushions of the carriage, and looked about him with the languid indifference of a king and the arrogance of a megalomaniac.

It was Leopold, King of the Belgians.

When Berselius's eyes fell upon that face, when he saw before him that man whom all thinking men abhor, a cold hand seemed laid upon his heart, as though in that person he beheld the dead self that haunted his dreams by night, as though he saw in the flesh Berselius, the murderer, who, by consent, had murdered the people of the Silent Pools; the murderer, by consent, who had crushed millions of wretched creatures to death for the sake of gold; the villain of Europe, who had spent that gold in nameless debauchery; the man whose crimes ought to have been expiated on the scaffold, and whose life ought to have been cut short by the executioner of justice, many, many years ago.

It was thus at one stroke that Berselius saw his other self, the self that haunted him in his dreams, saw it clearly, and in the light of day.

The terrible old man in the carriage passed on his way and Berselius on his.

When he reached home, in the hall, just as he was handing his hat to a servant, Maxine appeared at the door of the library. Her beauty, innocence, and sweetness formed a strange vision contrasted with that other vision he had seen near the Madeleine. Was it possible that God's world could hold two such creatures, and that God's air should give them breath? For a week or ten days after this, Berselius remained in his own suite of apartments without leaving the house.

It was as if the sight of Leopold, so triumphantly alive, had shown him fully his own change and his weakness had demonstrated to him clearly that he was but the wraith of what he had been.

CHAPTER XXXVIII
THE REVOLT OF A SLAVE

The day after that on which Berselius had seen Leopold, Madame Berselius, moved by one of those fits of caprice common to women of her type, came back suddenly from Trouville.

She knew of her husband's return, but she knew nothing of the injury or of the alteration that had come in him until Maxine, who met her at the station, hinted at the fact. Berselius was standing at the window of his private sitting room when Madame Berselius was announced.

He turned to greet her; even as he turned she perceived the change. This was not the man who had left her a few months ago, strong, confident, impassive; the man who had been her master and before whom she had shrunk like a slave. Intuition told her that the change was not the change wrought by sickness—Berselius was not ill, he was gone, leaving another man in his place. They conversed for some time on indifferent matters, and then Madame Berselius took her departure for her own apartments.

But she left the room of Berselius a changed woman, just as he had returned to it a changed man.

The slave in her had found her freedom. Utterly without the capacity for love and without honour, without conscience and with a vague superstition to serve for religion, Madame Berselius had, up to this, been held in her place by the fear of her husband. His will up to this had been her law; she had moved in the major affairs of life under his direction, and even in the minor affairs of life everything had to be surrendered at his word.

And now she hated him.

She had never hated him before, she had admired him; indeed, as far as her power of admiration went, his strength had appealed to her as only strength can appeal to a woman of her type; but now that his strength was gone hatred of him rose up in her heart, petty yet powerful, a dwarf passion that had been slumbering for years.

When the engine seizes the engineer in its wheels, when the slave gets power over his master, cruel things happen, and they were to happen in the case of Berselius.

Madame's rooms were so far away from the rooms of her husband that they might have been living in different houses. There was none of the intimacy of married life between this couple; they met formally at meal times, and it was at *déjeuner* on the morning after her return that she showed openly before Adams, Maxine, and the servants her contempt for the man who had once held her in subjection. Without a rude word, simply by her manner, her tone, and her indifference to him, she humbled to the dust the stricken man and proclaimed the full measure of his disaster.

As day followed day the dominance of the woman and the subjection of the man became more marked. Madame would, if the spirit took her, countermand her husband's orders; once, with absolute rudeness, she, at table and before the Minister of Foreign Affairs, who was a guest, turned to ridicule a remark which Berselius had let escape. The flush that came to his cheek told Maxine that her father's sensibilities were not dead—he was dominated.

Nothing could be stranger than this reduction of a man from greatness to insignificance. The old Berselius dying, bound in chains, would have mastered this woman with one glance of his eye. The new Berselius, free, wealthy, and with all his material powers at command, was yet her creature, an object of pity to his daughter and of derision to his servants.

Eight days after her return Madame Berselius, now free and her own mistress, left Paris for Vaux on a short visit to some friends, little dreaming of the momentous event that was to cause her return.

CHAPTER XXXIX
MAXINE

On the night of the day upon which Berselius had paid his visit to M. Cambon, Adams, seated in the smoking room at a writing table before a broad sheet of white paper covered with words, suddenly took the paper, tore it up, and threw the pieces in a wastepaper-basket.

He had been trying to put in language the story of the Congo as it had been revealed to him.

It was all there in his mind like a tremendous dramatic poem: the great sunlit spaces of the elephant country watched over by the vultures, the eternal and illimitable forests old as Memnon, young as Spring, unwithered and unbroken by the suns and rains and storms of the ages; the river flooding to the sea, and the people to whom this place belonged, and the story of their misery and despair.

When he contrasted what he had written with what was in his mind, he recognized the hopelessness of his attempt. He had not the power to put on paper more than the shadow of what he had seen and of what he knew.

To represent that people under the heel of that Fate was a task for an Æschylus.

Sitting thus before the picture he could not reproduce, there rose before his mind another picture he had seen that day. It was a large photograph of the Laocoon. He had seen it in Brentano's window, and, now, with the eye of memory, he was looking at it again.

That wonderful work of art washed up to us by the ages, that epic in marble, expressed all that words refused to say: the father and the children in the toils of Fate; the hand upholding for a moment the crushing coil of the serpent, the face raised to a sky devoid of God or pity; the agony, the sweat and the cruelty, all were there; and as Adams gazed, the python-like lianas of the forest became alive in his mind, the snake-like rubber vine twined in coils, circling about and crushing a nation and its children, remote from help and from God, as Laocoon and his sons.

Ages have passed since the sculptor of that marble laid down his chisel and gazed at his completed work. Little dreamt he that thousands of years later it would stand as a parable, representing civilization in the form of the python which he had carved with such loathing yet such loving care.

Adams, in the grasp of this startling thought, was recalled from reverie by a sound behind him.

Someone had entered the room. It was Maxine Berselius.

They had seen very little of each other since his return. Adams, indeed, had purposely avoided her as much as it is possible for one person to avoid another when both are dwelling in the same house.

The pride of manhood warned him against this woman who was rich and the daughter of the man from whom he received a salary.

Maxine knew nothing of the pride of manhood; she only knew that he avoided her.

She was dressed entirely in white with a row of pearls for her only ornament. She had just returned from some social function, and Adams as he rose to meet her noticed that she had closed the door.

"Dr. Adams," said the girl, "forgive me for disturbing you at this hour. For days I have wished to speak to you about my father. I have put it off, but I feel I must speak—what has happened to him?"

She took a seat in an armchair, and Adams stood before her with his back to the mantelpiece and his hands behind him.

The big man did not answer for a moment. He stood there like a statue, looking at his questioner gravely and contemplatively, as a physician looks at a patient whose case is not quite clear.

Then he said, "You notice a change in your father?"

"No," said Maxine, "it is more than a change. He is quite different—he is another man."

"When we were hunting out there," said Adams, "Captain Berselius had an accident. In trying to rescue a servant he was caught by an elephant and flung some distance; he hurt his head, and when he recovered consciousness his memory was quite gone. It slowly returned——" He paused, for it was impossible to give details, then he went on—"I noticed, myself, as the memory was returning, that he seemed changed; when he had fully recovered his memory, the fact was obvious. He was, as you say, quite different—in fact, just as you see him now."

"But can an injury change a person like that?"

"Yes; an injury to the head can change a person completely."

Maxine sighed. She had never seen the dark side of her father; she had never loved him in the true sense of the word, but she had respected him and felt a pride in his strength and dominance.

The man who had returned from Africa seemed to her an inferior being; the wreck, in fact, of the man she had always known.

"And this happened to him," said she, "when he was trying to save a servant's life?"

"Ah," said Adams, "if you could have seen it, you would have called it something even higher than that—it was a sublime act."

He told her the details, even as he had told them to Schaunard, but with additions.

"I myself was paralyzed—I could only cling to the tree and watch. The fury of that storm of beasts coming down on one was like a wind—I can put it no other way—like a wind that stripped one's mind of everything but just the power of sight. I can imagine now the last day, when the sun shall be turned into darkness and the moon into blood. It was as bad as that—well, *he* did not lose his mind or nerve, he found time to think of the man who was lying drugged with hemp, and he found courage enough in his heart to attempt to save him. He was fond of the man, for the man was a great hunter though an absolute savage, without heart or soul.

"Without heart or soul——" Adams paused. There was something about Maxine Berselius that made her different from the ordinary woman one meets in life—some inheritance from her father, perhaps, who knows? But through the sweetness of her nature which spoke in voice and expression, through her loveliness and her womanliness, there shone a light from within. Like the gleam from the lamp that lives in an opal, this mind-brightness of Maxine's pierced the clouds of her beauty capriciously, now half-veiled, now shining forth. It was the light of that flame which men call originality. Maxine saw the world by the light of her own lamp. Adams, though he had seen far more of the world than she, had seen it by the light of other people's lamps.

The Hostage House of Yandjali would have told Maxine infinitely more than it told Adams. She would have read in Meeus's face a story that he never deciphered; she would have seen in the people of the Silent Pools a whole nation in chains, when he with his other-people-begotten ideas of niggers and labour only saw a few recalcitrant blacks. It wanted skulls and bones to bring him to a sense of the sorrow around him; the sight of these people would have told Maxine of their tears.

This instinct for the truth of things made her a reader of people. Adams had interested her at first sight, because she found him difficult to read. She had never met a man like him before; he belonged to a different race. The man in him appealed powerfully to the woman in her; they were physical affinities. She had told him this in a hundred ways half unconsciously and without speech before they parted at Marseilles, but the mind in him had not appealed to the mind in her. She did not know his mind, its stature or its bent, and until that knowledge came to her she could not love him.

As he stood with his back to the fireplace after that pronouncement on the spiritual and moral condition of the Zappo Zap, his thoughts strayed for a moment with a waft of the wing right across the world to the camping place by the great tree. Out there now, under the stars, the tree and the pool were lying just as he had seen them last. Away to the east the burst elephant gun was resting just where it had been dropped; the bones of the giraffe, clean-picked and white, were lying just where the gun had laid them; and the bones of the man who had held the gun were lying just where the leopards had left him.

Adams knew nothing of this triangle drawn by death; he still fancied the Zappo Zap alive and deadly. Stirred into speech by that thought he went on:

"A cannibal—a creature worse than a tiger—that was the being for whom your father risked his life."

"A cannibal?" said Maxine, opening her eyes wide.

"Yes; a soldier of the Government who was detailed to act as our guide."

"A soldier—but what Government employs cannibals as soldiers?"

"Oh," said Adams, "they call them soldiers, that is just a name. Slave drivers is the real name, but the Government that employs them does not use the word slave—oh, no, everyone would be shocked—*scoundrels*!"

He spoke the word with suddenly flashing eyes, uplifted head, and a face as stern the face of Themis. He seemed for a moment fronting some invisible foe, then, smothering his wrath, he went on:

"I lose control of myself when I think of what I have seen—the suffering, the misery, and the wretchedness. I saw enough at first to have made me open my eyes, but the thing was not shown to me really till I saw the bones of murdered people—people whom I had seen walking about alive—lying there a few weeks later, just skeletons; a little child I had talked to and played with——"

He stopped and turned to the fireplace and rested his elbow on the mantel. He had turned his back on Maxine, and volumes could not have said more than what was expressed by that abrupt stoppage of speech and turning away.

The girl scarcely breathed till the man turned from the mantelpiece and faced her again. There was no trace of emotion on his face, but the trace of a struggle with it. Maxine's eyes were filled with tears.

"I am sorry," said he, "that I should have dragged this subject before you at all. Why should I torment your heart as well as my own?"

She did not reply for a moment. She was tracing the vague pattern of the carpet with her eyes, her chin resting on her hand, and the light from above made a halo of the burnished red-gold hair that was her crowning charm.

Then she said, speaking slowly, "I am not sorry. Surely if such things are, they ought to be known. Why should I turn away my face from suffering? I have never done so in Paris, and I have seen much of the misery of Paris, for I have gone amongst it as much as a girl can, but what you tell me is beyond what I have ever heard of, or read of, or dreamed. Tell me more, give me facts; for, frankly, though I believe you, I cannot yet fully realize, and with my mind fully believe. I am like Thomas; I must put my fingers in the wounds."

"Are you brave enough to look at material evidence?" asked Adams.

"Yes; brave enough to face the suffering of others if not my own——"

He left the room and in a few minutes later returned with a parcel. He took from it the skull he had brought with him through everything to civilization.

Maxine's eyes dilated when she saw the thing, but she did not turn pale, and she looked steadfastly at it as Adams turned it in his hands and showed her by the *foramen magnum* the hacks in the bone caused by the knife.

She put out her finger and touched them, then she said, "I believe."

Adams put the skull on the table; curious and small and ferocious and repellent it looked. One would never have imagined the black face, the grin, and the rolling eyes of the creature to whom it had once belonged. One thing only about it touched the heart with sadness—its size.

"It is a child's," said Maxine.

"Yes; the child I told you of—all that remains of it."

He was about to wrap the thing up again when the girl interposed.

"Let it lie there whilst you tell me; it will bring things nearer to me. I am not afraid of it—poor, poor creature. Tell me all you know—tell me the worst. I am not a young lady for the moment, please, just a person listening."

He took his seat in an armchair opposite to her, and resting his elbows on his knees, talking just as if he were talking to a man, found the words he could not find when, pen in hand, half an hour ago, he had tried to express himself in writing.

He told of the Hostage House at Yandjali, and the wretched creatures penned like animals eating their miserable food; he told of M'Bassa and the Hostage House there, with its iron rings and chains; he told how all over that vast country these places were dotted, not by the hundred but by the thousand; he told of the misery of the men who were driven into the dismal forests, slaves of masters worse than tigers, and of a task that would never end as long as rubber grew and Christ was a name in Europe and not a power; he told the awful fact that murder there was used every day as an agricultural implement, that people were operated upon, and suffered amputation of limbs, not because of disease; and that their sex and age—those two last appeals of Nature to brutality—had no voice; he told the whole bitter tale of tears and blood, but he could not tell her all, for she was a girl, and it would be hard to speak even before a man of the crimes against Nature, the crimes against men, against women, and against children, that even if the Congo State were swept away to-morrow, will leave Belgium's name in the world's history more detestable than the names of the unspeakable cities sunk in the Dead Sea.

Maxine listened, entranced, swayed between the terror of the tale and the power of the man who was telling it.

Ah! if he could have spoken to Europe as he spoke to her; if he could have made Europe see as he made her see, what a whirlwind of indignation would have arisen; but he could not.

It was the magnet of her sympathy that marshalled the facts, clad them in burning language, and led them forth in battalions that stormed her mind and made her believe what seemed unbelievable. Without that sympathy, his words would have been cold and lifeless statements bearing little conviction.

When he had finished, she did that which a woman never does unless moved by the very highest excitement. She rose up and paced the floor thrice. Without speaking, she walked the length of the room, then she turned to Adams.

"But this must cease."

"This shall cease," said he, "if I can only make myself heard. To-day—to-night—just before you came in, I was trying to put the thing on paper—trying to put down what I have seen with my own eyes, and heard with my own ears, but the ink seems ice. What I write seems nothing, nothing beside what I have seen. The mere statement that so many were killed, so many were tortured, conveys nothing of the reality. The thing is too big for me. God made it, I suppose; but I wish to God I had never seen it."

Maxine was standing now with her hands resting on the back of an armchair. She seemed scarcely listening to what her companion was saying. She was listening, but she was thinking as well.

"You cannot do everything yourself," said she, at last. "You must get others to help, and in this I can, perhaps, assist you. Will you go to-morrow and see Monsieur Pugin? I do not know him personally, but I know a friend of his. I will send him a note early to-morrow morning, and the servant can bring back the letter of introduction. You could call upon him to-morrow afternoon."

"Who is Monsieur Pugin?"

This question, showing such a boundless ignorance of every-day French life and literature, rather shocked Maxine. She explained that Ary Pugin, the author of "Absolution" and twenty other works equally beautiful, was above all other men fitted to bring home to France the story of this great sin. "Absolution," that masterpiece, had shown France her cruelty in the expulsion of the religious orders. France had read it weeping, drying her tears with one hand and continuing the expulsion of the religious orders with the other.

That, however, was not Pugin's fault; he had done his best. It was not his fault that logic and sentiment are so largely constituent of the French nature, making between them that paradox, the French mind.

"I will go and see him," said Adams, when the girl had explained what Pugin was, what Pugin did, and what Pugin had written. "A man like that could do more with a stroke of his pen, than I with weary years of blundering attempts to write. I can never thank you enough for listening to me. It is strange, but half the weight of the thing seems to have passed from my mind."

"To mine," she replied. Then, with charming *naïveté*, she held out both hands to him.

"Good night."

As he held the door open, and as she passed out, he realized that, during the last few months, his faith in the goodness of God—the old simple faith of his childhood—had been all but stolen by ferocious and fiendish hands from his mind, and that just now, in some miraculous way, it had been returned.

It was as though the gentle hands of Maxine had put it back.

Maxine, when she reached her own apartments, turned on the electric light in her sitting room, and sat down at once to write to the friend who was a friend of Pugin's.

This friend was Sabatier.

She had studied art under him, and between artist and pupil lay that mysterious bond which unites craftsmen. For Maxine was great in knowledge and power, and above all in that instinct without which an artist is at best an animated brush, a pencil under the dominion of mechanical force.

As she wrote, she little dreamed that the sympathy burning in her heart and moving to eloquence her pen, was a thing born not from the sufferings of an afflicted people, but of the love of a man. A child of her mind begotten by the man she had just left, and whom, that night, she had learned to love.

CHAPTER XL
PUGIN

Pugin lived in the Boulevard Haussmann. He had begun life quite low down in the Parisian world on the quays as apprentice to Manasis, a jew book-dealer, who has been dead twenty-five years, whose money has been dispersed, whose name has been forgotten, of whom nothing remains on earth but the few hours a day of time filched from him by Pugin.

Pugin had a hard and bitter fight for twenty years before he obtained recognition. The garret and starvation act had been unduly prolonged in the case of this genius, and it seemed a mystery where and how in the ruined city which is at the heart of every city, in that *cour des Miracles* where the Bohemians camp, he had found, like a crystal vase, his exquisite style, preserved it unbroken by mischance or shock of fate, and carried it safely at last to the hands of Fame.

He was very rich now, very powerful, and very fortunate. Charitable, too, and ever ready to assist a fellow-worker in straitened circumstances, and to-day as he sat reading in the cool recesses of his library, and listening to the sound of the Paris he loved floating in with the warm June air through the open window, he felt at peace with all the world and in a mood to do justice to his bitterest enemy.

The striped sun-blinds filtered the blaze outside, letting pass only a diffused and honey-coloured twilight; a great bowl of roses filled the room with the simple and deep poetry of summer, the story of the hedges and the fields, of orchards shot through with the voices of birds, of cattle knee-deep in cool water where the dragon-flies keep up their eternal dance to the flute-like ripple of the river amidst the reeds.

Pugin, his book upon his knees, was enjoying these pictures of summer woven by perfume, when a servant entered and handed him Adams's card and the letter of introduction written by Sabatier.

He ordered the visitor to be shown in. Adams, when he entered, found himself before a small man with a big head; an ugly little man, with a look of kindness and a very gracious and charming manner.

To Pugin Adams seemed a giant. A giant bronzed by unknown suns, talking French indifferently well, and with a foreign accent. An interesting person, indeed, but a being quite beyond his range of knowledge.

Pugin, in physical matters, was timid as a rabbit. He had never travelled farther than Trouville or Ostend, and when he indicated a chair, and when these two sat down to talk to each other, the mastiff-man felt instinctively the presence of the rabbit-man, and was at a loss how to begin.

Not for long, though. Bluffly, and with little grace enough, but with earnestness and a cunning one would never have suspected, he told of Maxine's great admiration for the author's work, and how she had suggested the enlistment of the said author in the crusade against crime which he, Adams, was endeavouring to raise.

Pugin listened, making little bows, sniffing the lettuce which the mastiff-man had so cunningly placed before his nose.

Then honestly and plainly and well, Adams told his tale, and the rabbit held up its hands in horror at the black doings disclosed to it. But it was horror divorced from sentiment. Pugin felt almost as great a revulsion toward the negroes upon whom these things were done as toward the doers.

He could not see the vast drama in its true proportions and its poetical setting of forest, plain, and sky. The outlandish names revolted him; he could not see Yandjali and its heat-stricken palms or M'Bassa burning in the sun.

But he listened politely and it was this that chilled the heart of the story-teller who instinctively felt that though he had shocked his hearer, he had not aroused that high spirit of revolt against injustice which converts a man into a living trumpet, a living axe, or a living sword.

Pugin would have been a great force could his sentiment have been awakened; but he could not see palm trees.

"What would you have? You cannot grow baobabs on the Boulevards."

"*Ma foi!*" said he, "it is terrible what you tell me, but what are we to do?"

"I thought you might help," said Adams.

"I? With all the power possible and goodwill. It is evident to me that should you wish for success in this matter, you should found a society."

"Yes?"

"There is nothing done in a public way without coöperation. You must found a society; you may use my name. I will even let you put it on the committee list. I will also subscribe."

Now Pugin was on the committee lists of half a dozen charitable and humanitarian concerns. His secretary had them all down in a book; but Pugin himself, lost in his art and the work of his life, had forgotten their very names. So would it be with this.

"Thanks," said the visitor.

Pugin would lend his purse to the cause, and his name, but he would not lend his pen—simply because he could not. To every literary man there are dead subjects; this question was dead to the author of "Absolution"—as uninspiring as cold mutton.

"Thanks," said Adams, and rose to take his leave. His rough-hewn mind understood with marvellous perspicuity Pugin's position.

"And one moment," cried the little man, after he had bidden his visitor good-bye and the latter was leaving the room. "One moment; why did I not think of it before? You might go and see Ferminard."

He ran to a desk in the corner of the room, took a visiting card and scribbled Ferminard's address upon it, explaining as he wrote that Ferminard was the deputy for —— in Provence; a Socialist it is true, but a terrible man when roused; that the very name of injustice was sufficient to bring this lion from his den.

"Tell him Pugin said so," cried he, following his visitor this time out on the landing and patting him on the shoulder in a fatherly manner, "and you will find him in the Rue Auber, No. 14; it is all on the card; and convey my kind regards to Mademoiselle ——, that charming lady to whose appreciation of my poor work I owe the pleasure of your visit."

"Nice little man," said Adams to himself as he walked down the Boulevard Haussmann.

He found Ferminard at home, in an apartment smelling of garlic and the south. Ferminard, a tall, black-bearded creature, with a glittering eye; a brigand from the Rhone Valley who had flung himself into the politics of his country as a torpedo flings itself into the sea, greeted Adams with effusion, when he read Pugin's card; gave him cigarettes, and shut the open window in honour of his guest.

He worked himself into a state of indignation over Adams's story; as a matter of fact he knew the whole thing well; but he was too polite to discount his visitor's grievance, besides it gave him an opportunity to declaim—and of course the fact that a king was at the bottom of it all, added keenness to the arrows of his invective.

As Adams listened, delighted to have awakened such a trumpet; as he listened to Ferminard thundering against all that over there, speaking as though he were addressing the Chambre, and as though he had known Africa intimately from his childhood, he noticed gradually and with alarm that the topic was changing; just a moment ago it was Africa and its luckless niggers; the Provençal imagination picturing them in glowing colours, and the Provençal tongue rolling off their disabilities and woes. One would have fancied from the fervour of the man that is was Ferminard who had just returned from the Congo, not Adams.

Well, a moment after, and Africa had quite fallen out of the discussion. As a child lets a Noah's Ark fall from its hands—elephants, zebras and all on to the floor whilst he grasps for a new toy—so Ferminard let Africa tumble whilst he grasped for Socialism, found it and swung it like a rattle, and Socialism went the way of Africa as he seized at last that darling toy—himself. The speech, in its relationship to the subject in point, was the intellectual counterpart of the cry of those mechanical pigs which the street venders blow up, and which, standing on a board, scream in the face of Oxford Street, loudly at first, and then, as the figure collapses, weakening in voice to the buzzing of a fly.

Ferminard was, in fact, a great child with a good heart, a Provençal imagination, a power of oratory, a quickness in seizing upon little things and making them seem great, coupled with a rather obscure understanding as to the relative value of mountains and mole-hills. A noise maker of a first-class description, but useless for any serious work. *Feu de bruit* was his motto, and he lived up to it.

It is only when you try to enlist men on your side in some great and holy cause, that you come to some knowledge of the general man's weakness and want of holiness—your own included. Adams, during the fortnight that followed his visit to Pugin, had this fact borne in on him. All the thinking minds of the centre of civilization were so busy thinking thoughts of their own making, that it was impossible to attract their attention for more than a moment; from Bostoc the dramatist to Bastiche the anarchist, each individual was turning his own crank diligently, and not to be disturbed, even by Papeete's skull.

With such a thing in one's hand, picked up like some horrible talisman which, if not buried, will eventually cast its spell upon human thought and the future of the world; with such a thing in one's hand, surely the Church would present itself to the mind as a court of appeal.

But as the Roman Catholic Church had actually put its broad back against the door of the torture chamber, and was, in fact, holding it tight shut whilst Papeete's head was being hacked from his body, it would scarcely be logical to bring out the victim's skull hoping for redress. Other denominations being of such little power in France, Adams determined to leave the attempt to rouse them till he reached England, whither he determined to go as soon as Berselius's health would permit him.

One evening, a fortnight after his visit to Pugin, on his return to the Avenue Malakoff, Maxine met him in the hall.

He saw at once from her face that something had happened.

Berselius was worse; that afternoon he had suddenly developed acute neuralgia of the right side of the head, and this had been followed almost immediately by twitching and numbness of the left arm. Thénard had been summoned and he had diagnosed pressure on the brain, or, at least, irritation from depressed bone, due to the accident.

He declared himself for operation, and he had gone now to make arrangements for nurses and assistants.

"He will operate this evening," said Maxine.

"And Madame Berselius?"

"I have telegraphed for her."

CHAPTER XLI
THE RETURN OF CAPTAIN BERSELIUS

Berselius, for the last fortnight, had been going back, slowly going from bad to worse, and keeping the fact to himself.

Sulphonal, trional, morphia, each tried in turn had no power to prevent him from dreaming. Sleep as soundly as he would, just as he was awaking, the black blanket of slumber, turned up at a corner or an edge by some mysterious hand, would reveal a dream or part of one.

There was nothing in these dreams to terrify him when he was dreaming them; in them, he was just the old brave Berselius that nothing could terrify, but there was often a good deal to terrify him when he awoke.

Many of them were quite innocent and as fatuous as dreams are wont to be, but even these innocent dreams fretted the soul of the waking man, for in every scrap and vestige of them he recognized the mind of that other personality.

After the first few days, his intellect, so severe and logical, began to lose its severity and logic, and to take up sides with his heart and to cry aloud against the injustice of this persecution.

Why should he be haunted like this? He felt no trace of remorse now for the past; the sense of injustice swallowed all that. Every day seemed to drive that past further off, and to increase the sense of detachment from that other man and his works; yet every night a hand, like the hand of some remorseless chess player, put things back in their places.

With the falling of the curtain of sleep he became metamorphosed.

Then came the day when the evil he was suffering from declared itself in a physical manner and Thénard was called in.

Thénard found his patient in bed. His mind was quite clear, but the pupils of his eyes were unequal; there was numbness in the left arm and want of grip in the hand. He had been prepared for the change evident in Berselius's face and manner, for Maxine had told him in a few words of the accident and loss of memory, and as he took his seat by the bedside he was about to put some questions relative to the injury, when Berselius forestalled him.

Berselius knew something about medicine. He guessed the truth about his own case, and he gave a succinct account of the accident and the loss of memory following it.

"This is due to the result of the injury, is it not?" said Berselius, pointing to his left arm when he had finished.

"I am afraid so," said TThénard, who knew his patient, and that plain speaking would be best.

"Some pressure?"

"So I imagine."

"Oh, don't be afraid of speaking out. I don't mind the worst. Will an operation remove that pressure?"

"If, as I imagine, there is some pressure from the inner table of the skull on the brain, it will."

"Well, now," said Berselius, "I want you to listen to me attentively; ever since that accident, or, at least, since I regained memory, I have felt that I am not the same man. Only in sleep do I become myself again—do you understand me? I have quite different aims and objects; my feelings about things are quite different; my past before the accident is ruled off from my present—that is, when I am awake.

"When I dream I become my old self again—is that not strange?"

"No," said Thénard, "every man is double. We have numerous cases where, from accident or other circumstances, a man's personality changes; one side of his nature is suppressed. There is one strange point about your case, though, and that is the waking up of the suppressed personality so vividly during sleep; but in your case it is perhaps not so strange."

"Why not?"

"Because, and excuse me for being personal even though I am complimentary, your personality as I knew you before your accident was so profound, and vivid, and powerful, that even though it is suppressed it must speak. And it speaks in dreams."

"So!—perhaps you are right. Now tell me, if you operate and remove the pressure, may I become myself again?"

"You may."

"Even after all this time?"

"The mind," said Thénard, "has nothing to do with time. At the Battle of the Nile, a sea captain, one of those iron-headed Englishmen, was struck on his iron head with fragment of shell. He lost his memory. Eight months after he was trephined; he awoke from the operation completing the order he was giving to his sailors when the accident cut him short— —"

"I would be the same man. I would not be tormented with the other self which is me, now?"

"Possibly—I do not say probably, but possibly."

"Then," said Berselius, "for God's sake, operate at once."

"I would like to wait for another twelve hours," said Thénard, rising and re-examining the slight dent of his patient's skull.

"Why?"

"Well, to see if things may be cleared up a bit, and the necessity for operation be removed."

"Operate."

"You know, in every operation, however slight, there is an element of danger to life."

"Life! what do I care? I insist on your operating. Not another night shall pass— —"

"As you will," said Thénard.

"And now," said Berselius, "make your preparations, and send me my secretary."

At twelve o'clock that night, Maxine was seated in the library, with a book which she had been vainly trying to read face downward on the floor beside her.

Thénard, his assistant surgeon, and two nurses, had arrived shortly after ten. Operating table, instruments, everything necessary had been brought, set up, and fixed by Thénard's own man.

Adams had no part in the proceedings except as a looker-on. No man could assist Thénard in an operation who was not broken to the job, for, when operating Thénard became quite a different person to the every-day Thénard of lecture room and hospital ward.

That harsh voice which we noticed in him in the first pages of this book when on entering the lecture room of the Beaujon he could not find his coloured chalks, came out during an operation, and he would curse his assistant to the face for the slightest fault or fancied fault, and he would speak to the nurses as no Frenchman ever spoke to Frenchwoman unless with deliberate intent to insult. When the last stitch was in, all this changed; nurses and assistant forgot what had been said, and in the ease of released tension, worshipped more than ever the cadaverous genius who was now unwinding from his head and mouth the antiseptic gauze in which he always veiled them when operating.

The clock on the mantel pointed to a few minutes past the hour, when the door opened, and Adams came in.

Maxine rose to meet him.

She read both good and bad news in his face.

"The operation has been successful, but there is great weakness." He rolled an armchair for her to sit down, and then he told her as much as she could understand.

Thénard had found a slight depression of the inner table of the skull, and some congestion and thickening of the dura mater. It all dated from the accident. There would, without doubt, have been severe inflammation of the brain, but for Berselius's splendid condition at the time of the accident, and the fact that Adams had bled him within an hour of the injury. Thénard had relieved the pressure by operation, but there was great weakness.

It was impossible to say what the result would be yet.

"Has he regained consciousness?"

"He is just recovering from the anæsthetic."

The girl was silent for a moment, then she asked where Thénard was.

"He has left. He has to operate again to-night on a case which has just called for him by telephone. He asked me to tell you that everything possible has been done. He will call in the morning, and he has left everything till then in my hands."

"I shall not go to bed," said Maxine. "I could not sleep, and should my father want to see me, I shall be ready."

"Yes," said Adams, "perhaps it will be better so. I will go up and stay with him, and I will call you if it is necessary."

He left the room, and Maxine took up the book she had dropped, but she could not read. Her eyes, travelling about the room, rested here and there on the trophies and the guns and the wild implements of destruction collected by the hunter, who was now lying upstairs, like a child dandled on the dark knees of death.

The books on philosophy, natural history, oceanography, and history, in their narrow cases contrasted strangely with the weapons of destruction and the relics of the wild. The room was like a mirror of the mind of Berselius, that strange mind in which the savage dwelt with the civilized man, and the man of valour by the side of the philosopher.

But the strangest contrast in the room was effected by Maxine herself—the creation of Berselius—his child, blossoming like a beautiful and fragile flower, amidst the ruins of the things he had destroyed.

When, after daybreak, Adams came to find her, she was asleep.

Berselius, awaking from a sleep that had followed the effects of the anæsthetic, had asked for her.

Thénard had fixed upon the white marble bathroom adjoining Berselius's sleeping chamber as his operating theatre, and after the operation the weakness of the patient was so great, and the night so hot, they determined to make up a bed for him there, as it was the coolest room in the house.

It was a beautiful room. Walls, pillars, floor and ceiling, of pure white Carrara marble, and in the floor, near the window, a sunk bath, which, when not in use, was covered by a grating of phosphor bronze, showing a design of sea serpents and seaweed. There were no basins or lavatory arrangements, nothing at all to break the pure and simple charm of this ideal bathing-place whose open French window showed, beyond a balcony of marble, the tops of trees waving against the blue sky of early morning.

Berselius was lying on the bed which had been arranged for him near the door; his eyes were fixed on the waving tree tops. He turned his head slightly when Maxine entered, and looked at her long and deliberately.

In that one glance Maxine saw all. He was himself again. The old, imperious expression had returned; just a trace of the half-smile was visible about his lips.

The great weakness of the man, far from veiling the returned personality, served as a background which made it more visible. One could see the will dominating the body, and the half-helpless hands lying on the coverlet presented a striking contrast to the inextinguishable fire of the eye.

Maxine sat down on the chair by the bed. She did not attempt to stroke the hand near her, and she smothered whatever emotion she felt, for she knew the man who had returned.

"Your mother?" said Berselius, who had just sufficient voice to convey interrogation as well as words.

"She has not returned yet; we telegraphed for her, she will be here to-day."

"Ah!"

The sick man turned his head again, and fixed his eyes on the tree tops.

The hot, pure, morning air came through the open window, bringing with it the chirruping and bickering of sparrows; a day of splendour and great heat was breaking over Paris. Life and the joy of life filled the world, the lovely world which men contrive to make so terrible, so full of misery, so full of tears.

Suddenly Berselius turned his head, and his eyes found Adams with a not unkindly gaze in them.

"Well, doctor," he said, in a voice stronger than the voice with which he had spoken to Maxine. "This is the end of our hunting, it seems."

Adams, instead of replying, took the hand that was lying on the coverlet, and Berselius returned the pressure, and then relinquished his hold.

Just a handshake, yet it told Adams in some majestic way, that the man on the bed knew that all was up with him, and that this was good-bye.

Berselius then spoke for a while to Maxine on indifferent things. He did not mention his wife's name, and he spoke in a cold and abstracted voice. He seemed to Adams as though he were looking at death, perfectly serenely, and with that level gaze which never in this world had been lowered before man or brute.

Then he said he was tired, and wished to sleep.

Maxine rose, but the woman in her had to speak. She took the hand on the coverlet, and Berselius, who was just dozing off, started awake again.

"Ah!" said he, as though he had forgotten something, then he raised the little hand of Maxine and touched it with his lips.

Then he asked that his wife should be sent to him on her return.

Alone, he closed his eyes and one might have fancied that he slept, yet every now and then his eyelids would lift, and his eyes, unveiled by drowsiness, would fix themselves on some point in the room with the intent gaze of a person who is listening; so in the forest, or on the plain, or by the cane brake had he often listened at night, motionless, gun in hand and deadly, for the tiger or the water buck.

Half an hour passed and then from the adjoining room came a footstep, the door opened gently, and Madame Berselius entered. She was dressed just as she had traveled from Vaux. She had only just arrived, to find death in the house, and as she looked at the figure on the bed she fancied she beheld it indeed.

Closing the door gently she approached the bed. No, it was not death but sleep. He was breathing evenly and rhythmically, sleeping, apparently, as peacefully as a child.

She was about to turn away when, like a bather who has ventured into some peaceful tropic rock pool wherein lurks an octopus, she found herself seized and held. Berselius's eyes were open, he was not asleep. His gaze was fixed on hers, and he held her with his eyes as the cat holds the bird or the python the man.

He had been waiting for her with the patience and the artfulness of the hunter, but no game had ever inspired such ferocity in him as this woman, vile and little, who yet had abased him to the earth.

He was dying, but what beast full of life is more dangerous than the dying tiger?

As Berselius gazed at the woman, she, with all her will urging her body to retreat, approached him. Then, her knees touching the bed, she fell on her knees beside him and his hand fell on her shoulder.

Holding her thus, he gazed on her coldly, dispassionately, and critically, as an emperor of old might have gazed on a defaulting slave. Then, as though his anger had turned to disgust, as though disdaining to waste a word on her, he struck her full in the face with the back of his right hand, a blow that caused her to cry out and sent her groveling on the marble floor, where a moment after the nurse on duty, attracted by the cry, found her.

Berselius was dead, but the mocking smile on his lips remained, almost justified by the words of the nurse imploring the woman on the floor to calm herself and restrain her grief.

Whatever his life may have been, his death affected Adams strangely. The magnetism of the man's character had taken a strong hold upon him, fascinating him with the fascination that strength alone can exercise. And the man he regretted was not the ambiguous being, the amended Berselius, so obviously a failure, but the real Berselius who had returned to meet death.

CHAPTER XLII
AMIDST THE LILIES

One day in March, nine months later, at Champrosay, in the garden of a little cottage near the Paris road, Maxine Berselius stood directing the movements of an old man in a blue blouse—Father Champardy by name, and a gardener by profession.

On the death of her father, Maxine had come to an arrangement with her mother, eminently suited to the minds and tastes of both women.

Maxine absolutely refused to touch any part of the colossal fortune left by her father. She knew how it had been come by, and as she had a small fortune of her own, a very small fortune of some ten thousand francs a year settled on her by an uncle at her birth, she determined to live on it, and go her own way in life.

Art was to her far preferable to society, and in a little cottage with one woman for a servant, ten thousand francs a year were affluence.

Madame Berselius, who had no scruple in using money obtained in any way whatsoever, fell in with her daughter's views after a few formal objections.

Gillette had furnished the cottage as only a French firm can furnish a cottage, and the garden, which had gone to decay, Maxine had furnished herself with the help of Father Champardy.

Adams, after the death of Berselius, had lingered on in Paris to settle up his affairs, going back to the Rue Dijon and taking up his old life precisely at the point where he had broken it off.

But he was richer by three things. Two days after Berselius's death, news came to him from America of the death of an uncle whom he had never seen and the fact that he had inherited his property. It was not very much as money goes in America, but it was real estate in New York City and would bring in some seven or eight hundred pounds a year. He was richer by the experience he had gained and the Humanity he had discovered in himself, and he was richer by his love for Maxine.

But love itself was subordinate in the mind of Adams to the burning question that lay at his heart. He had put his hand to the plough, and he was not the man to turn aside till the end of the furrow was reached. He would have time to go to America, in any event, to look after his property. He decided to stay some months in England; to attack the British Lion in its stronghold; to explain the infamies of the Congo, and then cross the Atlantic and put the matter before the American Eagle.

He did.

For seven months he had been away, and every week he had written to Maxine, saying little enough about the progress of his work, and frequently using the cryptic statement, "I will tell you everything when I come back."

And "He will be back to-day," murmured Maxine, as she stood in the little garden watching the old man at his work.

The newness and the freshness of spring were in the air, snow that had fallen three days ago was nearly gone, just a trace of it lay on the black earth of the flower beds; white crocuses, blue crocuses, snow-drops, those first trumpeters of spring, blew valiantly in the little garden, the air was sharp and clear, and the sky above blue and sparkling. Great masses of white cloud filled the horizon, sun-stricken, fair, and snow-bright, solid as mountains, and like far-off mountains filled with the fascination and the call of distance.

"Spring is here," cried the birds from the new-budding trees.

The blackbird in Dr. Pons's garden to the left, answered a rapturous thrush in the trees across the way, children's voices came from the Paris road and the sounds of wheels and hoofs.

A sparrow with a long straw in its beak flew right across Maxine's garden, a little winged poem, a couplet enclosing the whole story of spring.

Maxine smiled as it vanished, then she turned; the garden gate had clicked its latch, and a big man was coming up the path.

There was only Father Champardy to see; and as his back was turned, he saw nothing and as he was deaf, he heard nothing. The old man, bent and warped by the years, deaf, and blind to the little love-scene behind him, was, without knowing it, also a poem of spring; but not so joyous as the poem of the sparrow.

"And now tell me all," said Maxine, as they sat in the chintz-hung sitting room before a bright fire of logs. They had finished their private affairs. The day was two hours older, and a sunbeam that had pointed at them through the diamond-paned window had travelled away and vanished. The day was darker outside, and it was as though spring had lost her sportive mood and then withdrawn, not wishing to hear the tale that Adams had to tell.

In Adams's hand Papeete's skull had been a talisman of terrible and magical power, for with it he had touched men, and the men touched had disclosed their worth and their worthlessness. It had been a lamp which showed him society as it is.

The life and death of Berselius had been an object lesson for him, teaching vividly the fact that evil is indestructible; that wash yourself with holy water or wash yourself with soap, you will never wash away the evil being that you have constructed by long years of evil-doing and evil-thinking.

His pilgrimage in search of mercy and redress for a miserable people had emphasized the fact.

The great crime of the Congo stood gigantic, like a shadowy engine for the murdering of souls.

"Destroy that," said the devil triumphantly. "You cannot, for it is past destruction; it has passed into the world of the ideal. No man's hand may touch it; it is beyond the reach like the real self of your friend Berselius. Sweep the Congo State away to-morrow; this will remain. A thing soul-destroying till the end of time. It began small in the brain of one ruinous man, God whom I hate! look at it now.

"It has slain ten million men and it will slay ten million more, that is nothing; it has ruined body and soul, the stokers who fed it and the engineers who worked it, that is nothing; it has tangled in its wheels and debased the consciences of five nations, that is nothing. It is eternal—that is everything.

"Since I was flung out of heaven, I have made many things, but this is my masterpiece. If I and all my works were swept away, leaving only this thing, it would be enough. In the fiftieth century it will still have its clutch on man, yea, and to the very end of time."

Cause and effect, my friend, in those two words you have the genius of this machine which will exist forever in the world of consequence, a world beyond divine or human appeal.

In England, Adams had found himself confronted with the dull lethargy of the people, and the indifference of the Established Church. The two great divisions of Christ's Church were at the moment at death grapples over the question of Education. Only amongst the Noncomformists could be found any real response to the question which was, and is, the test question which will disclose, according to its answer, whether Christianity is a living voice from on high, or an echo from the Pagan past; and a debased echo at that. Debased, for if Adams could have stood in the Agora of Athens and told his tale of horror and truth, could Demosthenes have taken up the story; could Leopold the Barbarian have been a king in those days, and have done in those days, under the mandate of a deluded Greece, what he has done under the mandate of a deluded England; what a living spirit would have run through Athens like a torch, how the phalanxes would have formed, and the beaked ships at Piræus torn themselves from their moorings, to bring to Athens in chains the ruffian who had murdered and tortured in her name!

To complete the situation and give it a touch of hopelessness, he found that others had striven well, yet almost vainly in the field. Men working for truth and justice as other men work for gold, had attacked the public with solid battalions of facts, tabulated infamies; there had been meetings, discussions, words, *palabres*, as they say in the south; but the murderer had calmly gone on with his work, and England had put out no hand to stay him.

But it was not till he reached America, that Adams found himself fighting the machine itself.

One great man with a living voice he found—Mark Twain—and one great paper, at least. These had raised their voices calling for Justice—with what result?

Two side facts the skull of Papeete showed to the searcher, as a lamp shows up other things than the things searched for. The deadness of the English Church to the spiritual, and the corruption of his own countrymen.

When he had finished, it was dark outside. The firelight lit up the little room. Glancing through the diamond-paned window at that happy interior, one would never have guessed that the man by the fire had been telling the girl by his side not a love story, but the story of the world's greatest crime.

Maxine, whose hand was resting on the hand of her companion, said nothing for a moment after he had ceased speaking. Then, in a half-whisper, and leaning her forehead on his hand, "Poor things," sighed Maxine.

So attuned were her thoughts to the thoughts of her companion, that she voiced the very words that were in his mind, as gazing beyond his own happiness and a thousand miles of sea and forest, he saw again the moonlight on the mist of the Silent Pools, and the bleached and miserable bones.